She lived for every day that she saw him...

It wasn't just his looks, though they thrilled her. And it was in spite of his secrets, which fascinated her. It was because of his jests, his humor, his rich, slow voice, his slow, curling smile. Those half-lidded, knowing eyes that avoided hers when she caught him watching her.

Amber wasn't a fool. She knew what desire was; she'd been wanted before, and she swore the man wanted her. But she knew as sure as the sun would rise that Amyas wanted to marry Grace. It didn't mean he was evil or cunning, or even that he'd ever betray Grace. It just meant that he desired Amber. He'd tried to hide it, but she was sure he knew she knew. He tried to keep his distance. It must have been as awkward for him as it was for her.

But there it was, and whatever it was, Amber also knew her life would be hellish from now on. Because she wanted him, too. How many years could she bear it?

And what could she do *but* bear it?

Other **AVON ROMANCES**

Coming Soon

And Don't Miss These
ROMANTIC TREASURES
from Avon Books

EDITH LAYTON

ALAS, MY LOVE

AVON BOOKS

An Imprint of HarperCollinsPublishers

AVON BOOKS
An Imprint of HarperCollins*Publishers*
10 East 53rd Street
New York, New York 10022-5299

Copyright © 2005 by Edith Felber
ISBN: 0-06-056712-0
www.avonromance.com

First Avon Books paperback printing: April 2005

Avon Trademark Reg. U.S. Pat. Off. and in Other Countries, Marca Registrada, Hecho en U.S.A.
HarperCollins® is a registered trademark of HarperCollins Publishers Inc.

Printed in the U.S.A.

10 9 8 7 6 5 4 3 2 1

*In memory of my gorgeous Georgie Girl:
bright and beautiful,
steadfast and true
as the stars she watches from now.*

Acknowledgments

With thanks to two erudite Englishpersons, Robert Holland and Miranda Bell. Each helped me find the real Amyas: one with words and one with music.

You and I and Amyas, Amyas you and I,
to the green wood must we go
Alas! You and I, my life, and Amyas
The knight knocked at the castle gate,
the lady marvelled who was thereat
To call the porter he would not blin;
the lady said he could not come in
Alas! You and I, my life, and Amyas
The portress was a lady bright,
Strangeness that lady bight
She asked him what was his name,
he said, "Desire, your man, madame."
Alas! You and I, my life, and Amyas
She said, "Desire, what do you here?"
He said, "Madame, as your prisoner."
He was counselled to brief a bill;
And show the lady his own will.
Alas! You and I, my life, and Amyas
Kindness said she would it bear,
And Pity said she would be there.
Then how they did we cannot say;
we left them there and went our way.
Alas! You and I, my life, and Amyas

—Cornysshe song, circa 1515

Prologue

London, 1800

It was dark, and it was still. He dared not breathe. He held his breath until he felt he might burst. He couldn't hear anything but the blood drumming in his ears. But he knew the qualities of silence, and it was too quiet out there. Still, he finally had to let a shudder of air hiss out of his lungs. A breach of the silence, but no more than a mouse might sigh. It was necessary.

It was too much.

His head was grasped in a vise; his hair jerked so hard his scalp lifted. His head came up, and he was forced to follow.

"Got you!" The man panted in triumph. "Now you'll pay!" He hauled the scrambling boy out of the hole and pulled him away by his hair. "Oh, now I've got you, you piece of impudence, you devil, you villain," he crowed as he dragged the screeching, spitting boy into the light.

Twist and turn as he might, the boy couldn't pull free. The man hadn't just grabbed a hank of hair; he had most of it in his meaty hand. The boy heard laughter and catcalls and got a fleeting glimpse of the customers looking at him as he was dragged into the middle of shop like a skinned rabbit held aloft by the ears. The light and the pain made his eyes swim. But he could see the butcher's angry face too well.

"A heel of pork marching off by itself yesterday," the butcher thundered at him. "A sausage today! Nibbling away me profits bit by bit, day by day. Did you think I was blind? Or daft? Oh, you villain, you *will* pay!" The man panted as he rummaged on a sawdust-covered table with one hand and held the struggling boy in the other.

"Why not just hand him over to the Runners?" a woman's voice asked.

"Aye, I will that," the butcher muttered. "But first I've a lesson to learn the wretch. Hiding in me wall, like a rat, creeping out of a night to steal me blind. Oh, I'll show him good!"

He flung the boy down so he could seize up a cleaver. The boy, frantic now, bounced up and ran. He was grabbed by a hand and hauled back. That hand was pinned to a block by the butcher's own hard hand. The cleaver rose—and fell.

The boy neither screamed nor screeched. The butcher frowned, raised his hand, and looked down. But before he could raise the cleaver again, the boy realized he was free. A second later he was gone, flying out the door of the shop, trailing blood.

The butcher pursued, but the boy disappeared into the milling crowd that was always in the streets at the market of a morning.

He ran and ran, and only then did he cry out. He held his hand and sobbed and sobbed. . . .

"Wake up, Amyas! It's only a dream," another boy's voice whispered, as a hand shook his shoulder.

He sat up sharply and looked around wildly. Then he relaxed.

"Yes, lad, it was only a dream," a man's deep voice said softly. "Don't worry, you're safe with us."

Amyas lay back again, his heartbeat slowing. It was all right. This was familiar, it was real, he was safe. He was in a cell in Newgate Prison, on a heap of straw that he shared with two other boys and the man. Tomorrow he would be taken from this place in chains to begin a long journey. He'd been sentenced to transportation to New South Wales. He'd leave in the morning, but he was on familiar ground now, and among friends.

"Aye. It was only a dream," he reassured them, flashing a smile so the youngest boy wouldn't look so worried. "I get it from time to time," he explained. "A thing that happened years ago, when I was just a tyke working a kid lay. Funny, but I still dream about it when I get scared. I suppose I am, a bit, about tomorrow. Not to worry. I'll be fine now."

"But you're still a boy, Amyas," the man said. "So leave the worrying to me. We'll do. We'll be leaving England, but will survive the trip. We'll get to the Antipodes and will flourish there. You'll see. And then we'll come home, in triumph. We *will* come home again. Just stay with us. With me and my son, and your brother, of course. In unity there is strength."

Amyas nodded. He knew that. He believed this man. The fellow seemed honest, in his fashion. He was strong and smart, and safe to trust, because he didn't fancy lads either. He had a son, too, and was good to those who helped him. Amyas and his brother had helped them both. They knew Newgate, after all, and for all the man's cleverness and strength, he'd needed someone to tell him how to get on during his first days there so he could keep his shirt, and his son, and his own life safe from the other prisoners. And so now they were a unit, the four of them. A gang had a better chance than any man or boy alone.

Amyas settled back down in the straw and curled in a knot, knees to chest. He closed his eyes. Only then did he unclench his hand. He unfurled it like a bruised flower opening to the sun and slid it under his other arm. He kept it close to his body, next to his heart, and the secret blade he'd hidden there. He would sleep now because he was comforted; the man had only said truth.

Amyas thought what he always did these days as he gave himself up to sleep, so he could get through the night. "We'll come home, in triumph. We *will* come home again." The words hummed through his mind, simple as a rosary, potent as a prayer, with even more faith and hope in it for him.

They were throwing him out of England. But they wouldn't be hanging him, and that was something. Although the journey was said to be a dire one and the land he was going to was halfway round the world and inhospitable, he'd survive it as he'd survived so much before. And he would prosper. One day he would be able to steer his own destiny, and men and women would look up to him. And one day he would come back again, too.

Then he'd be able to go home, at last. He'd have to find it first, of course, but he would, he promised himself. And on that promise, he slept, dreamlessly, until morning, when he would begin his long journey.

Chapter 1

London, 1816

"It's time I went home," he said.

The room was dark and hot, and stank of smoke and too many men crammed together for too long. The windows were covered with thick draperies, so no one could see out. But one man knew what time it was. Amyas St. Ives filled his pockets, pushed back from the gaming table, and announced he was leaving.

"Aye, with all our money," another gamester at the table grumbled as he eyed the diminished pile of coins in front of him.

"Leave the lad be. He had the Devil's own luck with the dice," a thickset gentleman muttered, looking up at

7

the departing man with bleary eyes. "We'll even up the score next time, St. Ives." Then he blinked against the guttering candlelight and groaned. "Damme if the play didn't run so deep it stole my wits. Forgot the hour entirely. Must be dawn or past it." He fumbled, trying to dip two fingers into a waistcoat pocket that was stretched tautly over his ample stomach. "Damme if I ain't been robbed," he exclaimed. "My watch is gone!"

Amyas paused, reached into his own pocket, and drew out a golden watch. He flipped it to the seated man. "Here it is. You lost it, all right, to me. Remember?"

The other men laughed as the heavyset fellow turned red. "No, no," he protested, handing back the watch. "Now I remember, lost it fair and squarely. It's yours, St. Ives. I'll win it back tomorrow night."

"Keep it," Amyas said. He stretched his long limbs and stifled a yawn. "At least, keep it safe for me. Because we won't meet at a table again for a long time. As I said, I'm going home."

A dark young man sitting at the table suddenly looked up from counting his winnings.

"Aye," Amyas told him. "All the way home. I'm going back to Cornwall, gents. London town won't see me soon again."

"You, rusticate for long? In a pig's eye," the thickset man said on a laugh. "Ain't a Hell or a bawdy house big enough to keep your interest in a backwater like that for long. Don't know why you're going at all, come to think on. Nobody we know lives there, and I didn't think you did. You always win, so I know you ain't got pockets to let neither, so you ain't going there on a repairing lease . . . Unless you're getting shackled?" he added, looking up with interest. "Who's the lucky girl?"

"I may find out," Amyas said lightly. "That, among other things. Give you good night. I mean, good morning, gentlemen."

Amyas shook hands with the thickset man, sketched a bow to the others, and left the room. He took his hat and cape from a footman, then left the gloom of the private gaming Hell and trotted up a short stair to the street.

The dark young gentleman who had been at the hazard table fell into step beside him. "Amyas," he said, "you're not, really. Going to Cornwall, I mean."

"Oh, but I am," Amyas said, blinking against the sudden gray light. He took a deep breath. "Even London smells good at dawn, doesn't it? Lord! I've missed filling my lungs with clean, sweet air. I'm ready to leave town for more reasons than even I knew."

"I also long for the smell of open fields sometimes. But Cornwall? You've got to be joking."

"No jest, Daffyd," Amyas said, as they walked up the street together. "You knew I always meant to go there one day. So why not now? We've sorted out things here, and the future is ours, at last. We're back in England, with no debts, no worries. We've seen our friends restored to their rightful places. We've got plenty of money and respectability, or at least, the best kind money can buy."

"Money and friendship," Daffyd corrected him.

"Yes, well, being friends with an earl helps wonderfully. We're not exactly acceptable, but we're admitted to most high places."

"Because they don't know what we are. They'd toss us out the door if they knew we were convicts."

"We *were*," Amyas agreed. "And what of it? We're not now. And we're not lying about who we are."

"We're not telling, neither."

Amyas shrugged. "Why should we? Look, we were in and out of the nick a few times in our youth, true. And it's only bad luck I picked a pocket that had a pound note in it and showed it to you. They nabbed you for holding it and me for lifting it, and it was transportation for us, true. But you were eleven and I had only a year or so more to my name."

"Old enough to be hanged," Daffyd muttered. He was a dark, trim young man of medium height, with a thin, aristocratic nose, shining blue-black hair, and startlingly blue eyes

"Aye," Amyas said. "But we were lucky. We did our time and earned our pardons, and now we're not convicts. Now we're only gents of indeterminate origin."

"We're determinate enough for the Quality," his companion said glumly. "They know we don't have 'names.' Men with names use them. Them what don't are looking for trouble. Don't look at me like that," he told Amyas. "It's what some gentry mort told me the other night, when she didn't recognize my name. She looked like she expected me to devour her, too."

"And did you?"

The dour face broke into a grin. "No. But she wanted me to. It was as much fun disappointing her as obliging her would have been. No, more, I think. She was dead respectable. If I'd had her, there'd have been enough weeping, wailing, and bemoaning to raise the dead, or at least her family, ten seconds after. She was a society virgin. Having her would have got me a bucket of tears down my neck and another stretch in Newgate, or a quick wedding. That would be worse. I don't want marriage with the likes of her, nor would she with me, if she'd a brain in her head."

"You're too sour, Daffy, always were."

"Too realistic, you mean. Look you, Amyas. You and I, we're considered low because we *are* low. We may be rich now, and a bit educated. But we ain't well-bred, and there's no getting around it. We can talk like gents because we've the gift of mockery. But don't be fooled like those we're fooling. We come from the gutters, and we're lucky not to be back in them—not to mention on the gallows, which is where we were bound before we met up with good fortune."

He shook his head. "A chance in a million we'd be thrown into Newgate with a fellow who inherited an earldom. But we took the chance when it came our way, not that any of us knew it then. It was the best bargain we ever made. We taught him how to get on in chains, he taught us manners and letters. But you can't teach blood. We're a pair of mongrels, Amyas, you and I. Mongrels who were convicts, transported to the Antipodes and come back rich, against all odds. And no matter what money we have or manners we ape, if the nobs knew, they wouldn't have the time of day for us. They might box with Gentleman Jackson and learn cursing from coachmen, hang around taverns with the rabble, and fancy common wenches as mistresses, but that's only amusement. They don't want such as us in their homes."

Amyas raised a tawny eyebrow. "I never heard you say so much at once. Been brooding about it, have you?"

Daffyd nodded and rolled his shoulders. "Suppose I have. It's been fun living with the Quality, but it's starting to make me itch."

"Exactly," Amyas said. "Which is why I'm going."

"No," Daffyd said. "Were that it, I wouldn't open my mummer. But the thing is, you're looking for something that isn't there."

"You don't think I had a mother and father?" Amyas said pleasantly enough, though Daffyd saw a muscle knot in the side of his lean jaw.

Amyas St. Ives was an amiable-looking man, but Daffyd knew just how lethal he could be if provoked. Amyas was a tall, loose-limbed fellow, with thick, sun-streaked gold hair. He was athletic and well made, but walked with a slight hitch in his long-legged gait. These days, so soon after the war, that wasn't unusual in any man of military age. But whether it was war or worldly experience that had caused it, that wasn't the only reason he looked as though he'd been around the street a few times.

The lean tanned face might have been classically handsome before his nose had been broken, and spectacularly. That nose was flattened at the bridge and artistically bent. Rather than disfiguring him, it added interest to an already striking countenance. His jaw was long, but the full lips were shapely, and his sleepy eyes were ringed with dark lashes. When he opened those eyes they were wide, and turquoise blue.

He was dressed as befitted a gentleman, in a tight blue jacket, high white neckcloth, silken waistcoat, fitted buff breeches, and polished half boots. He usually wore kid gloves and carried a walking stick, though he never removed his gloves and never used the stick. Still, though he was got up like a man of style and fashion, his entire manner seemed careless. He was laconic. Life seemed to amuse him. But obviously not at the moment, in spite of his faint smile.

His companion was tense and seemed to walk on his toes. Amyas's change of expression didn't account for that, and Daffyd was wary.

"I know you didn't hatch from an egg," Daffyd said curtly. "It just never mattered to me who your kin was, or I'd never have been so quick to call you brother all those years ago. I've seen you through a lot since, some mad starts, too. But I tell you it's daft for you to go hunting for your parents when all you've got to go on is your first name."

"Only a name, but a significant one," Amyas said, holding up one gloved finger. "How many men do you know called Amyas? None, nor ever met one, right? I had the name before I got to the foundling hospital; they said I knew it then, though not much else. It's from an old Cornish folk song. That's why I took the name 'St. Ives' to go with it. It's in Cornwall. Now, if I add my age to my real name, it shouldn't be that hard to find my origins. I've hunted up harder things. All I have to find is a family who had an infant boy that year and named him Amyas."

"It's a fool's errand," Daffyd said brusquely. "Cornwall's too big. Like trying to find one shell on a beach. Maybe she who gave you up had good reason and kept you secret as a clam. Ever think of that? So how will asking now, almost three decades later, tell you anything? You were found in London, a long way from Cornwall. Maybe your ma's from London. Maybe she just thought it was a nice name because she heard it in a song. Give it up, save your time and energy."

"For what? More gambling, whoring, and drinking?" Amyas asked quizzically. "Lovely fun, but I've had enough. I need some diversion from diversion," he said with a smile. "The war's over, Napoleon's stashed on Elba, so there's no need for me to ferret out news for His Majesty anymore. I've won my pardon and have more money than I can think of things to spend it on. What shall I do? Hang around London and find new things to gamble on and new brothels to spend my nights in? Let the earl entertain me? I won't ask more of him. Our brother's a newlywed; should I sit in his parlor? Or maybe you think I should go back to New South Wales? I may, in time. But not yet."

"Come with me," Daffyd urged. "I know just how you feel. I'll hunt up some cousins. I've a notion to go out on the road again for a spell myself."

"Daffy, my brother, you may find traveling with your gypsy cousins a treat. I found it interesting, but no offense, not something I long to do again. I like a roof over my head that doesn't rattle when the rain comes down, a soft bed that only moves when I want it to, and softer females to help me make it move. The one time I so much as smiled at one of your gypsy lasses, I almost lost my smile, and my head, for it. No, thank you."

Daffyd's smile was a white flash in the rising light. "You wanted more than a smile. Gypsy lasses are as virtuous as society ones, though no one but gypsies believe it."

Amyas smiled, too. "Oh, I believe it now. But I'm off to Cornwall," he said with decision. "A new world to explore. I haven't been many places."

Daffyd made a scornful sound.

"No, no," Amyas said. "Think about it. The first place I remember was that foundling hospital. We two met in the streets of London after, but we never went farther than those few streets, though they seemed the world to us then. We did go to the Antipodes. But traveling in chains in the bottom of a prison ship isn't exactly sightseeing, unless seeing rats and corpses is considered such. When we won our freedom, I was able to travel and see New South Wales, true. And I did, working for Geoffrey—I mean, the earl. But deserts and forests, mines and shores start to look the same after a while."

"You traveled when you agreed to work for Army Intelligence," Daffyd protested. "Though I never knew why they called those lackwits that."

"No argument there," Amyas said mildly. "But I had to think of getting information or giving it while watching my back, and not the sights. Here in London, when I was young, I was too busy looking for food to see anything else. I never really got to explore for my own sake, not in my whole life. Except for that trip with your cousin this spring," he said ruefully. "And then I only saw open roads and fields. I want to see Cornwall. This is my chance. Who knows what tomorrow will bring?"

"That's a Newgate lag talking," Daffyd said with a frown. "Never knowing where his next meal or chance to pinch some lolly for one is coming from. Never knowing when he's going to be hanged, or if he's free, when he'll be nabbed. You have to start thinking like a gent."

"Exactly," Amyas said triumphantly. "If I'm going to stay in England and play the gent, I ought to have some idea of the country I'm living in. And," he added softly, "if I can get an idea of where I came from, so much the better."

"It's not enough to know who you are?" Daffyd asked.

Amyas stopped in the middle of the street. There was none of the usual laughter in his eyes as he looked at his adopted brother. "But I don't. You know who your father was, Daffy. You may not have liked him, but you knew him. Christian didn't know his father was going to inherit an earldom, but he knew damn well who he was. Most men do. You just said a man with a name uses it. You have one, Daffy. It might not be Quality, but it's yours. I don't have that. I might as well have crawled out from under a rock, so people think when they hear I was a foundling. As though it was my fault I have no name except the one I remember, and no family except for those who chose to call me brother and son. We've lived in gutters and prisons, you and I. We live in the best places now. So you know what I say is true wherever we go."

Daffyd scowled and looked down at the pavement.

"None is held in such contempt as one who has no name," Amyas said. "Worse than contempt, it's as though I were nothing. I want to be something. Let me at least try."

"Don't see as how I can stop you," Daffyd muttered.

"Don't know as how you could," Amyas agreed, with his usual smile. He drew a gold watch from his pocket. "But I'm not setting out for Cornwall right now. I've things to get done before I do. So, I'll see you at dinner, at my place?"

"So you will." Daffyd's eyes narrowed as he looked at the watch. "That's the one I saw you give back to Fanshawe at the gaming table!"

"It is," Amyas said airily. "But you didn't see me take it back again when I shook his hand and said good-bye, did you? Neither did he. Here, give it back to him," he said, as he handed it to Daffyd. "Tell him you found it on the floor or some such. He's too buffle-headed to be anything but grateful. Here, don't look at me like that! I wasn't trying to rob him—I did that fine enough at the hazard table. Just trying to see if I lost my touch. I haven't," he said with satisfaction. "See you at dinner, then." He lifted a finger to his forehead in a salute and, swinging his walking stick jauntily, strolled off into the rising day.

"It's a big place," Daffyd said, as he and Amyas leaned over the map they'd spread on the table after their finished dinners had been cleared. They were in a comfortable parlor in a flat in one of London's better districts. It was clearly a bachelor establishment, because though it was neat, there were no flowers on the tables or ornaments of any kind. The paintings on the walls were of horses, and a cheroot lay smoldering in a bowl on the table. No female would have allowed that.

"You could spend the rest of your life tramping those moors, climbing cliffs, and riding the shores," Daffyd said, jabbing a finger at each feature he mentioned. "There's a prison on the moors. Dartmoor. No one wanted to go there, remember? Worse than Newgate, they said. Back of nowhere. Even if you escape, you don't get far."

He traced the borders of Cornwall with one finger.

"Aside from the moors in the middle, there are villages hugging the shores, north and south. There are steep cliffs there, caves in them, too, so secret only them that know them can find them. It's so wild, they once had cannibals there! Lived there for generations. S'truth!" he said, crossing his heart.

"I asked around today, and so I was told," Daffyd went on. "Fishermen and farmers live there now. What have you got to say to them? Much good it would do even if you did. The people are close as clams, at least to strangers. Half of them work the smuggling lay. God knows what the other half do; they don't talk to anyone but their own." His dark blue eyes were intense as he looked at Amyas. "Give it up. There's worse than not knowing where you came from. Sometimes, knowing is worse."

Amyas shook his head. He kept staring at the map. "I've a notion I'll find something there, Daffy. I don't know what it is, but I swear I can feel my thumbs tingling: pricking, like the witch said in that play we saw at Drury Lane the other night." He laughed, but Daffyd didn't. "Ah, don't worry. I know it's a long chance and a dim one, but I was always one for playing against the odds. What am I gambling, after all? Only a few weeks. Little enough to lose in search of a dream, don't you think?"

He straightened, put his hands on the small of his back, and stretched.

"I'll take the summer to roam around asking questions. I'll write from each place I visit, so that if those cannibals get me, you'll know where to search for my bones. Hope I'm tasty," he added, with a smile.

"You take life so easy, then you get caught up in a mad chase like this," Daffyd said, shaking his head. "But if you only mean to go for two months, so be it." His glance grew shrewd. "You told those flats we were gaming with you might choose a bride on your travels. Never say."

Amyas laughed. "Never's a hard word. Soon as you say it, you find you don't mean it. So I don't say it. I'm not searching for a bride . . . exactly. But I wouldn't mind finding one."

Daffyd's dark brows rose.

"Aye," Amyas said lightly. "Well, why not? I've got enough money to buy an abbey, yet I live in these simple rooms without a maid or a footman. I wouldn't have anyone at all, because you know I can do for myself, but Old Gibbs is a perfect gentleman's gentleman for me—maybe because I'm no real gentleman and neither is he. He was a good enough bloke in the old days and needs work now. So he sees to my clothing, brings food in from the cook shops, and keeps the place neat. I can't bring myself to hire on more, but it would be a natural thing to do if I had a wife to keep in style."

"But finding a bride in Cornwall, of all places," Daffyd said. "You can't mean that. You have your pick of women here in London."

"No, I don't," Amyas said, looking at the map again. "I'm an ex-convict, a man with no name, and maimed, to boot—or rather to foot. I walk with a hobble, and have other 'interesting reminders of my past on my person'—as our adopted father once put it." He grinned. "A highborn lass wouldn't look at me twice."

"Liar," Daffyd said. "They look at you right enough."

"But that's all they can or will do. At least the decent ones. I'm not talking about ones who are looking for sport."

"Well, there are thousands of others here in London," Daffyd protested.

"Yes. But not ones of good families and breeding," Amyas said quietly. "And I've a notion to marry one of those. Maybe I'll find her in the countryside. Strikes me they won't be so toplofty there."

Daffyd stared. "*You?*" he asked. "Looking to marry up?"

"Why not?" Amyas said. "It would be hard for me to marry down." He laughed at Daffyd's expression. "I don't expect to find a lady willing to be my bride. But a good solid merchant's daughter or a rich tradesman's niece is often as well-bred as a lady, and won't look for so high in a mate. I'm a realist. Whatever I find out about myself, I don't think I'm a lost prince or heir to a title. That doesn't happen except in books."

He held up a hand. "Aye, I know Geoffrey turned out to be an earl, but though he didn't expect to, he always knew it *could* happen. I know better. Even if I find it, I doubt my name will amount to much, and I want my children to have better than I did." He smiled. "That wouldn't be hard. But I want them better in all ways. And finally having a family wouldn't be bad either."

"You have me," Daffyd said. "And Christian and the earl."

"I know, and I'm grateful. But I mean a big family, a real one, a family born, not made. I want my children protected six ways out of seven, should anything happen to me."

"I can't argue with that." Daffyd sighed. "So. I can be packed by daybreak."

"Oh no!" Amyas said in alarm. "You don't approve of my mission, you don't really want to go to Cornwall, and you don't like the gentry. It would be a disaster for both of us. No, thank you. And I do thank you, because I know what a sacrifice you're willing to make. I'll do fine on my own. I'll be back before autumn. Wish me well, that's all I want."

"That, without saying," Daffyd said, holding out his hand, "But I'll say it. Good luck."

Amyas extended a gloved hand, and they shook, solemnly.

"Now," Amyas said, "shall we see how many gold watches I can win tonight?"

Daffyd shrugged "Why not? You'll have to keep time on your travels so you know when it's time to come home."

"Home?" Amyas asked quizzically. "Is London that?"

"If it isn't London, then what is it?" Daffyd asked in return.

"*That*," Amyas said, "is just what I want to find out."

Chapter 2

He fell in love right away. Amyas rode down long lanes by the sea, and everywhere he turned the sight delighted him. It had been that way since he'd crossed the Tamar and had gone into Cornwall. He was sure he'd felt that moment even before he'd seen it on his map. That was how in love with the place he was. He stopped at inns or farmhouses, and sometimes slept in haylofts. Whether the nights he spent were comfortable or not, his heart remained light. He was, he realized, truly enchanted.

The high, jagged cliffs, the rolling hills, the rocky shores, the sudden glimpse of hidden beaches that opened themselves to spectacular views of the sea as he rode past them: If he had to come from anywhere, he thought, this was where he wished it was. Not only because he saw a likeness in his mirror to so many of the fair-haired strangers he saw, but because it was as though the land itself was in his bones.

Or so he hoped.

"Folly, of course, to think this is where my mother came from," he told the vicar of St. Edgyth, as he'd told many such men since he'd come to Cornwall. "But a kind folly, I think," he added, flashing his winning smile, "because this is where I'd like to find her family."

"That's flattering, Mr. St. Ives," the vicar said. "And I hope it's so for your sake. But I must have her maiden name or I won't find her in my register. If she wasn't born here, that would be the next best way to find any mention of her. Although, in truth, I can't recollect seeing a 'St. Ives,' either. You are certain she wasn't married here?"

"No," Amyas said truthfully, before he invented more. "It's too bad I never knew my father, and that she died so young, and that both their families were so small. Worse luck still that my father's sister never referred to her by her first name. It's another pity that my dear aunt, the last of my father's family, at least so far as I know, passed away before I was old enough to ask more."

He lied with the ease of familiarity. Lies were a tool he'd used before. And these were ones he'd told other vicars, innkeepers, many more men he'd met on the road since he'd come to Cornwall. The language he heard spoken as he ventured farther into

Cornwall defeated him, of course. But most people he met were too polite to speak their murmurous tongue in front of a stranger. Their accents when they spoke English might be thick, but he soon understood, because he had an "ear." Given time he could understand most dialects. The one he heard here was soft, sounding more Irish than foreign to him. And vicars and barkeeps usually spoke so that everyone could understand them.

"But surely you can look to see if there are any other Amyases in your register?" Amyas now urged the old man. "Or perhaps remember if you've heard tell of one in the district? It's an unusual name."

The old man shook his head. "So it is, and so I'd have noticed it. The records go back to 1560; I suppose I could look again. But I'm almost positive that I've only heard the song, alas." His smile was sad. "Yes, very like the song it is, too, isn't it? 'Alas, you and I, my life, and Amyas.'"

They stood quietly for a moment. The day was soft and breezy, a warm wind ruffled the scarlet poppies' petals on the hill, and scattered Amyas's golden hair. In spite of all the flowers, the scent was of the sea they could see glinting silver and blue in the distance. The churchyard they stood in was filled with dark tombstones, filed to wafers by the passing years and chafed thinner by constant sea winds.

"Alas, indeed," Amyas said. His smile was genuinely regretful. "This is a lovely village. I'd have liked my roots to have been here. Well, then I must move on. I'll go on to see St. Michael's Mount, then wend my way back to London along the north coast road. I'll traipse the moors when I can, but I feel this is where I belong. I feel it in my blood . . . foolish, isn't it?"

"No, no," the old man assured him. "It may well be so. I wish you luck in your search. Have you a place to stay for the night?"

"I thought the inn in your village," Amyas said. "Do you recommend it?"

"Heartily," the old man said with relief, pleased that he could do something for this amiable stranger. "You might find more modern comforts if you ride on, but the Jolly Eel is a clean establishment, and the innkeeper's wife is a wonderful cook. All the local lads go there of an evening. Perhaps they could help in your search. Most are simple fishermen, but they've lived here for generations and know other families along the coast."

"A fine idea," Amyas said, bowing. "Thank you for your help."

"I did nothing," the old man protested. "Should you like to stop with me a while and have some sherry? The sun is lowering."

"Thank you. But I think I should hurry on to secure my lodgings before the sun sinks any lower."

The old man laughed. "Little fear of not doing so, sir. We were once a bustling port, but not many travelers stop here now. Times change. The sea keeps changing the coast, and people change their destinations. I've lived here for decades and never saw the inn filled, though they say it was hard to get a room there in its prime. That was a long time ago. Other ports now get the shipping, and the tourists. Visitors on their way to St. Michael's Mount stop at St. Mawes, or rush on farther and rest at the turn in the coast they call the Lizard before they get to Land's End. We are, I'm afraid, a forgotten village."

"You shouldn't feel bad," Amyas said. "You should be glad of the peace and quiet."

"Ah, but you're from London, so the peace of this place is a novelty to you. Not many outsiders appreciate it. We are far too quiet for this modern age, I suppose."

"Not for me," Amyas said, then, as though it was just a sudden thought, continued, "I'll stay at the inn and look forward to a good talk with the local folk . . . but . . ." He hesitated. "I have noticed that people in these parts seemed disinclined to talk to a stranger." He raised a gloved hand before the vicar could speak. "Now, I know Cornwall has a wild coast, and don't doubt that revenue officers masquerade as whatever they can to wheedle information out of innocent men. But I'm looking for nothing but information about my lost family.

"The earl of Egremont is my foster father, and will vouch for me," Amyas added. "I promise you, I'm no part of the government and haven't been since the late wars—except for paying my taxes. Speaking of that—I think there isn't a bottle of my wine in my cellars that ever saw a tax stamp! Like most men in London, I've never asked my wine merchant about it. I just pay my bill and he sends me fine French wine. I don't ask where he got it, only that I get it, and if that's a crime, why then, throw me in prison."

It amazed even Amyas that he could say that with a straight face, so he hurried on, "And if that's a crime, prison will be too full of my fellow Londoners to take me in. My interest in this district is only in its past. But how do I convince the local folk of that? I hate to dine in stony silence, with every man's back turned to me. Believe me, that has happened."

"Yes." The vicar sighed. "I can see it might have. You're right. That well may be why we don't have more visitors. Our local folk are less than friendly to strangers. It is true we have a certain reputation for smuggling, but that was long ago," he added hastily, looking around as though there might be someone else on the hillside with them, apart from the birds in the treetops. "Our menfolk support themselves by fishing or farming. But sometimes the fish don't run well, and the weather kills crops, and there's need . . ."

The vicar fell still, obviously thinking deeply. "And yet, tourists make for good industry, too," he mused aloud. "Just look at the towns they flock to, not one of them without something to sell. And all does sell; visitors will even buy seashells and bits of driftwood with the name of the town painted on them! I've seen it . . ."

He eyed Amyas, seeing a well-set-up young gentleman of obvious means and manners, resplendent in his high beaver hat, tailored jacket, white linen, tan gloves, buff breeches, and high, riding boots. Amyas stood tall, holding his gold-headed walking stick, his clothing unstained by hours of riding. Even his horse seemed to gleam. The old man seemed to come to a decision.

"I'll send a note round to the inn," the vicar said, "and to my parishioners. I have some influence here, though I seldom use it except in matters of morals. But this pertains to that, too," he murmured, talking to himself again. "Welcoming a stranger is something we ought to do as a matter of course. But if it could also help the livelihoods of some folk here, why, it would only be good business sense. And so I shall tell them. Don't worry, Mr. St. Ives," he said decisively, looking at Amyas, "I doubt you'll find yourself without company this night!"

The taproom at the Jolly Eel was crowded that night, packed with local men and some of their women. They were a hard-bitten lot. Life on and near the sea had burnished their faces as brown as the wood on the old mahogany bar and carved almost as many niches on each of them, for the lines of their smiles and frowns to settle in. Their language, when they spoke English, was as salty as the air that blew through the open door and windows, opened to let out the smoke from peaty fire in the hearth.

A gentleman from London would stand out in such a crowd, even surrounded by people. Amyas did. He was also left out, literally, because while the babble of voices was loud, few in the crowded room spoke to him. When they did, he found none of them had ever known anyone with a similar name, though several could hum or sing a few bars of the old song. It was clear that no matter what the vicar's decree, few entirely believed he wasn't an excise man, or didn't have some other ulterior motive. He couldn't blame them. He wouldn't have trusted himself if he were one of them; he looked like a swell nob in a crowd of peasants.

Amyas was annoyed with himself. He could have dressed in less elegant clothes and fit in better. He decided he'd change when he got on the road again so he could go into the next village in less conspicuous clothing. He was wondering how long he should stay and drink before he went to bed when a more urbane voice than he'd heard so far that evening addressed him.

"Mr. St. Ives," the hearty voice said, "allow me to introduce myself. Hugo Tremellyn, at your service."

Amyas looked up to see a stocky, dark, middle-aged man looking at him. Amyas's trained eye immediately saw that though the man was heavy, it was mostly muscle beneath his clothing. He was broad in both shoulder and beam, and had a pleasant, broad, tanned face. He was dressed well, if casually, in loose-fitting jacket and breeches, with a kerchief around his throat, in the style of a country gentleman.

"The vicar sent a note, asking us to greet you civilly, and assuring us you weren't bent on making mischief," Tremellyn said in a deep bass voice. "I came to make your acquaintance." He stuck out a thick callused hand, and Amyas took it. Then the man stepped back and studied Amyas from head to boot tops. He smiled wider, showing strong white teeth. "He also told us about your business here. Now, myself, I never met any Amyas but you. But my fleet can be seen from here to Penzance, 'round the Mount and to Newquay, following the fish, and my men go to many ports. I'd be pleased to make inquiries for you."

Amyas returned the smile and stifled an inward sigh. Now he'd have to make excuses for leaving so soon. He'd no intention of lingering here waiting for word from the local squire or whatever the fellow was. He already itched to be on the road again.

"I *have* heard the name used in conversation, y'see," Tremellyn added, with a frown, "although for the life of me, I can't remember where or when."

Amyas stood up straighter.

"Tell you what!" the fellow said with animation, "Why not drop round for luncheon at my house tomorrow? I'll have more of a chance to think on it, and we'll have a chance to talk."

"That would be kind of you," Amyas said.

"Good, good," Tremellyn said with pleasure. "We take our meal at two. And so you must take the road out front and ride toward the sea. Go two miles until you see a stone gatehouse, from the old days. When you get there, just go right and take the winding road on past it. Ours is a stone house high on the hill, with nothing but the sky around it and the sea below. Two, then?"

Amyas nodded, "That would be fine."

"Good, good," Tremellyn said, "Now I must be off. My girls will be wondering about me being out so late. I've a lovely daughter; two lovely young girls at home, in fact, who'll be happy to meet you," he added, on a wink. "We don't get many strangers hereabout, y'see."

Amyas retained his smile with difficulty and stifled a groan. Two lovely daughters. He knew what it meant when a father said that. The pair probably looked like the pike their father caught and conversed in giggles. But he'd suffered worse, for less. "Thank you," he said pleasantly, "I'll be there." *And soon gone*, he added to himself.

He had few hopes, but it was hard for Amyas to be depressed about his appointment when he rode out to keep it the next day. He tilted his head to the sky and felt the sun on his face as he rode past the old stone gatehouse. The view seemed to go on forever, and the world looked wide and warm. Sunlight glinted off the endless sea in the background, a few clouds that

meant no harm scudded past on high, and the world
smelled so fine, Amyas thought he'd have been hum-
ming on his way to meet the hangman. So two eager
unwed daughters didn't trouble him much, no matter
how provincial, ugly, or foolish they might be.

Tremellyn's house was impressive, though it
wasn't a manor or a mansion. Made of gray stone,
with a stout roof, not thatched like others in the area,
it spread out on the hilltop, dominating it. It wasn't a
gentleman's house, or a manor, but it looked the
home of a successful man. Amyas relaxed. He'd
learned how to behave in a gentleman's house, but
knew he'd be more comfortable in this one. *If*, that
was, the daughters weren't too obvious. He had no
doubt their father had invited him home for them.
The problem was that whatever they were, he could
only be polite and try not to raise any expectations.

He could dally with duchesses, and had done, and
play with lower-class lasses of all ages, and enjoyed
doing it, too. But he couldn't spare even a lingering
glance for a respectable burgher's daughter. Not if he
didn't want to find himself at the altar with a
prospective father-in-law behind him, a pistol pressed
against his kidneys.

Amyas rode up the drive to Tremellyn's house. A
collection of dogs came racing out to confront his
horse, and were whistled back by an old man, working in the garden. The old fellow tipped his battered
hat, and herded the dogs to a stable to the back of the
house. Amyas was impressed; Tremellyn had enough

blunt to hire a gardener. He was further impressed when a boy came out of the stables to take his horse. A stable, hired help to keep it, here in the middle of nowhere? Tremellyn had money. Amyas wondered if it came from boats, fish, or smuggled goods. He'd feel more at home if it was contraband that made the man rich.

A neat young maid showed him into the house, took his hat, and led him to a sunny parlor. Tremellyn awaited him there, as did a young woman. Amyas was impressed, again.

He'd been expecting a room filled with hand-hewn furniture, embellished with seashells as ornaments, with maybe a few landscapes hung on whitewashed walls. Instead, the salon was as handsomely furnished as any drawing room in London. The couches and chairs were graceful and gilded. The floors were covered with imported carpets; the walls were papered, and hung with fine portraits of lords and ladies from centuries past. Amyas knew worth, and he knew swag, and his estimate of Tremellyn rose higher. The portraits weren't of any Tremellyns of Cornwall, unless the family descended from noble families on the Continent. This was fine art.

And, he noticed as the young woman rose from her chair, the living lady was very fine, too.

"Mr. St. Ives," Tremellyn said, greeting him, "welcome. Allow me to present my daughter, Grace."

Grace Tremellyn sank in a curtsey. Amyas bowed, but didn't take his eyes from her. She was dark as her father, but shapely. Young, maybe a mite too young for him, he thought. He was seven-and-twenty now, or so he estimated. At least he was sure he hadn't breached thirty as yet, but she looked no more than seventeen, if that. Then he remembered that some of the Quality married off their females young, especially if they bloomed as pretty and early as this one. She wore a pink gown, and curtseyed like a lady born. Her long-lashed eyes fixed on Amyas as she rose. And when she did, her sudden smile produced twin dimples in her fair cheeks. Amyas found himself suddenly much more interested in the Tremellyn household.

"Grace, here's the gentleman who's searching for his lost family," Tremellyn said. "Sit down, sit down," he told Amyas, indicating a chair. "I told my girls about you, sir, and they are all sympathy. We know the worth of family here in Cornwall. Tremellyns have been here as long as the sea itself, and I myself can name all my ancestors back to the year dot."

Amyas couldn't resist the urge to take Tremellyn down a notch, and not only because anyone bragging about their families always set his back up. He took a chair, sat, smiled, crossed his legs, and looked up at the portraits. "Your kin, sir?" he asked innocently.

"Lord, no!" Tremellyn laughed. "My people didn't have the time or the notion, or the money to sit back and pay some fellow to paint them. They were too busy trying to stay afloat. No, I'm a self-made man, St. Ives, and proud of it. These handsome folks," he

said, hitching a thumb at the portraits on the wall,
"had the ease and the coin to get famous artists to
paint them. But their descendants didn't have the
wits to keep them in the family. Not I. What I have, I
made, and I hold. And spend where it does the most
good. The girls like the pictures, and so do I."

"As do I," Amyas said, appreciating his host even
more.

Grace Tremellyn showed her dimples again.
"Yours is such a romantic story, Mr. St. Ives," she said
in a wispy little voice that he had to strain to hear.
"Just think! Trying to trace your family by your
Christian name! It *is* an unusual one. And names do
run in families. I have heard it before, and so I told
my father. It was Will Penhall of the Blue Lady, out of
Coverack, who mentioned a crew member of his by
that name, I'm sure of it. Remember, Papa?"

Amyas stilled.

"It may well have been him," Tremellyn said, con-
sidering. "But I'm not so sure it was. We'll find out.
How long are you staying in the area?" he asked
Amyas.

Amyas thought quickly. Grace Tremellyn was smiling at him, her father looking hopeful. He didn't
know if Tremellyn remembered who had been named
Amyas, or even if he knew anything of the sort. But
the house was fine, the man had means, the family,
though not noble, was old as the granite cliffs the
house rested on. And the girl was lovely. He could do
worse.

"I certainly can stay on long enough to learn more," Amyas said. "My time, after all, is all my own."

"That so?" Tremellyn said, looking interested. "You've no work to get back to then?"

Amyas decided to look insulted as he answered, in his best imitation of a nobleman's drawl, "No, sir. I have not. I let my investments work for me."

"Very wise, very wise," Tremellyn said, as his daughter smiled even more sunnily at Amyas.

Amyas smiled back at her. *Well, why not?* he thought. He'd seen prettier, and doubtless had known wittier women, and certainly known more sensually appealing females. But he was ready to take a wife, and this girl was charming, and well brought up, and moneyed. And by God, he loved this place!

"Ah! You're late, but welcome." Tremellyn said, looking up to the doorway behind Amyas. "St. Ives, here's our Amber. Amber, here's the gentleman I was telling you about."

Amyas turned his head, and for all his practiced manners and all his guile, he could not for the life of him have spoken one sensible word then. He could only stare at the young woman who stood there.

If Cornwall was all he had hoped to find as his lost homeland, then Amber was all he'd ever wanted in a woman. It was only that he hadn't known it until just that minute. He rose to his feet slowly, too impressed and befuddled to do more than stare at the newcomer.

She was tall for a woman. But the perfect height for

him. Her curling hair, all the colors of blond the sun
could turn it, was pulled back from her face. And
what a face, he thought as he stared. Her complexion
was fair, yet also blushed by the sun, tinted peach
high on her cheeks and forehead. Her eyes were clear,
wide enough for him to see all the changeable colors
of the sea in them as she stared back at him. She had
a straight nose and full rosy lips. Her figure was lush,
with high breasts that made him feel a surge of pure
lust. She wore, he noted belatedly, a blue gown. With
an apron over it. Amyas's breath stilled. He looked
his question at his host.

"Amber is our gift from the sea," Tremellyn said
fondly. "She was found, an infant, on the shore after a
wreck. We get many treasures that way, including the
sea amber her hair reminded me of. I took her home
and she's been like a sister to Grace ever since. And
now she's grown she insists on taking charge of the
kitchen."

"And our lives," Grace added, with a giggle.

Amber smiled at her, then looked back at Amyas. "I
didn't know my first name when I came here," Amber told him. "So there isn't even that to use to find
my family. I'd love to help you find yours, Mr. St.
Ives." Her smile had understanding in it. "We may be
able to. This is the land of the lost and found, as I
should know."

"Thank you," he said calmly, though he felt cold
and cheated. It was really too bad. She was a
foundling with neither name nor history, like him-

self. She was exactly what he did not need. He wanted to marry wisely and well. He had to put the whole notion of anything to do with her from his mind. He'd done such before and could do it again. After all, a man who followed his body and not his brain was a fool. He wouldn't have lived so long if he'd been one. The world was filled with desirable females. He needed more in a wife.

"And I came to tell you luncheon is ready," Amber said.

Amyas turned from her. "Tell me about this other Amyas, please," he asked Tremellyn's real daughter.

Chapter 3

$\sim$

Amber couldn't remember the last time she'd been so angry. She'd been thinking about it for hours. She finally gave up. She needed fresh air. She stopped pacing, threw a shawl over her shoulders, and left her room, taking the short stair down to the kitchen. Amber shushed the old dog that rose from his bed of blankets by the stove to greet her, signaling him to lie down again. He sank back, giving her a reproachful look. But this wasn't the time to go strolling with old Ness. She wanted to be utterly alone. She went to the back door, threw it open, and paced out into the night. And stopped.

A bulky shadow of a man stood by the fence in the moonlit garden, his uplifted head a darker silhouette against the starry sky. The scent of pipe smoke was strong on the salt air.

"Thought you'd come out here," Hugo Tremellyn said calmly, his words accompanied by a puff of smoke.

Amber's shoulders slumped. "That transparent, was I?"

"To me, aye. The fellow's lucky you didn't brain him with the soup tureen. I recollected what you did to young Jim Morgan when he grabbed your book and threw it in the well. Coshed him with the bucket, no less."

Amber smiled in spite of her mood. "Well, I've stopped reacting like that. I was terrified that I'd killed poor Jim, but he only saw double for a day or two. I've learned how to be a lady since. But it's not at all gratifying."

"I should think not," he said amiably.

"The fellow has a right to prefer Grace," she said a little desperately. "Any sane man would. It's just that . . ."

". . . that his eyes near fell out of his head when he saw you, and then he turned to ice when he heard you weren't my daughter," Tremellyn said. "I know. I saw."

She came to stand beside him. "Think he's after money?" she asked softly, as she gazed up at the stars. "He seemed well set up."

"So a fortune hunter would seem," Tremellyn said. "But he looked liked the real thing to me. Not a gent born, maybe, but a man of means, nonetheless." He took a deep draw at his pipe, his next words coming out with the smoke. "He may want to know about us more than about our Gracie, I'm thinking. He could be snooping about the neighborhood trying to get news of the lads."

She nodded. "But if he was after information, then why not try me? Especially once he heard I'm not related to you. If it's news of the local shipping business he's after, why not try to find a wedge he could pry open for information? Here I am, a foundling taken in out of charity, with no name or family of my own here or anywhere. I'd sooner cut off a foot than speak a word that could be taken out of turn about anyone. But he doesn't know that—or us, after all."

Tremellyn frowned, took the pipe out of his mouth, and probed at the bowl with a thick, callused finger. Amber knew that meant he didn't want to speak just yet. She continued.

"I doubt he's an excise man, or works for His Majesty," she said, trying to make her voice sound casual. "Vicar wouldn't have sent him if he thought anything like, and Vicar's observant. So I'm thinking that it might only be the usual: The fellow doesn't want anything to do with a nameless wench. He might have looked at me, but then he froze over when he found out I was an orphan. Seeing how I live with a decent family and am treated like family, he likely realized I wouldn't want to play in the hay with any wandering stranger."

"You were working in the kitchen," Tremellyn mused. "Could be he thought you were used like a servant or treated like one."

"Huh!" she huffed. "You set him straight when you started complaining about my taking over your kitchen. No, if he's looking for a bride, Grace would be his choice."

"No matter that you made his eyes water?"

"Grace is just as easy on the eye, you know." She fell silent.

"Fancy him?" Tremellyn asked quietly.

"How could I? I don't know him," she said on a shrug. "I admit when I came into the room and he stared at me like he recognized me, my heart leapt."

Tremellyn stirred.

Amber added quickly, "Not out of instant love, Mr. Tremellyn! I thought he might have recognized me, is all. I mean, I thought that he might know my mirror image." She laughed, weakly. "I've always fancied that if I had a family, I might have a twin, or a sister, or look just like my mother. That's a common dream amongst foundlings, I hear." She wrapped the shawl more tightly around her shoulders. "So yes, I'd hopes. But when he heard what I was he turned away and proceeded to ignore me, politely, for the rest of the night. That's what made me angry. Why look at me like that, then treat me as if I was serving the meal instead of just supervising the serving of it?"

"Jests aside. Do *you* think we treat you like a servant?"

"Oh no, Mr. Tremellyn!" she said in obvious surprise, wheeling around to face him. "My taking charge of household matters is my decision, as you said. You treat me like a daughter, and have done since the day you found me on the beach. Even though it must be difficult at times, since I'm so officious."

"Officious?" he asked on a chuckle.

She nodded. "I'm a nag and a scold, and I know it. No, don't try to be polite, even Gracie agrees, if with a loving smile. But that's Gracie. She's forgiving. I have a year or two on her, or so everyone estimates, but I've always clucked after her like a broody hen, from the first, haven't I? All the servants say so. She was my living doll to play with and manage. I took her as such from the day I first saw her in her crib. I suppose it was because I needed someone to love."

She shrugged, and went on softly, "All I had was the waterlogged shift on my back and the word 'mama' on my lips when you found me, and that, hardly spoken right, you said. You gave me everything else: my name, and good food, the clothes on my back, the roof over my head, and an education. I can read and write as well as sew and cook, and manage accounts. I don't mind doing it for my family, which is what you and Grace are to me. So I've always tried to earn my keep by making the place comfortable for you."

"You have done that."

She nodded, pleased. "But you got more than you

asked for, I'm afraid. I'm a natural manager, and an utter despot, and I know it. In fact," she said, looking off into the night, "I always wondered if my possessiveness about you both isn't what accounted for you not marrying again."

He started.

"Well," she said quickly, "remember how I tormented poor Widow Stephens that time she came to dinner? She never came here again."

They both were still, thinking about the widow. Both were also remembering how Tremellyn had nevertheless kept up an intimate relationship with her for many a year, though she refused to set foot near his house ever again.

"A bucket of fish guts raining down on a person when she steps over your threshold will do that," Tremellyn finally said.

Amber made a choked sound. Then Tremellyn laughed aloud, so she joined him. She supposed he could laugh about it now, since the widow's reign as his mistress had ended a long time ago. He'd other romantic interests in the village since, which Amber and Grace pretended not to know about.

"But apart from that," he said, "you've nothing to feel guilty about. You filled my house with laughter, took over the running of it as soon as you could walk and talk, and you've been a true friend and sister to Grace. I never want to think of you staying on here because you think you owe me."

"I stay on because I don't want to move on," she

said simply. "You've made it that comfortable for me."

"Not even to set up your own house?" he asked, looking at her sidewise. "Pascoe Piper's been paying particular attentions these days."

She snorted. "Huh! He's been paying them and getting nothing back for a while now. Nor will he."

"He's a fine-looking lad and a good captain."

"So he is, though he catches more bottles of fine French wine than mackerel these days."

"Most of the lads do. The sea's a harsh place to make a shilling, and so as long as the traffic isn't anything treasonous, who's to complain? You never have. Are you starting now?"

Her eyes widened. "Oh no, never!"

Now he nodded. "Nor have any of us who live off the sea. Spies and suchlike are things we don't deal with, nor never would, but free trade's another thing entirely. Prinny doesn't need our extra pennies to build another dome on his palace."

"It's not that," she said. "Pascoe wants what he doesn't understand. I can't be the kind of wife he wants. Nor is he the right man for me. Anyway, I'm happy here. Why should I leave? Unless you want me to," she said quickly. "I'd leave on a second if you did."

"And who would run my house and watch my Grace?"

He gazed at her where she stood next to him, arms wrapped in her shawl, bathed in the moonlight. She was barefoot, yet still almost his own height. She wore a robe over her nightdress, and it was entirely proper, as she always was, because she was buttoned to her neck and covered with a shawl. Even so, no man could forget the graceful supple form beneath. Her amber hair was braided for the night and gleamed in the moonlight, her braid a shining coil the midnight light turned to soft rose. The eerie light also showed the purity of her skin, though her eyes were shadowed and leached of color, and held mysteries that they never did in sunlight.

"But should you ever want to move on," he said slowly, "never think you owe us anything. You've paid in full."

"I couldn't have," she said, shaking her head. "When I think of the fate that could have befallen me! A nameless waif wandering the beach at dawn, after a shipwreck, with nary a trace of who birthed her ever found? I could have been thrown in the workhouse, or worse."

She hesitated. This was such a different conversation to be having with Mr. Tremellyn. Quiet, comfortable; alone in the night, they spoke like comrades. It wasn't that he'd ever been unapproachable; he'd always been as kind and generous to her as to his own daughter. But he'd been more of a judge and jury to his girls than a companion. Yet tonight, it seemed they talked like two old friends. She relished it.

She was more than grateful to Hugo Tremellyn, she loved and respected him. Most people did. He was a favorite in the community, known to be free with his jests when he went to the inn of a night, and considered a strict but just employer by the many men who sailed his small fleet. He wasn't a handsome fellow, being on the portly side, as Grace always teased him, with blunt, weathered features. But some women were attracted to his bluff manner. He was considered a good catch but had never remarried, preferring to carry on his love life in private with available widows, or women known to earn an extra coin at the intimate trade.

He was easygoing with both his daughter and Amber, leaving most of their upbringing to nurses and maids, then employing governesses until they had learned to read, write, and speak like ladies born.

But tonight, in the broad wild moonlight, he and Amber stood and gossiped like equals. She thought it might have been that he was being kind to her because he'd seen how hurt she'd been by the reception she'd gotten from Amyas St. Ives. She'd tried to conceal her instant attraction to the fascinating stranger, then the pain of the insult when he'd snubbed her. But Hugo Tremellyn had seen both. She was touched by his sympathy and honored by his accepting her as an adult.

And so then, because this was such an unusual, grown-up conversation to be having with the man she'd come to think of as her father, and because the night allowed more intimacies than the day, she had the courage to tell him what she'd always wished she could.

"I'm sorry I never met your wife," she said softly, "but glad in a way, that you missed her and decided to take me in to keep Grace company, and she, only a babe in arms. Is it wicked for me to be glad that you were lonely? If so, I'm sorry, but I don't like to think about what might have happened to me if you hadn't been."

"Then don't think about it. And don't thank me, neither. Now," he said with decision, "what's to do with the young man? Should we let him come courting our Grace?"

She was pleased to be asked her opinion, even if that opinion pained her. "I think we should let things go on. You can't know what's on the hook if you don't let the line play out." He smiled at her turn of phrase, as she'd hoped. "And don't forget," she added, "Gracie is as clever as she's kind. If he's a rogue, she'll see it, and so will we."

"And if he's not?" he asked mildly, though he watched her carefully.

She shrugged again. "Then she's got another suitor to consider." *And if I have to watch and yearn because of it*, she thought, with a hollow feeling in her stomach, *so be it. That won't be anything new.*

They stood in the silence a while longer and watched the stars wheel overhead, until the dampness of the night reminded them it was time to go to bed. Then she gave him a civil good night and went back to her room, her heart lighter, though her mind was still troubled.

And he stood in the night and watched her go,

and stayed watching where she'd gone for a long time after.

"What were you two talking about so long?" Grace asked curiously the moment Amber crept back into her room and shut the door behind her.

She was tucked into Amber's bed and sat up to greet her.

Amber chuckled and slipped out of her night robe. She clambered into her side of the bed. "Nightmares?" she asked on a yawn, as she pulled up the covers.

"Oh no, just too excited to sleep."

Amber smiled. The Tremellyns were well-off; Grace had her own room and her own bed. But she'd invaded Amber's bed in the middle of the night since she could toddle: for company in thunderstorms, to talk about disturbing dreams, complain about lessons or punishments, or just so she could gossip about the day to come or the one they'd just passed.

They lay back on their pillows and talked in hushed voices. Tremellyn had often come upon them so, years ago, and smiled, and called them his Snow White and Rose Red. Grace was dark as her father, but lovely as her late mother was said to have been, with soft straight ink black hair, and dark Gypsy eyes. Though she looked as though she would be the wilder of the two, she was gentle and domestic, as happy to set a seam in the parlor as to sit in the garden.

Amber was impulsive and moody, as wild as any

Gypsy, though she looked like an aristocratic lady with her pale complexion and bright hair. That honey-amber-colored hair had long since been transformed by the sun into a medley of gold, peach, and bronze. If it hadn't been for Grace's constant watching and warnings, her skin would have been sunbitten, too. Amber rode, but preferred to walk along the shore for hours, hunting for lost treasures. Grace said she was still looking for traces of her lost family, and Amber wasn't sure she was wrong.

They both liked books that told stories, and both dreamt of the world beyond their doorstep. It was only that Grace was content to dream, and Amber wanted more. But, as Amber often said, that might have been because Grace knew where she belonged.

"Wasn't he handsome?" Gracie asked, after Amber blew out their lamp.

Amber didn't ask whom she meant; strangers were rare. "No, he was attractive. That's different."

Gracie made a rude sound. "Attractive's better, then. Just look at Elias Ingram. Handsome as he can stare, but so boring you don't care." She giggled. "We could make a poem of it."

"Aye, we can," Amber said, "and so add: Amyas St. Ives is looking for wives."

Grace was still for so long that Amber turned on her side, thinking her friend had gone to sleep.

"That was awful," Grace finally said into the darkness. "How he looked at you, then, when he found out who you were, he never looked at you again. I mean, his face when he first saw you! My stomach turned all fluttery, and he wasn't even looking at me. Do you suppose that he's so toplofty he thought you were a servant, no matter what Papa said, just because you weren't a daughter of the house?"

"I suppose he wants nothing to do with me, for whatever reason. And much I care!" Amber said, pretending a yawn so Grace wouldn't press the subject.

But Grace was attuned to her feelings, and always had been. "Amber? If he comes courting . . . shall I turn him away? I would never encourage any fellow you might care for. Remember Tom Jennings? I knew you liked him a little, and I didn't see him again, or ever mind not doing so. And look at poor Blanche Jennings today! I was lucky I followed my heart on that, because he's the worst husband to her."

"But he could have been the best for you," Amber said roughly. "So never do something so foolish again. You and I are not alike, nor are our destinies."

And that was why I never let you see how I felt about a fellow again, Amber thought, *because every one of them passed me over for you, even if they'd looked at me first. A woman without a family isn't marriage goods hereabouts. If I'd let you know how I felt about any of them, you'd never have a fellow to walk out with of an evening. There were some I was interested in . . . but after Tom, I never let you know. There were some who tried for my favors, if not my hand, and I never let you know that, either. No more than I'd let your father know, because he'd do more than feel bad about it. He'd kill them.*

"That's nonsense, my dear," Amber said aloud, more harshly than she'd intended.

"So, you wouldn't mind? Not that he'd come courting me! My goodness, Mr. St. Ives may be off on his quest to find his family by tomorrow," Grace said. "But if he stays, and if he calls again . . . Though I wonder if I should care for a fellow who took a family name so seriously, but if he came calling . . ."

"You should walk out with him, of course," Amber said. "How else will you know how you feel about him? You're queen of the district, with more beaux than hairs on your head, but marriage is forever. There's no crime in taking your time to decide."

"And it isn't as though you have no beaux either," Grace said comfortably. "If Pascoe gets much more ardent, we'll have to throw a bucket of water on him, Papa said. And Pascoe's such a good-looking fellow! Clever, too. Papa says he'll own his own fleet by the time he's thirty. That's why he doesn't care if you're a Tremellyn or not; he doesn't have to look for a dowry. Not that Papa wouldn't provide one," she added quickly. "But Pascoe doesn't know that, does he? He just likes you. He's never shown any other girl such attention, at least, any decent one. He keeps on, too, no matter how cool you are to him or what his mother says."

And if his mama didn't kill me, Pascoe's demands would, Amber thought sadly. But all she said was, "I'm in no hurry to wed, and certainly not Pascoe. Unless—you want me gone?"

Grace sat bolt upright, protesting. Amber smiled in the darkness. She'd successfully turned the subject. Bad enough if she had to watch Amyas St. Ives court her darling Grace, worse if she had to discuss it before it happened.

"I know, Grace. I'll feel free to stay here, single, until I'm ninety," she finally grumbled, as she burrowed into her pillow. "Now, will you be quiet and let me go to sleep?"

But Amber lay awake long after Grace's peaceful breathing told her that she was lost in sleep. She kept reassuring herself, telling herself she could deal with seeing Amyas St. Ives's vivid blue eyes fixed on Grace in that intent way of his. She could bear seeing those gloved hands gently cupping Gracie's elbow as he escorted her out, his honey-colored head bent to catch Grace's every whisper, his wide shoulders next to hers as they went out the door. She could act as though she was simply delighted, she had to.

Amber had always been able to do that for Gracie. She would do anything for the people she loved.

Chapter 4

~~~~⌒◯◯⌒~~~~

Grace Tremellyn's complexion was camellia-petal pure even in sunlight; her smooth jet hair was swept back and tied at the nape of her neck, exposing her dainty ears. Pearl earbobs were set in those little ears, and a cameo on a silver chain lay at the base of her throat. She wore a white gown with capped sleeves, like any well-bred young girl in London, and she was toting a parasol, too. Her gown might be for an ingénue, but her neat figure was womanly. She sat quietly beside him on the driver's seat of his rented gig, and Amyas was pleased.

Or at least, he was, so long as he didn't glance into the backseat.

He smiled at Grace Tremellyn. "So, as I understand it," he told her, gesturing with his whip, pointing to the horizon over the head of his team, "I can drive you along the coast road, but only so far as the turn at the bend there in the distance?"

She ducked her head. "But it is a long drive."

He leaned toward her. "Not long enough," he breathed, lowering his voice for her ear only.

She looked up at him, startled.

The back of his neck prickled.

"So," he said blandly, as though he hadn't said that, "we must turn around at the end of the road, even though we have the formidable Mistress Amber in the backseat to watch and make sure I don't overstep my bounds any more than I drive a foot over the boundary your father set?"

"Aye." Grace giggled.

There was no matching sound from the backseat.

"Lord!" Amyas said. "The Queen isn't watched so close, I don't think. Not that I blame him, but is your father this careful of his daughter all the time? Or could it only be because I'm a foreigner?"

Grace's averted cheek turned pink. "Because he doesn't know you yet, sir," she said softly.

Amyas nodded. "Good thinking," he said, as he picked up the reins and started down the drive. "So I'll have to remedy that, won't I?"

She turned to look at him full in the face for the first time since he'd called on her this morning. "Are you staying long enough to do that?" she asked with more spirit than she'd shown since then, too.

"I didn't think I'd stay on so long at first," he said,

looking deep into her dark eyes, "but I find the scenery too beautiful to leave."

He saw her irises widen before she looked down in confusion. Then she turned face forward, and he saw how rosy her cheek was.

He was amazed. He'd only begun his flirtation, just reconnoitering, really. His words had two meanings; his eyes had spoken only one of them. It was a delicate balance: an innocent remark, or one that could be construed as such, combined with a smoldering look. He'd flirted just enough to interest her, while not enough to raise any expectations he couldn't meet.

After all, he didn't know the girl. Her shyness could disappear the moment he turned down that curve in the road—which might be why her father forbade it. Amyas wanted to see if she was good bride material, but wasn't a fool. He hadn't asked for anything from her, much less her hand.

Grace didn't say anything. And the silence from the backseat was deafening.

He immediately corrected himself.

"Well, I can't blame your father," he said in a hearty voice. "He has only my word for who I am and what I intend."

Since that was true, Amyas felt on firm ground now. He always tried to tell the truth. Lies were too easy to forget, and if truth was told creatively enough, it wasn't exactly a lie. Most magistrates didn't see the finer points of that, but women usually did. The difference, Amyas had learned, was that women *wanted* to.

Amyas hoped she'd believe him. Grace Tremellyn was a gentleman's daughter, even though that gentleman wasn't noble and only lorded it over a tiny village on the brink of the sea next door to nowhere. But how many real ladies would Amyas get a chance at? And Cornwall had begun to stir echoes in his heart.

But Grace was shy with him. He sought an innocent question to get her talking again, to find out if she'd anything to talk about. A pretty wife was fine, but he'd only take a witty one. Marriage was for a long time, and he'd rather not stray to find his pleasures. He'd never seen a lasting loving marriage, but wanted to believe in the possibility. Even his mistresses had to be clever, and ease of conversation was as important to him as gaining his ease in a bed.

He drove down the drive from Tremellyn's house in silence until they passed the old stone gatehouse, near the main road. "Does anyone live there?" he asked.

"No," Grace said. "We used to play there when we were children. Remember, Amber?"

"Of course, I do," Amber said from the backseat. Her low-pitched voice made the small hairs on the back of Amyas's neck stand up. The woman had the damnedest voice, he thought, all velvet and bedready, yet clear and strong. He couldn't see her, but he couldn't ignore her, and her voice made him want to talk to her. But he was courting her sister . . . no, if Grace was really her sister, he'd be courting Amber instead.

Amyas stifled a sigh. This all might be fruitless.

He had to ignore Amber, the elder nonsister and Tremellyn's found treasure, or give up the notion of courting Grace Tremellyn altogether. But that was proving difficult. He wished he could turn to see her, but he didn't want to raise expectations in that quarter. Not for her, or for himself.

He spoke to Grace again. "Your father doesn't let the gatehouse out to a tenant? Odd. He doesn't seem like the sort of fellow to let a chance to turn an honest coin get away."

"But he says he couldn't stand having strangers on his land, knowing his business," Grace said. She ducked her head again, and whispered, "And he says he needs the place for his grandchildren, someday."

So she was just a pretty little ninny, Amyas thought with regret, looking at the way the sunshine made her hair gleam blue-black as she bent her head. She couldn't even talk about the possibility of giving her father grandchildren without getting embarrassed. Amyas appreciated innocence, had sympathy with bashfulness, but no patience with timidity. The timid got eaten. He'd seen it too often. He himself might have had to prey on the foolish in his past, but he wanted no part of that in his future. He wanted to marry well, but wished to marry happily. So this charming little woman was probably not for him, nor he for her.

Tremellyn's daughter had made limping conversation when he'd come to call on her just now, and he'd hoped once away from her father's fond eye that her personality would assert itself. But maybe she didn't have one.

It was true that Amyas was more used to women who acted and spoke roughly. But since he'd come to London, and more specifically, since he'd come into money, he'd had more than polite conversation with women who were born ladies, even if they didn't act like them. Lady or convict, wellborn or street-raised, he liked a lass with something to say. Tremellyn's daughter didn't say much at all, even when she spoke.

But it was a beautiful day; the sea lay glistening before them. He was willing to try to make the outing pleasant for her, even though he'd given up on her.

"And Amber needs a place to read," Grace went on. "When she's home she's always got some work to do; it's only when she leaves the house that she can relax, she says. The gatehouse is old, but sound, even though no one lives there. Sitting in it is better than sitting on the grass, too, because the dew gets everything damp, and there's a fireplace there that she can light when it rains or when the mist is too heavy on the ground." She turned her head. "Isn't that so, Amber?"

"Yes," Amber said repressively, as though she didn't want to take part in this conversation any more than Amyas wanted her to.

But Grace refused to leave her out.

"Amber does our household books, too," she told

Amyas. "She tallies them so well no one would risk overcharging us a penny, even if they dared try Papa's temper. She runs our house so well we don't need a housekeeper either, though Papa insists on having a cook and maidservants, so that Amber can have some time to herself."

"Likely so that he wouldn't have to taste my stew again, or my porridge," Amber chuckled. And then, as though remembering her position as chaperone, she closed her mouth and said not another word.

The silence grew. Amyas mightn't want to include her, but he couldn't decently let her exclude herself.

"What other treats were you saving Mr. Tremellyn from, Miss Amber?" he asked her, looking steadily ahead, as though he had to watch his docile horse carefully as it trudged down the straight and empty road.

"Apple tarts," Amber snapped. "But Grace is our baker. Why don't you tell Mr. St. Ives about the treats you baked for the church fair, Grace?"

"My scones or my seed cakes?" she asked.

"Those, and the rest," Amber said patiently.

"But you know there are those who say Mrs. Penrose's pastries are better," Grace said.

Amyas could swear that he could hear Amber's muted sigh of exasperation above the sound of the carriage wheels rattling over the road, the surf in the distance, and the wild gull's cries.

"They aren't better than yours," Amber said.

And so Grace prattled happily on about her recipes

as opposed to the famous Mrs. Penrose's recipes, and the recipes of a dozen other females Amyas had never heard of and never wanted to.

The girl, he decided, as Grace told him how too much sugar was bane to a crust, wasn't simple or even stupid. She was just very young, and also very obviously unaware of him as a man. That put an end to the last meager hope he'd had that he could form a liaison with her. He gave a mental shrug. There were other villages. His search had just begun.

He gazed at the view; the sea looked as endless as his freedom. It also looked empty—except for a ship he noticed entering his field of vision on his left, sailing parallel to the shore. Amyas tensed. Then he relaxed, reminding himself he didn't have to board it. He never had to screw his courage to the utmost degree again and pretend composure he didn't feel in order to force himself to step onto a ship. He didn't have to sleep with his eyes open so as to fend off the dreams the rocking berth would give rise to. He didn't have to feel his stomach roil, not with seasickness, but the worse sickness he felt at being trapped with nothing but sea around and beneath him. Never again.

He let the Tremellyn girl's prattle wash over him like the warm spring sunlight, and gazed out to the horizon, taking pleasure in the view, if not the company.

The company was watching him, though. Amber tried to look at the sea, but her eyes slid from it to study the back of the man in front of her. After all, she saw the sea all the time. It wasn't often that she got a chance to see something like Mr. Amyas St. Ives. She hadn't wanted to, not this close, and not this morning. But Grace had begged her to come along after St. Ives sent a note to ask her out for a drive. And Mr. Tremellyn had looked surprised by the way Amber had kept refusing. So here she was.

Grace needed a chaperone, and Grace needed a husband, and so, of course, however she felt about it, Amber had no real choice but to be there. At least she didn't have to face him. She sat behind the courting pair, like a a shadow, which was what she was supposed to be. An observant shadow.

She gazed at the back of his head and frowned because she didn't seem to be able to look anywhere else.

Amyas St. Ives wore a high beaver hat. Few men in the village ever wore such, not even for funerals. The very idea made her smile. A fellow would hardly put on such a topper to catch fish! She couldn't suppress the sudden giggle that bubbled up in her throat, envisioning the fishermen of Cornwall going to sea each morning in high beaver hats.

"Did you say something, Amber?" Grace asked, spinning around.

"No, I just coughed," Amber lied.

St. Ives turned his head as well, looking ready to be amused. Too ready, Amber thought. She wished Grace would talk about something other than recipes. She must be boring the fellow silly. It was clear to Amber that Grace was burying him under a heap of information about glazes and crusts because he impressed and overawed her, and when she got nervous she chattered like a scolding squirrel.

He looked forward again. Grace returned to her recipe recitation, leaving Amber alone to study her driver some more. He was dressed this morning in a well-tailored blue jacket and dun breeches. But his thick honey-colored hair was a jot too long; it escaped to overlap his high white neckcloth.

He said he didn't travel with a valet, but Amber didn't think that was why his hair was overlong. His whole attitude was casual. While his clothing was immaculate, it wasn't precisely neat. He was obviously a man who would always choose comfort before fashion. But he was better dressed than any fellow she'd ever seen outside of the occasional gentleman's magazine Mr. Tremellyn brought home.

He smelled like sandalwood, too; she got a whiff every time the breeze blew past him. Most men she knew smelled like workingmen: of sweat and smoke, salt sea, wet wool, and fish, of course. Mr. Tremellyn smelled like pipe smoke and soap.

St. Ives spoke the way she supposed a real gentleman would, too, drawling lazily, as though nothing was important enough to enunciate. His whole manner was languid. But his eyes, those beautiful clear blue eyes, were always alert. His mouth was a wonder: well shaped, with such plush lips he'd look feminine if it weren't for the strength of his face and that poor broken and bent nose of his.

Amber was very glad she sat behind him. Bad enough she saw the tanned contours of his lean cheek, the strong hands in their neat kid gloves holding the reins, a long leg stretched out, boot resting on the floorboard, extended to show that muscular thigh . . . Odd, that a man who limped would have such strong and well-shaped legs. . . .

She sat up as though a pin had pricked her.

"Amber?" Grace asked, turning to look at her again. "Are you all right?"

"Oh. Fine. A bee came too close," Amber invented, flapping at the air with her hand as she reminded herself: *not for me, not for me, not for me.*

He was for Grace, but Grace was behaving badly. She wasn't a fool or a bore, but it would be hard for the fellow to know that. It was time for Amber to be more than a chaperone. She had to be a matchmaker, or at least, see if a match were possible. She took a deep breath. It was the last thing she wanted to do, but she had her obligations.

"Tell us, Mr. St. Ives," she said, "what do you think of our little village so far?"

That's how it's done, she silently told Grace. *Ask him about himself.*

St. Ives began to compliment the view, their charming village, and present company.

"Do you live in London all the time?" Amber asked, as soon as he stopped to draw breath.

"Oh no, I've only recently returned from abroad," he said.

"Where were you?" Grace asked hesitantly, stealing a glance at Amber, who nodded back to her.

"I was traveling on business," he said, and told them about France, and how it looked now that Napoleon had left Paris.

But they knew about that. Most of the men they knew wouldn't talk about what they took from France and brought to England, but they would tell tales of how the people there were recovering from the war.

"I was in Spain before that," he said, with an entertainer's sense of losing his audience. "Italy, too, and Portugal . . . and once," he said with a curious smile, "I went to the Antipodes as well."

"No! Tell us about that." Grace exclaimed, just as Amber blinked and asked, "Why?"

"Why, on business, of course," he said, answering Amber first. "His Majesty's business," he added, with that curious smile playing about his lips.

So then he told them about how wide and empty of people the land was, how their winter was England's summer, and what strange beasts he'd seen. When Amber showed interest, he told them about animals with pockets, and little green birds that could be trained to speak like men.

They stopped the gig at the end of the road, beside a stony patch of beach, just before the forbidden turn. Amyas stepped down and offered a hand to Grace.

"We can't ride farther, but surely we can walk

along the strand?" he asked, though he looked at Amber as he said it. So did Grace.

Amber nodded. Grace took his hand, and stepped down. He offered Amber his hand too. They didn't look at each other as she got down from the gig.

Amber felt foolish and a little sad as she trailed behind them as they picked their way along the stony shore. He was so big and handsome and Grace so small and neat, they could have made a handsome couple. At least, they would have if Grace had leaned on that strong arm he offered, or looked up at the dark gold head bent to hers, or thanked him when she almost stumbled on the stones and he steadied her. Instead she'd shied away from his merest touch. As it was, they looked as mismatched as Amber felt misplaced.

It might have been those lowering thoughts that blinded her. Amber stubbed her toe on a slick rock the low tide had exposed. She slipped. When she tried to right herself, she fell. She landed flat on her hands and knees, her big toe throbbing so loud it deafened her. Her knees and palms were stinging, her gown was rucked up, her rear in the air, and her dignity in tatters.

Strong hands raised her as easily as she'd fallen. "Have you hurt yourself?" he asked.

"Yes. Ouch. Oh, blast!" she said through angry tears. "Oh, bother!" she said in confusion and annoyance at herself. "I'm sorry."

She brushed down her skirts, and hopped on one foot, trying to pick up her other foot and get a look at it. She staggered. "Oh, damna . . ." She clenched her teeth and damned in silence as she hopped in place, trying to overcome the pain so she could think again.

She found herself scooped up in his arms, and he strode back to the gig with her, Grace trotting at his side. It was embarrassing, and wonderful, and dreadful, and so she concentrated on not crying, and tried not to think of how easy it was for him and how good it felt to her.

He put her on the backseat of the gig, took her foot in his hand, stripped off her slipper, and stared at her toes. "Can you move them?" he asked.

She gritted her teeth and wriggled her big toe, and though it hurt, it hurt less than it had, and she could bend it. She sighed in relief. "Not broken," she said, then saw that her skirt had flown up to expose a shredded knee, which was only then beginning to ooze blood. "Oh, bother!" she said, and bit back tears as she looked down at her stinging palms and saw the same thing happening to them.

"Poor Amber, you're all cut up!" Grace exclaimed.

"But I'll do. My dignity hurts more," Amber said, with a rueful smile. "Thank you," she said, not looking at St. Ives.

"You're welcome," he said, as coolly. "Well, we'd best get you home, and quickly." He put two hands on Grace's waist without asking and lifted her to the

seat as easily as he vaulted up himself. He turned the
gig, and sent the horse trotting back along the road.

No one spoke.

Amber was in too much pain, and suffering too
much embarrassment.

Grace was too worried about her adopted sister.

And Amyas was trying to forget and subdue his reaction to Amber. He'd been making dull conversation
with Grace when he'd heard Amber exclaim and
turned back to see what had happened. He'd known
right away she wasn't hurt badly. But seeing her on
the ground, that pert little derriere stuck up in the air,
he'd felt like doing anything but rescuing her.

She wore a simple flowered frock, and her amber
hair had been tucked beneath her bonnet. But when
she'd fallen, her bonnet had flown off, and her gown
had flown up. God, he thought almost angrily, but
she was a sumptuous-looking woman! Rounded and
supple and well formed. She wore a shift, so his view
wasn't as complete as he wished, but he'd seen
enough; even her legs were shapely, her thighs firm.
He'd looked away as soon as he could, in order to
preserve her modesty and his reputation. That wealth
of hair tumbling down around her shoulders, all the
shades of her namesake, bright and beguiling! It was
almost the same shade as his own, but curling and . . .

Amyas suddenly thought of what Daffyd would
have to say about that. He'd said it once, years before,
about a bar wench Amyas had been wooing. "That

fond of yourself, are you?" Daffyd had mocked. "Like that Greek lad, Narcissus? Now me, I like contrast in my females, so I don't think I'm making love to my fist."

Amyas had teased him, mocking his scrap of learning in order to avoid the subject. But he'd given up the wench.

Now he realized Amber did look like him, in coloring at least. She was also fair-skinned, with blue eyes, and bright many-colored hair. She was also a foundling, literally found, here, in Cornwall. He'd picked up scraps of education in his travels. Both he and Daffyd had an old sot for a tutor once, in prison, who had told them wonderful stories in exchange for bread. Amyas had sought more out when he began to read books later. He couldn't help remembering another old Greek story now. About an orphan boy who riddled a Sphinx and killed a king and married his widow—only to discover she was really his own . . .

Amyas sat up straighter. That was nonsense. Amber was too young to be his mother, of course. And almost every other person in the vicinity had his coloring. It was one of the things about the area that made him so comfortable, making him feel as though he was part of some big family.

Being found wandering the streets of London or being found on a lonely shore made little difference. No one had come to claim either of them. So she, in truth could be . . . she might be . . .

The odds that she actually was his sister were more

infinite than the stones on that damned beach where she'd fallen. Still, he felt queasy at the thought.

Amyas's inconvenient lust was squelched like a campfire doused with water. In fact, his skin crept. He felt guilt and disgust. Ridiculous, but good! he thought. Guilt and disgust were better than saltpeter. He didn't want to be attracted to Miss Amber No Name. He wanted to find a wellborn wife, so he could start a respectable, decent, and envied life.

So he was tempted to a tumble with her. What of it? He could and would deal with that. But gently, because none of it was her fault. And, he thought with the inconvenient humor that was his curse and salvation, they might be relatives, after all.

He let out breath he hadn't known he was holding. "We'll be back soon. How are you feeling?" he asked Amber.

"I'll do," she repeated, then, as though realizing that sounded cold and ungrateful, added, "If I'd taken a tumble like that a few years ago, I'd have made nothing of it. I used to scrape my knees all the time. I'd cure them by dashing into the sea. Remember, Grace? You were always horrified. I don't blame you. The shock of the cold salt water would make my knees sting a positive symphony. I'd howl along with it. But the water was so cold it took my pain and my breath away, and I'd feel better when I dashed out again. I ought to have done that this time, too," she said on a weak laugh. "Too bad growing up makes us such cowards, isn't it?"

She ruined her brave speech by sniffling.

Amyas looked back at her. Grace had retrieved her bonnet for her, but Amber only held it in her lap. Her skirt was kilted up to expose her bleeding knees. The breeze scattered her hair around her flushed face; that lovely face was screwed up with pain and the effort of dealing with it, until she saw him look at her. Then she lowered her bonnet over her naked knees and raised her head high. One glittering tear escaped her. It trickled down her cheek, and she pretended it wasn't there.

And he was lost again.

Chapter 5

Pascoe looked deep into her eyes. "Your eyes," he said, as though the words were forced from his lips, "I wouldn't be here except for those eyes." He saw her recoil, and added quickly, "I'm not trifling with you. I have too much respect for Tremellyn for that."

Amber sighed. "And for me?"

He looked confused, which was rare for him.

"Pascoe," Amber explained patiently, "I know you respect Mr. Tremellyn. But the point is, I don't think you respect me."

"What?" he exclaimed. The room seemed to grow still behind him, so he lowered his voice, and said furiously, "Did you fall on your head, or your knees, girl? Why would I be here declaring myself if I didn't?"

"Is that what you're doing? I thought you had to speak to Mr. Tremellyn first."

"He knows what I'm after," Pascoe said. "Nor am I fool enough to ask a man before I ask the woman. And he isn't your father, after all."

"So he isn't," she said sadly. "But why ask me at all?"

"Look in the mirror, lass," he said.

"Now that is foolish. The thing is, Pascoe, you want a wife, and that's not the same as wanting me." She lowered her voice. They weren't alone.

They sat in the Tremellyn front parlor, Amber with her legs out straight because it hurt too much to bend her knees, even if she could with all the bandaging on them. Her feet were up on a chair, a lap rug over her legs for decency's sake. She was receiving guests to-day, the day after her tumble on the shore. It wasn't a bad accident, and she wasn't more than stiff and bruised. But Hugo Tremellyn was respected, word got around quickly, and it was a very small village. Neighbors had come calling when they heard about her mishap. Amber had gotten flowers to solace her, as well as pots of soup, cakes, bottles of wine, and now, Pascoe Piper. She'd been dismayed when he'd entered the room.

"I heard Miss Amber came a cropper," he'd said, as he removed his cap, all the while staring at Amber. "It's too choppy for fishing today, so I thought I'd use my daylight hours to visit the invalid instead."

No one argued that it wasn't too choppy for fish-ing, because it didn't matter. Everyone knew he wasn't interested in hauling anything with scales these days, and that he wouldn't be going out whatever the weather, because he'd come home from a trip across the Channel the night before.

Now Grace entertained one of Pascoe's crew, a lanky blond youth who had come with him, along with two of her female friends. They sat at the other end of the room. Though the girls slid glances at him, Pascoe was intent only on Amber.

She'd been surprised, then a little anxious when she'd seen Pascoe come in. He wasn't wearing his working clothes. He wore a thick dark sweater over his shirt, and dark trousers, as he usually did. But everything was clean and fitted well instead of hanging loosely, and he wore shoes and not boots. He also smelled of soap and bay rum, rather than fish. Amber had to admit he was attractive. But his attractiveness had never been the problem.

Pascoe Piper had straight brown hair and light brown eyes. A blade of a nose and severe cheekbones dominated his tanned face. A bit above middle height, he had wide shoulders and was all lean muscle, like any man who labored on the sea. He had brutal good looks, but was said to be a fair man. He was certainly an ambitious one. Pascoe captained his own boat and had plans for another. Though he didn't speak much, he spoke well enough because he practiced. He'd changed his native accents as best he could as soon as he'd learned some people had difficulty understanding him, because he wanted to be able to trade with ease on more than just this coast. The local girls fluttered when they saw him, but Amber didn't.

Pascoe had hinted at his interest in her before, whenever they chanced to meet. There was no other way he could, because she refused to walk out with him. But now she was receiving guests, and so he was taking the opportunity to let her know she was also receiving a real offer. She had to let him know she wasn't interested, as kindly but firmly and clearly as she could.

She decided to put the blame on herself, where it belonged. There was nothing wrong with Pascoe, just that he was wrong for her. He wasn't cruel or mean-spirited, but he was strong-minded and forceful to a worrisome degree. She supposed it was because he was pampered by his mother and fawned over by women, and men seemed to obey him naturally. Amber suspected he'd never think of any man as equal to his own worth, let alone any female. She didn't know if she wanted to be treated exactly as an equal, but she certainly didn't want to be thought of as inferior by the man she'd choose to spend the rest of her life with.

But those had only been nebulous feelings. Now that she'd met Amyas St. Ives, she realized that thinking a fellow was attractive was very different from feeling it right down to her bones.

She refused to think about that now. It was enough that she knew she didn't want Pascoe. She tried to tell him he didn't want her.

"You want a wife to cook your meals, bear your children, and ... entertain you," Amber told him, trying for an oblique mention of the marriage bed. It wasn't oblique enough. Pascoe stopped looking as though he was going to interrupt her and just grinned. But she persisted. "You don't know me. If you did, you wouldn't want me."

"What's there to know?" he asked, smiling widely now. He had very white teeth. "I've seen you grow from girl to woman, and like what I see."

"That's just it," she said. "I am more than what you see. All women are. I'm a moody creature. I like to walk along the beach when I'm brooding, even at night. I enjoy a rousing discussion more than I do mending a quilt. I like reading a book most of all. And when I do, I forget the time and place. If I had a husband, he'd have to learn to like his dinners over-cooked, or raw, because I'd forget what I was cooking if I got to a good part in a book."

He laughed. "You wouldn't need to read any books for pleasure with me around." His smile was proud as he added, "And if you think I don't have the brass to set my wife up in fine fashion, think again. I can hire a cook same as Tremellyn. But I can save my money, because my mam is the best cook in these parts, and she'd cut off my hand if I tried to pay a hired cook one penny. So my wife would never have to lift a finger in the kitchen."

Amber tried not to grimace. The thought of living under the same roof as his little busybody mother would be enough to put her off marrying Pascoe even if she were madly in love with him. Fortunately, she wasn't even sure she really liked him. He'd ignored her when she was a child, and only paid attention to her when she came to womanhood, eyeing her as he did all the women in the village. They were thrilled to receive his attentions. She hadn't been. That might have been a mistake, she thought now. She suspected the more she ignored him, the more he wanted her.

She had to change that, but cleverly. They lived in a very small village, after all. Long, burning looks were easier to tolerate than a man with hurt feelings.

"I don't think we'd suit, Pascoe," she went on. "You need a wife who can share your interests."

He looked at her as though she was a child who'd said something adorable. "If I wanted someone to hunt and fish with, I'd be asking a man to marry me. I'm looking for a wife, and mother for my children."

"Well, but I don't think I'd suit you there either," she said with desperation. "I like children well enough—but only if they're likeable." Incurable honesty made her add, "I expect I'd be mad about my own, but I don't find all infants charming, so I don't sigh over every babe and want to cuddle it. The thing is, Pascoe, you want a soft woman, a domestic creature, a nice, gentle female. Me? I like to talk politics, and I love to argue. Your mother *is* a fine cook, and she keeps your house so clean you could eat off her floors, as she says. You need someone like her, and yet also someone who could get along with her . . . by which I mean not someone argumentative, like me. You want someone sweet, docile, and domestic.

"In fact, Pascoe, when you come right down to it," she said, tilting her head as she considered it, "Grace is more in the line of what you're looking for. She'd be a wonderful wife." She smiled. "But every lad in the neighborhood knows it, so I don't know how good your chances are. You'll have to get a bouquet and stand in line."

There! she thought, sitting back. *That should get his competitive juices flowing.*

It did, but not as she wished.

"Nothing good comes easy," he said, nodding, as he clapped his two hands on his knees, and prepared to rise. "I'm willing to wait. I'm not giving up. I have to convince you, is all. And I will."

"But why me?" she almost wailed.

He looked at her with surprise. "Are you daft? You're the prettiest maid in the village. Nay. Not pretty. Never that. You're . . . a magnificent-looking female, and so say all. You've a few odd notions, but a good man, children, and your own home and family will soon knock them out of you and calm you down."

She was too shocked to be politic. She would have leapt to her feet if she could. As it was, she raised her chin. "I have a home, Pascoe," she said angrily. "And Mr. Tremellyn is a good man. And Grace is like my sister. I may not have a name of my own, but I do have a home!"

"Softly now!" he said, with a grin. "What a hornet! I never denied that. Nor do I care that you don't have a name, though I can tell you that many a lad who lusts for you does. But they don't have the money to afford to wed where they will, nor the name to support them for marrying a no one if they did." Now he lifted his chin. "My name goes back to the beginnings of time here, and our children will have respect because of it, wherever you came from. I'd like to meet the man who says not."

"Your mother might," Amber said desperately.

He looked thoughtful. "Aye, but she'll do as I say."

And though he was attractive and paying her an honor, Amber felt a chill, and finally knew why she always knew she had to say no to him.

"Don't fret about it," Pascoe said. He touched the tip of her nose with one finger and grinned at her, before he straightened and swaggered back to say goodbye to Grace.

The door swung open again to admit another visitor.

Amyas St. Ives gave his beaver hat to the maid and entered the room. The sight of how he was dressed was enough to kill all conversation. He wore casual clothing, but still had on a well-fitted jacket, his neckcloth was still tied in the latest fashion, and today he carried a silver walking stick in his gloved hand. It wasn't that he looked like he didn't belong in Tremellyn's elegant parlor, his appearance just made everyone else look as though they didn't.

"Oh, Mr. St. Ives!" Grace said, coloring prettily as she jumped to her feet. "How kind of you to call. Amber's doing very nicely. Everyone says it's because of how quickly you got her home yesterday."

"I'm happy to hear it," Amyas said. "I'm pleased to see you suffered no lasting injury," he told Amber, with barely a glance at her. His gaze shot back to Grace. "But I also came to see how you were faring, Miss Tremellyn."

Grace's face grew pinker. "Very well, as you can see," she said. "In fact, poor Amber's misfortune has brought me good company today. Let me present Pascoe Piper, captain of the *Agatha*, a fine ship indeed. And here is Tobias Bray, one of its crewmen, and Miss Ingram and Miss Hooper, neighbors and friends. Everyone, this is Mr. St. Ives, who is visiting our village."

Amyas and Pascoe looked at each other, and nodded. Amber, watching them, thought they also looked as though they were different species. She guessed they were the same age, neither yet thirty, but languid Mr. St. Ives and earthy Captain Piper didn't seem to belong in the same room. They seemed to think so, too.

"Ah," Pascoe said, tucking his thumbs in his belt and studying Amyas. "St. Ives, the fellow looking for his family, is it? There's no one by that name here."

Amyas smiled. "No, nor did I expect to find one here today. I just came to pay a call."

"Well, I've paid mine," Pascoe said with a smug, possessive glance at Amber. "I'm sorry I didn't have a chance to chat with you, too, Miss Tremellyn," he added to Grace, "but your sister ... I mean, your friend Amber took up all my visiting time."

Amyas's expression grew stiff.

"Pascoe," Amber protested in her clear, carrying voice, "don't blame your bad manners on me. It isn't too late to mend them. Grace is still here, and the tide hasn't gone out."

Pascoe's face grew even darker, but he flashed a smile. "So it hasn't. I won't rush off then. Miss Tremellyn, forgive me."

"Of course I will!" Grace exclaimed.

Amber hid her smile as Grace began to chat with Pascoe, asking him about two subjects he couldn't resist: his mother's health and his boat's condition. That left their elegant London visitor standing, with nothing to say to anyone. It was clear he'd wanted to talk with Grace, but was too well mannered to cut into the conversation she was having with Pascoe. He didn't know the others, and they seemed too in awe of him to speak to him. The only other person there that he knew was Amber.

Her smile slipped, and she felt a little sick when she saw him glance at her and hesitate, obviously reluctant to come chat with her. That puzzled her. He mightn't be interested in courting her, but why should he try to avoid her? She hadn't offended him.

But he didn't hesitate long. "Miss Amber," Amyas

said in a drawl, as he approached her chair, "how are you?"

Second-best, and not even that for you, she wanted to say. But she tried to frame a polite reply. She was shocked to see he wasn't even looking at her. He was looking instead at an invisible spot on his pristine blue sleeve, trying to brush it away. She had manners. But she also had a limit.

"How am I?" she asked sweetly. "I am stuck here, in this chair, because though I feel fine, my knees don't. They won't bend. Mr. Tremellyn had to carry me downstairs, and no one will let me stand up, even if I could. That's how I am, Mr. St. Ives, thank you for asking. Now, you've done the pretty and can go back to Grace and the others, thank you very much."

His head came up. "I'm sorry," he said. "I really am. So let me rephrase my question. May I sit here, next to you and talk a little while?"

She nodded, suddenly very sorry she'd let him know he'd hurt her feelings. She had a terrible premonition he could do much more of that.

He sat in the chair Pascoe had just left. "I'd never have suggested a walk on the shore if I'd thought you'd take a tumble," he said. "So it's my fault, and I'm sorry for it."

"You didn't know I'd be so clumsy," she said.

"You weren't. Grace, that is, Miss Tremellyn, was holding my arm, or she might have slipped as well. You ladies will wear thin slippers."

"Well, we wouldn't if you'd told us we were going

for a long march," she snapped, before she could stop herself.

He threw up one gloved hand in surrender. "Right again. I shouldn't have been so impetuous. But I'm spoiled. We men wear boots, so I didn't stumble, even with my bad leg."

She looked down, not knowing if he cared to discuss his injury.

"It's an old wound," he said.

"From the war?" she asked.

His smile was wry. "From being in His Majesty's toils, yes. But that's boring stuff. I'm not usually a fellow who likes to talk that much about himself, and yet all I've done since I got to Cornwall is natter about my family, my history, and my search. You must be sick of it."

"Oh no," Amber said, delighted he was going to ask her some questions about herself at last.

"So, tell me," he said, edging closer to her, "do you think Grace blames me for your accident?"

Her head went up, and she looked at him before she could control the hurt surprise that sprang to her eyes.

He frowned at what he saw. He stared into her eyes, his own curiously naked in their own surprise. "Your eyes . . ." he said, as though reluctant, "You have such eyes. I've seldom seen their like." His generous mouth twisted as though he tasted something bitter, as he added, ". . . except in a mirror."

"Oh no," she said, feeling as though the breath had

been knocked out of her as she looked at him, "I don't have such long, dark eyelashes."

They sat and stared at each other, neither seeming able to find a safer thing to say, or a way to look away.

"St. Ives," a harsh voice interrupted. "I was just telling Miss Grace here that I think I heard your name before, after all."

Amyas shot to his feet. He faced Pascoe. "Indeed?" he said with barely controlled excitement.

"Aye," Pascoe said. "A St. Ives worked a herring boat near here, I'm sure of it. I just have to remember where."

"St. Ives isn't the name I'm looking for," Amyas said. "There are dozens of them. 'Amyas,' my given name, is rare, and the name that I feel could lead me to my family."

They were talking about names, but they might as well have been talking about when they were going to meet for a duel, Amber thought, because they stood as though faced off against an enemy, taking the measure of each other.

"Well, well, here's a nice sight," Hugo Tremellyn said, rubbing his hands together as he came into the room. "Company. I was just going over some papers, or I'd have been here to greet you myself. Hello, Pascoe, give you good day, St. Ives. And young Tobias, how are you? Miss Hopper, Miss Ingram, welcome."

Amyas and Pascoe turned to him. They talked about the weather, then the peace, and the latest news of the health of the old king. As time passed without them being spoken to, Grace's friends rose and left in a flutter of hasty good-byes, Pascoe's young crewman with them.

Their leaving stopped the conversation. "I must be going, too," Amyas said. "I didn't mean to overstay. I only came by to see how Miss Amber was faring, and of course, to pay my respects to Miss Tremellyn."

"Mighty kind of you," Tremellyn said. "You don't have to leave now, you know."

"Papa!" Grace said in embarrassment, "Mr. St Ives was just paying a courtesy call, and it has surely been over an hour. A morning call isn't supposed to last above a half hour."

Amber bit her lip. That was true, and it had been an hour, but Grace shouldn't have mentioned it, at least in front of her visitors.

"It seemed like five minutes," Amyas said gallantly, "but if it has been that long, I must go."

"Well, let's set a time to meet again when we don't have to watch the clock," Tremellyn said. "That is, if you're staying on at the inn and not moving on right away."

"I'm not going yet," Amyas said. "The inn is clean, the food is good, and this village is well located." He glanced at Grace as he added, "I've been thinking that instead of moving on I should make it my base of operations and ride out to make my inquiries every day."

"Good, good," Tremellyn said, "So, would you like to take your dinner with us Friday night? . . . And you too, Pascoe, if you're not at sea," he added belatedly, when he saw the captain's expression.

"I'd be happy to," Amyas said, bowing.

"Me, too," Pascoe said quickly.

"Good day then," Amyas said. "I'll come back tomorrow to see how things are, if I may?"

"Of course," Tremellyn said.

"I feel responsible for Miss Amber's accident," Amyas said. "I want to be sure there's no permanent harm done," he said, though his warm smile was just for Grace.

She smiled back at him. Her father beamed, and Pascoe seemed to relax. Still, Pascoe watched Amyas go to the door. He noted that when Amyas reached it, he looked back, and that look was only at Amber. He didn't have a smile for her. In fact, as he gazed at her, his face stilled.

She stared back at him.

Amyas seemed surprised when the maid came with his hat and stick. He blinked, frowned, and sketched a bow to those in the parlor. Then he clapped on his hat and left.

Pascoe's eyes narrowed until he saw the door shut closed behind Amyas. "Well, I'm leaving now, too," Pascoe said. "I'll see you tomorrow evening then." He nodded to Amber, put a finger to his forehead, and saluted Grace, then stopped in front of her father. "Mr. Tremellyn?" he said. "A word with you?"

"Why, certainly, Pascoe," Tremellyn said. "You never need ask."

"Will you walk with me a ways then?"

"What is it?" Tremellyn asked, after they went out the door.

Pascoe watched the back of Amyas and his horse as it cantered down the road before he spoke. "Just how well do you know that fellow?" Pascoe asked, hitching a shoulder at the departing guest.

"Not very, but he's amiable enough, and rich, I think. What's the problem? Oh! Well, and if you're thinking he's a revenuer, he isn't. I know where to ask, and I did, and he ain't, that's certain."

"There be worse than that, believe it or not," Pascoe growled. "Which one of your girls do you think he's courting?"

Tremellyn was still. When he finally spoke, it was with a shake of his head. "You don't mince words, do you? Well, aye. There's the rub. I don't know. Thought I did, but I still don't."

Pascoe nodded. "Well, here's a fellow who comes out of nowhere, talking swell and splashing around his blunt, making eyes at both your girls, and both of them showing him more dimples than there are in a fat lady's arse. And you, letting him run tame around the house? I'm surprised at you, Tremellyn, I am. So, if it's true that you know where to ask about his name, I'm thinking it would be smart to ask more, too. I think it would be wise if you asked around some more about that fellow, Mr. Tremellyn, I really do."

Tremellyn clapped Pascoe on the back, and laughed.

"I'm pleased that you care, and I'm sure my girls are, too. But don't worry about us. I can sail my own craft, lad, and come safe to harbor, too. I've got my eyes well opened."

But those eyes narrowed as he watched Amyas ride down the lane and back to the main road.

Chapter 6

The butcher visited him again that night. Amyas woke sitting bolt upright, his thoughts tangled, his body covered with a sheen of sweat, his heart still racing madly from running from the butcher.

"Damnation!" he said, and dropped his head into his hands.

At least no one was there to hear him shout out loud. He was sure he had, he'd had the dream often enough to be sure. But many men shouted when they met the monsters of their dreams. He knew that only too well. His own adopted brother bellowed so loud he woke the house when his nightmares were riding him. But maybe not any longer, now that he was wed to the woman of his dreams.

It was a nuisance that he still had the damned

dream, but not a shame. He'd been in prison and on prison ships, and had heard too many brave men fight imaginary battles in their sleep to be ashamed of it. They usually woke confused and still afraid, but he only woke relieved that it was a dream and angry because he'd had it again.

At least his dream was as explicable as predictable. The butcher always did the same thing to him, and he always got away, and the shock was always greater than the pain, though the horror was always worst of all. Because his nightmare was real, had happened. If he could ever convince himself it couldn't happen again, he supposed the dream would go away.

But the dream served a purpose other than to give his heart exercise. It always came when he was worried and unsure of his next step. It showed him that he had to think hard to make sure that it wasn't another misstep he was about to make.

Amyas rose and padded over to the bureau, poured water from the pitcher there into a basin, cupped his hands, and submerged his face. Then he shook his head to dash the water from his hair, washed his chest and body, reveling yet again in the luxury of his privacy. A prisoner would never dare sleep naked. He went to the window, cracked open the shutters, and stood and looked out into the darkness and let the cool night air dry him.

He had decided to court Grace Tremellyn. There was no reason not to anymore. She wasn't as foolish as he'd first thought, only young and unsure of herself. There was nothing wrong with that, it was a thing she'd grow out of, with help. He'd help her. Her lack of conversation had proved to be because she was too impressed by him to speak freely. That actually felt very good, though he was certain she'd grow out of that even if he didn't try to help her to. He grinned at the thought.

But she was sweet and very good-looking, with a proud old family name. Not aristocracy, which would be reaching too high, but not exactly merchant class either because when a merchant had been at it for centuries, that changed the designation. He liked her father very much, and he loved the place where she lived. He could build an even finer house for her, by the sea, and raise a family with a proud heritage to make up for his own shadowy beginnings.

He'd find a likely perch on one of the deserted crags that he'd seen. He'd build a home there, one where he could look at the sea for the rest of his life and know he never had to venture out on it again. There were many things he did just to prove to himself that he was free and could finally do them, and it was wonderful how good that always made him feel.

Yes, he thought on a yawn, feeling the first delicious waves of sleepiness begin to claim him as he thought pleasant things; that was a good plan. Even though he'd had the dream to warn him, he could see no possibility of a misstep in it.

And then he thought of the one problem with his

scheme and came awake again, in mind and, rampantly, in his treacherous body too.

There was Amber No Name: the glowing, tempting, clever and enticing nonsister of his prospective bride. Now, that was a fine problem, enough to give a man a lifetime of interrupted sleep.

But that cocky sea captain, Pascoe Piper, was courting her, and with any luck at all, she'd be gone from Grace's house and less important in her life by the time he walked her down the aisle. How many times did a man see his sister-in-law, after all? He didn't know, having never had or seen a real family go about the business of daily living. But he didn't think it would be too hard for him to avoid her.

So why didn't that make him happier?

He felt the pangs of desire, looked down, and realized the state he was in. Because he wanted her. There it was, and that was clear.

He shook his head. No, no, and no again. He'd had clever women, beautiful ones, too. Now he wanted a wife, and fine as Amber was, there were too many counts against the girl for him to consider her as a prospective wife.

She came from nowhere and was no one. And so was he. She was lovely, true. He thought of her face and her curving body, he'd held her in his arms, and knew the feeling of it too well for his present state. But she was scented with roses, soft and beguiling. Her hair had blown across his face and blinded him with gold. He was enchanted by all of her colors:

ivory, with gold, and amber, rose and peach, the hues of the intimate sex she teased him by reminding him of, the hues he longed to discover in her. There were those beautiful blue eyes, too.

She was all the colors of a ravishing sunset. But it wasn't only her looks. From the first, he'd felt a tug of yearning beyond desire. She was bright, many women were. But she was also quick; he'd seen her lips quirk when she refused to laugh at something he said that only she had caught and understood. She shared his sense of humor. She had so many similarities to him . . .

Exactly. His traitorous sex, which had been responding just to thoughts of her, shrank at the thought, even as his mind skittered away from it. She was very like him, and she might even be kin to him. There were dozens of reasons why that was a ridiculous thought, but the point was that he would and could never know if it might be true.

He had, he now realized, in some corner of his mind, come to agree with Daffyd. Amyas was a quaint old Cornish name, but in the weeks he'd passed here he'd come to see that he could spend months more, and the odds of him ever finding his origins because of it were little better than nil.

So he'd never know who he was. Amber would never know who she was. And above all, he wanted to marry a woman with an established family. With all she was, he could never have that of her. So why torment himself with thoughts of her at all? There were many women he'd wanted and couldn't have for one reason or another, and so had forgotten. That was the way of the world. A man certainly couldn't have every woman who attracted him. She was merely an inconvenient desire; he couldn't have her in any way.

So he wanted her. So what? He'd learn to deal with it. Why should he give up a lifelong dream because of one impediment?

Amyas scowled. He was distantly aware he might be rationalizing, putting himself in temptation's path because he didn't want to move away. He knew there were faults with his reasoning. But he didn't want to find them now. It was the middle of the night, and he was tired. Besides, marrying well and finding a place he belonged was too bright a dream, and he was too close to that, at least, for him to give up so soon.

He padded back to his bed and climbed into it. He punched his pillow, flipped it over, lay down, closed his eyes, and banished thought. He was a disciplined man who had conquered his fears and terrors all his life, or he wouldn't have lived this long. So in a few minutes he was sleeping.

But the butcher was there again before dawn.

"Thank you," Grace told him the next morning when he came to call. "But we can't go riding. I couldn't leave poor Amber."

"You certainly can," Amber said. "Poor Amber is all healed, or as near as. It's just that I don't want to go out in a carriage yet, and I know I don't want to go trotting along the shore yet either."

"Nor do I," Amyas told Grace. "Much as I love getting my boots sandy and salty, and though I love picking up females who tumble at my feet, I think I could find other ways to entertain you."

She giggled. "But I can't go with you unless Amber comes, too."

"Nonsense," Amber said. "You can take Nan. She'd love some time away from polishing the silver."

Amyas stood in the parlor, looking down at Grace. Amber sat in a great chair by the window. He thought Grace looked charming in a fashionable muslin gown, something green and white. It flattered her fair skin and ebony hair. Amber, Amyas saw in the one quick glance he gave her, wore something pink, and she glowed.

"Well, Nan could come with us," Grace said thoughtfully, "but she has to get the silver done. She's our maid," she explained to Amyas, "and usually doesn't have to work that hard, but we're going to great effort for the dinner party we're giving Friday night."

"Party? I thought it was merely myself and that Captain Pascoe I met here yesterday"

"So it was," Grace said, wrinkling her nose as she thought about it. "But Papa decided to make it into something more."

She looked adorable when she wrinkled her little nose, Amyas thought, and tried not to look over at

Amber. If Amber only looked adorable, he believed he could risk looking straight at her.

"But how rude of me," Grace exclaimed. "Won't you sit down?"

"I'd hoped we could go out," he said.

She ducked her head. "Not on such short notice, I don't think."

"You could go for a walk in the garden," Amber said curtly. "You don't need me to do that. I'll watch here from the window, and if Mr. St. Ives attempts to compromise you, I'll throw my teacup out the window at him and scream for Mr. Tremellyn to come running with a hatchet."

"Oh, a hatchet," Amyas said, finally looking over at her. "I'm good at fending those off. Better tell him to grab a pistol, too. It's hard even for me to dodge a bullet."

She grinned. He smiled back at her, until he reminded himself to look away, because Grace hadn't spoken.

She was frowning.

"I was only joking," he told her. "I'm tame as a lamb, and we'll walk under your sister . . . your friend Amber's watchful eye all the while."

"Oh, very well," she said. "I'll just go fetch my bonnet!"

She dashed away. And left him standing there, alone with Amber.

"You don't worry that I'll ravish you?" he asked her. "I mean, here we are, alone at last."

She laughed. "It does seem like a lot of bother over a simple walk, doesn't it? But you're a single gentleman, and Gracie has been brought up like a lady. You're from London and so probably think we're provincial, and I suppose we are. But the smaller the village, the louder the gossip."

"No, not really," he said. "London is, after all, only a collection of little villages. In London, your village is determined by the street you live on, who you were born to, and where you go. Each village is small, so the amount of gossip is the same." He didn't add that he belonged to none of them and only knew about the few streets he'd lived in long ago. He'd met the people of the class his adopted father and brother now belonged in. He felt at home with them wherever they were and sometimes socialized with their friends, but he knew very well he'd never belong in their set.

"But you didn't answer my question," he said.

She tilted her head. "Oh," she said. "About whether I worry about being alone with you? No, of course I don't. Why should I? You're a gentleman, and you are, after all, courting my . . . friend."

"Does that rankle?" he asked. "That I didn't say 'sister'?"

Her slight smile faded.

"I'm sorry," he said sincerely. "I didn't know what else to call you."

"Oh," she said. "I hadn't thought of that. You're right. I'm not actually her sister, though I tend to forget it, as do most of the people we know. I was raised as such."

"But she calls her father 'Papa' and you call him Mr. Tremellyn."

"So I do," she said. "Because he's not my father, though he's been like one to me."

She was so damned lovely today, he thought. The pink gown was more the color of roses, he saw now. She had a shawl over her shoulders, but the gown was low, and her skin was a pearly pink shade in the reflected light, all the way to the shadowed valley between her high breasts. Her hair was lit up by the sunlight, and got up in some arrangement that let long streamers of curls hang down at the sides of her face. He wanted to go over and push them aside so he could lean down and kiss that perfect pink mouth of hers.

He'd grown up in a world where sex was dealt with promptly and directly. As a boy in the lowest slums, he'd seen men and women copulating more often than he'd seen them dancing together. He'd come to manhood in the Antipodes, in a convict society, where sexual attraction was as acted on as soon as it was felt. If it could be, that was, for women were at a premium and charged accordingly. Since he'd left the prison colony and come to England he'd seen there was a different kind of pleasure in the way civilized men and women teased each other to distraction. They called it flirtation. But the women he'd met, of high birth and low morals, had never let it go on very long, which was a pity, he thought now. He rather enjoyed it.

He didn't know how to deal with desiring a well-brought-up, virginal, unattainable young female. It was lucky, he realized, that he didn't have to. Grace was charming. But she gave him no such problem.

"You and Grace can walk along the road in front of the house, then meander on back to where we have our vegetable and flower gardens," Amber said. "I won't be able to see the side of the house as you pass along that way. But I assure you I will be timing you until I see you appear again."

"But I have a limp," he said. "So you have to give me extra time to get there."

"Mmm," she hummed, as though she was really considering it, though he could tell from her tucked-in smile that she wasn't. "How long should I give you, do you think?"

"Well," he said, thoughtfully, "That depends on how long you think a well-brought-up young woman should let her suitor linger."

All hint of her smile vanished. "Suitor? Early days for such a declaration, Mr. St. Ives," she said, turning a serious face to him.

"Is it?" he asked. "You don't believe in instant attraction?"

She looked at him and didn't answer right away. "I do," she finally whispered. "Oh, I do. But," she added, picking up her head and glaring at him, "I don't believe a gentleman would act on it."

He nodded. "You're right, of course. So you see, there's nothing to fear."

She didn't say what he knew she was thinking. Was he actually a gentleman? He wasn't, but he didn't think she knew that.

"You're quick!" he said, when Grace appeared in the room again, flushed and smiling.

"And I'm not alone," she said gaily. "Look, my friends Mary Ingram and Elizabeth Hooper have returned, and with Tobias, as well." The two girls bobbed curtseys, and the gawky young fisherman bowed. Grace produced a pair of dimples as she smiled up at Amyas. "I think we would be too much of a crowd to go for a walk now, but we can take tea together, can't we?"

"If it was teatime," Amber commented.

Amyas nodded to Amber. "Just so. But another time, perhaps?" he asked Grace.

It seemed to Amyas that her two friends and the young fisherman were holding their breath until she answered. "Oh, indeed," Grace said merrily. "I'd be happy to."

"To what?" he heard the young man ask her, as she turned to her new guests again.

Amyas suddenly felt much older than he was, and altogether out of place. But he couldn't just leave. If he did, it would look as though he felt exactly the way he did.

"So, Mr. St. Ives, have you found out anything more about your namesake?" Amber asked him.

He turned to her gratefully. "No, not a word. I begin to think I won't after all."

"So you're giving up?" she asked.

"No. I'm going to keep looking. It's a long chance, but I really want to find some more family. You must know how that feels."

She nodded. "Oh, I do. But I won't. I have nothing but a splintered boat and my own self to offer as proof that I ever *had* a family. You have your memories of your mother and aunt, and records of your father's family, after all."

A good liar tells few lies, so there's less to remember, and Amyas was a very good liar. He had his answer in a second. "Yes, but the whole point was to try to find my mother's family."

Her smile was sad. "Pardon me, sir, if I say that that sounds a little greedy to me. I've nothing at all. Your memories seem an embarrassment of riches."

"But you haven't suffered for it," he said.

"Have I not?" Her voice grew low, her expression lost. Her lashes shuttered her eyes as she gazed down at her lap, and her voice grew so far away he had to move closer. "Do you know what it's like to look into every stranger's face hoping to see a resemblance? At some point, most children think they're lost or kidnapped princes and princesses, or so my governess once told me. But few pray they are lost fisherfolk's daughters. Or a farm wife's castaway. Or a servant girl's last hope for respectability, thrown away so she could find better work. I tried to put a better face on it. I learned all the stories: Moses put in the bulrushes, Oedipus the king found on a mountaintop . . ."

Amyas's eyes flew wide.

She sensed his shock and looked up. "Is that a rude thing for a well-brought-up woman to mention? The king did marry his mother, but it was an accident. It's more of a tragic story than a warm one, I think. And it is classic."

He smiled. "I don't take offense. But most of the classic stories are rude, I think, and warm. The gods and goddesses carried on just like the Prince and all his friends do in high society."

She grinned, as he smiled. They kept looking at each other. She was the first to look away. "But that's a sad story," she went on, as she fingered the knotted the edges of her shawl. "Still, I wouldn't even mind a sad story if I could find any hint of one about me or my origins. I never did, I never could."

He moved close to her chair, curling his hands into fists so he wouldn't reach out to her. "Have you tried? I mean, in recent years?"

"No," she said. "What would be the point? Even the wreckage of the boat they thought I came in is long gone, so how could any trace of my story remain? Mr. Tremellyn put notices in all the papers at the time. It was the talk of the whole village, and it's a village of seafarers, so I know the talk was spread. I come from nowhere, Mr. St. Ives. It's as if I came from the sea itself. I've grown to accept it."

"Like Venus," he breathed, looking down at her, catching his breath at the pink-and-gold beauty of her.

She looked up at him.

"She was born on the breast of a wave in the sea, and came to shore on a seashell," he said softly. "I saw a picture of it once, in a museum in Italy. She stood in the waves, on a scallop shell; her hair was the only thing that covered her. She was beautiful. You have the hair, and the face." His voice lowered as he added, irresistibly, "As for the figure, well, I'm too much of a gentleman to ask to see more . . ." He was about to add, "more's the pity," when another visitor was shown into the parlor.

He looked up. It was Pascoe Piper.

The two men nodded at each other. Grace danced over to greet the new guest. Although Pascoe had looked only at Amber as he came in the room, he had to turn his attention to Grace.

Just in time, Amyas thought with shocked relief. The interruption saved him. He stepped away from Amber the way a man would pull back from a precipice. He'd looked down at her and almost fallen. She'd lured him with her looks. Then she showed him a bit of her soul, and the emptiness there was much too much like that in his own. If he lingered with her, he'd have to court her. And if he married her, he'd be uneasy for the rest of his days.

But if he found whom he'd been named for, and it wasn't anyone who had anything to do with her . . . ?

No, Amyas thought, as he straightened. Even so.

He knew what he wanted. He knew what lust was. This fascination with Amber was just unfortunate sexual attraction. He was too randy, he'd been celibate too long, and she was a toothsome piece. He knew how such things went. The fascination with her would fade if the lust were ever sated, because that was the best part of it. And then where would he be? Cheated by his desires, wed to a woman who could give him nothing he needed.

"Forgive me," he said. "The classic myths really are warm. I hope I didn't offend. It was your coloring that reminded me of the picture. I really should go now," he said, taking out his watch and consulting it. "I'll be back."

"Yes, of course," she said, "You're coming to dinner on Friday, aren't you?"

"I am," he said as he looked at Grace. "But I've a stroll in the garden to claim, too."

"Yes," Amber said softly, and looked at Grace and Pascoe, too.

Amyas said good-bye and left her.

"I must go," he told Grace, "I don't want to overstay again."

"Oh my," she said, seeming genuinely upset, "and here I neglected you by talking to my older friends. Can you forgive me?"

"For what?" he asked. "I'll be back."

Chapter 7

It was an overcast day, with low scudding clouds driven by a squally wind. Amber glanced out a window in the gatehouse and realized those winds would soon whip fits of showers in from the sea. So she went to bring in extra wood; the fire in the gatehouse hearth was high enough, but she liked to be prepared.

She gathered the wood, but the door was torn from her hand by a sudden gust of wind, flung wide, and slammed back against the stones of the gatehouse wall. She struggled to pull it closed, especially since the rain she'd predicted was sleeting down, too. But she was overmatched, and soon drenched as well, as she fought to drag the door back and close it.

She was startled when the door was suddenly

pulled from her hands. It wasn't the wind this time. A pair of human hands dragged the door back with disconcerting ease and shut it firmly behind them. Amber stood in the cottage again, the man next to her. Neither said a word, but Amber's stomach grew cold, and her pulse began to race. She knew who he was without looking, from the size of him, and from the look of the long hands that had seized the door— the long, gloved hands.

She damned the fate that had made her go out to get more wood at just that moment. She'd left the house in plenty of time in order to avoid him, but he'd arrived much too early. She'd come here to avoid just such a meeting.

"Thank you," she said, without looking up.

"You're welcome," Amyas said as he bent to re-trieve the wood she'd dropped in order to do battle with the wind and the door. "Where do you want this?"

"By the hearth," she said.

He deposited the wood and looked around. It was a simple room with walls of hewn stone, but it had been made cozy. Colorful rag carpets lay on the stone-flagged floor, and the diamond-paned win-dows that weren't shuttered admitted light. There were paintings hung on the walls, two comfortable chairs by the fireside, and a table. A stove was tucked against one wall, there was a bed piled with bright coverlets against another. An old gray-muzzled dog lay in the center of the bed; he raised his head to look at the new arrival, and thumped his tail in greeting.

The fire in the hearth leapt high, banishing damp. Amyas was sure that when the weather was clear there would be a fine view of the sea. He nodded his approval, sending water spilling from the hood of his oilskin coat to puddle on the floor.

"You're early," Amber said, adding quickly, "that is, you usually call at eleven, and it lacks fifteen minutes to that."

"So I am," he said, glancing at the clock that sat on the stone mantel. "The grayness of the day fooled me into forgetting the time, I suppose."

Raindrops dewed his long eyelashes, surrounding his intense blue eyes with rainbow stars. She looked away.

"I came here to get away," she said awkwardly, in answer to his unspoken question. "I mean, to do some reading while the house was made ready for visitors. I may supervise the housekeeping," she added on a wry smile, "but I don't actually do it."

"No, Mr. Tremellyn made that clear," he said.

The wind whined as it slid around the house and rattled the shutters.

"So," Amber said too brightly, "have you had news about any other Amyases, Mr. St. Ives?" She knew it was a dull thing to ask the minute she said it. He'd hardly have gotten new word in a day. But she had to say something. He towered over her, and his nearness was making her nervous. Wet as he was, she could still almost feel the banked heat of the man.

She almost asked him to take off his dripping coat and come sit by the fire. Then she remembered that the right thing would be to ask him to leave, because he oughtn't to be standing alone with her in the gatehouse, or anywhere else. But that seemed both old-maidish and presumptuous. After all, he'd never been anything but cool and courteous to her. It was her own fault that she thought she sensed so much more in his eyes. If he were so attracted to her as she'd thought by the way he looked at her, he'd have acted on it by now.

In the week since he'd arrived, he'd paid court to Grace, coming to visit with her, stroll with her, even taking tea with her just the other day. But he didn't seem smitten. The way he looked at Grace was nothing like the way he looked at her. And it seemed he was always looking at her. That was why she'd planned to be out of the house today.

If he was as drawn to her as she thought, Amber wondered why he couldn't consider her as well as Grace if he was looking for a wife. He wasn't a titled gentleman after all, seeking a lady of similar rank. Even titled gentlemen married women of lesser station these days. Surely, the fact that she was a foundling couldn't matter that much now that he'd come to know her?

Why was he so attracted to her and yet also avoiding her?

Of course, she admitted his reaction to her could be all in her own mind. The man might appear to be looking at her because she was always looking at him! He might appear to be seductive only because she found him amazingly so.

He stood beside her now, silent as she was, waiting for her to speak even as she waited for him to. Amber shivered, and dragged her shawl tighter across her shoulders, forgetting it was as cold and wet as her thin, sopping gown. She shuddered again when she felt the clammy chill of it slide over her skin. She wished he'd say something.

"This is a snug place," he said.

"Oh, thank you. Yes, I try to make it so. I took it over when I was just a girl; I used to be hostess at tea parties here. The other guests were Gracie and our dog, Ness. He still loves it here, as you can see," she said, nodding at the old dog dozing on the bed. "This was my place. It was abandoned. I took bits and pieces from the attics to furnish it, food from the pantry for our parties, and acted as though I was giving Gracie a great treat by having her come to call."

She laughed, remembering. "What crust! It was her house, and her father's charity that was keeping me here. But she believed me entirely, and soon everyone else did, too. The governesses always knew where to find me. Finally, Mr. Tremellyn had the house cleaned and the roof fixed. He said it was a safer place for us to play than a makeshift house in a tree. As you see, it's still my retreat."

Her tone became wistful. "Right now, the view isn't so good because the rain's coming down too hard, and so is the evening. But when it's not you can see clear to the horizon. That's another reason I love this house, you can see far and wide, and still stay snug and hidden inside. Sometimes I come here to read in peace, but if I sit by the window I often find I've held an open book on my lap for an hour, because I've been seduced by the look of the sea. I love the sea. Do you, Mr. St. Ives?"

"I like to watch it, yes," he said slowly. "The truth is I'd rather watch it than sail on it."

"Do you suffer from seasickness?" she asked with interest. "Many fisherfolk do, though they'd rather drown than admit it." She grinned. "But it's hard to keep *that* a secret. They have to put up with a lot of good-natured jokes about it. Still, most say that after a day or two, when there's nothing left to give the sea but themselves, they can manage well enough. Those that can't move inland and find other occupations."

"No, I don't suffer from that problem," he said, and added, "It's only that my experiences at sea haven't all been happy ones."

"It can be terrifying during a storm. But I don't mind however rough it gets, and neither does my stomach." Her smile became wry. "Probably because I come from the sea, as you know."

"I asked that you forgive my foolish comments the other day, and I'll ask it again," he said seriously. "Of course, you didn't really come from the sea, Miss Amber, and no one thinks it."

"I didn't mean that! Or, at least, I did, but not because of anything you said. I don't mind it either, because I've heard that kind of thing all my life."

"But it must make you feel lonely," he said. "So I'm sorry I brought it up."

"Living on the shore is lonely, whoever you are," she said. "That's why Mr. Tremellyn took me in, to be a companion for Grace. His wife had just passed away, and life by the sea can be lonely for a child. This way, we had each other."

"But more so for you," he said, "because of the mystery of your birth."

"Oh, so you really do think I'm born of the waves?" She laughed before he could correct her again. "Don't let it trouble you, Mr. St. Ives. People who live near the sea talk about it most of the time. We discuss tides the way other folk talk about the weather, and the weather means more to us than whether or not we ought to wear a bonnet or carry a parasol. The sea is our life and our obsession. And because we live by it as well as off it, we're used to finding all sorts of things on the beach, living and dead, treasure and nuisance.

"So of course, there are folktales about infants from the sea. Venus arising from the waves isn't the first such story I heard, not by a long shot. There are selkies, who are supposed to be half seal and half human, but I don't change shape when I go into the water, I promise you! And there are stories about the sea king's daughters, too. But I don't swim well enough to claim that, either," she added, with a smile.

She looked up and saw him looking back at her. His hair was soaked, turning it into a dark honey color, with none of the usual bright gold the sun showed in it. He seemed to have moved closer, so close she could see how close-shaven his tanned skin was, and how clear. His eyes were half-lidded, and his gaze was on her. He wasn't smiling. His mouth was set firmly, but it parted on an indrawn breath . . .

A keening gust of wind whinnied down the chimney and made the flames in the hearth stagger. It woke Amber to the time and place, and her own place.

"But speaking of water—you're soaked," she said quickly, "You'll surely catch cold unless you get that dripping oilskin off."

He didn't answer, only kept looking down at her, but his gloved hands crept to his collar, to undo the buttons there.

"No, no. Please don't take off your coat. I'd ask you to stay, but I can't, you see," she said a little desperately. "I know you're not in the least interested . . . I mean, I know you're a perfect gentleman, but still and all, the circumstances, you see. We're alone. It wouldn't be at all proper."

He blinked. "No," he said, raising his head and

looking around the gatehouse as though seeing it for the first time. "No, of course not." He took a deep breath. "Lord, I've been remiss. My poor horse must feel like a sea horse now. I'd better get it into the stables, and myself over to the house."

He turned to the door, but paused and looked at her. "But how will you get back? It seems to have blown up to a storm now. We can ride double, you know. Or if the old hack had the wits to go back to the inn by himself, we can at least run to the house together. My oilskin's big enough for two; that is, it can act as a canopy for both of us."

She shook her head. "No," she said softly. "I'm staying here for the next few hours."

"You are? But, I thought . . . aren't you expecting Captain Pascoe? He's paid a call every morning I've been here"

"Well, he's only done that since you have!" she snapped. She realized how angry she sounded, and smiled. "At any rate, I expect he took his boat out this morning. The fish bite better in the rain."

Amyas raised an eyebrow, and she looked away at the fire. He'd eat Pascoe's next load of fish raw if that was the business the man was in now, and they both knew it.

"So you'll have the parlor all to yourself," she said. "Except for Grace's friends, of course."

Amyas nodded. "I see. I'm sorry you won't be there, too." He put his hand on the door handle and turned around again. "Maybe you'd like to invite Grace and me here instead? Like in the old days you were talking about?"

He smiled at her hopefully. She could swear she almost felt the physical pull of that warm, appealing smile.

Damn, and damn, and damn, she thought, thinking words she tried to never say aloud, because she was raised as a lady. And because she loved Grace. And because this man must never know how much she wanted him.

"No, not today," she said on a forced smile. "Perhaps, some other time."

When I can deal with it, she thought.

"I look forward to it," he said, ducked his head in a bow, opened the door, and left.

She stood still until she was sure he had gone on. And then she went back to the hearth, sat down, and stared into the fire.

The Tremellyn parlor was crowded with visitors when Amyas was shown inside.

"Give you a good day, though it isn't one," Tremellyn said, rising as he saw his newest guest being shown in.

Amyas saw Pascoe Piper getting up from a chair, too. Amber had said he'd be away at sea. Amyas couldn't ask why he was there without giving her away. He couldn't even inquire about her, in case they'd seen him coming from the gatehouse. She'd said she was staying there for the next few hours. Should he tell Piper? He decided that was the one thing he wouldn't do.

It was an awkward situation, but he'd been in them before. He'd let it play out without saying a word, to learn how much they knew and how much he was supposed to know.

A glance showed him Grace hadn't even seen him. She stood surrounded by young people, laughing at something Tobias, the gangling young sailor who crewed for Piper, was telling her. Amyas didn't feel like intruding. She'd see him soon enough.

Instead, he went to join his host and the captain, and stood before the fire with them, hoping the heat would take the damp from his clothing and the chill from his bones.

"A harsh day," Tremellyn said, taking his pipe from his mouth and gazing at its bowl. "Even Pascoe here stayed in dry dock."

"The fish don't run in the rain?" Amyas asked innocently.

Pascoe gave him a strange glance. "Aye, that they do," he said. "But not on both sides of the water, and I like to cast my nets far."

That was as close as he could come to admitting it was wine and not mackerel he was after. Amyas acknowledged it with a nod, pleased. The man seemed to trust him that far, at least. Probably because Pascoe finally realized he wasn't angling for Amber. He eyed Piper. The fellow was good-looking and probably was doing well with money, too. Why didn't she want him?

He thought of Amber, and his breath stilled. She'd looked bright as the firelight in the old gatehouse. Her gown had been rose, her shawl paisley, her hair the color of sunlight and sunset. The droplets of rain on her hair hadn't dimmed the spectacle of it. But rain had soaked the bodice of her gown. He'd looked down and seen the perfect outlines of her high, firm breasts. She was chilled, her nipples peaked and puckered. He'd had to look away so he could think of something to say.

She'd dragged the damp shawl over her shoulders to cover herself, but it must have been clammy, so she'd soon let it fall. When he'd looked at her again, her breasts were just as beautiful, but it was obvious she was no longer cold. Then he'd seen her nipples rise again—when she saw him looking at her. He'd found it difficult to look away. But he'd done it and looked into her eyes instead. Then it was even harder to look away.

What if Pascoe married her? It was time to stop fooling himself, Amyas thought sadly, she'd still be in his life if he married Grace. He looked around the elegant parlor with something like despair. He liked the house, the village, and Tremellyn, and Grace was charming. But there were other villages, other houses, other charming women without such temptresses in their families. . . . No. He realized that if Amber actually were in the Tremellyn family, he'd have no problems.

Amyas sighed. He thought it might be best if he moved on. He wondered if he could somehow still manage to have the best of it if he stayed. He wasn't a man who liked to give up.

"And so, you're ready for dinner tomorrow night?" Tremellyn asked him, breaking into his mournful train of thought. "Amber isn't here now, but she'll slay me if I don't remember to ask you if there's anything you don't eat. She's ordered the lamb, the beef, and the fowl, but there's still time to get something else before it's too late."

Too late, indeed, Amyas thought, and said, "I eat everything, Tremellyn. And hope I have the manners to eat that which I don't eat, too."

Tremellyn laughed.

"Speaking of Amber," Pascoe said, "where is she?"

Tremellyn looked at Amyas. Amyas remained silent. Tremellyn's gaze grew narrow.

"Oh, there and here, Pascoe," Tremellyn finally said. "Busy as a cat with her tail on fire. You know how a woman is when company's coming. We're having a few others as well tomorrow night, decided to make it an event. The vicar and his missus are coming, and Baron Bourne and his lady from up the coast, if they can make it, and I don't doubt they will. The nobility never turn down a free meal. Even young Tobias, your crewman over there is coming. Someone has to partner Gracie's girlfriends. It's grown into a social occasion."

Tremellyn smiled as he tamped down the bowl of his pipe. He shrugged. "And why not? It's been a while since we entertained, I mean, in style. You're in for a treat, St. Ives. Our Amber's preparing a feast."

Amyas bowed. "I don't doubt it, and I feel honored."

"What stuff!" Tremellyn's laughter was loud. "You're from London and close with an earl! You've seen dinner parties that put ours in the shade! With noblemen and ladies, even the Prince, I don't doubt."

Amyas smiled. "Yes. But that doesn't mean they were better."

Tremellyn beamed.

"Mr. St. Ives!" Grace said as she fluttered up to them. "My goodness! I didn't see you come in. How are you, sir?"

Feeling old, feeling foolish, feeling as confused as I really am, Amyas thought as he saw how pretty she looked in her blue gown.

"Fine, Miss Tremellyn, and how are you?" he asked.

They chatted about the weather and the upcoming dinner party.

Pascoe talked about something else with his host.

Tremellyn was standing, smiling as he watched St. Ives and his daughter together. They made a handsome couple: the tall blond gentleman bending his head to hear what the dark slender girl was saying.

Pascoe was watching them, too. "What do you really know about the fellow, though? He's got manners and seems to have money, and says he's looking for his mother's family. What else is he looking for? Who was his father? Where does he come from? Where was he raised?" Pascoe asked, sounding like the little voice in Tremellyn's mind that he'd been trying to ignore. "What exactly does he do with himself in London? And what did he do in the past? He talks and dresses like a swell, but what is he, really? I'm thinking you're buying a pig in a poke, Tremellyn."

"I'm not buying anything," Tremellyn said, frowning. "Nor is my Gracie, neither. She's just as kind to him as she is to every lad that comes courting. She smiles as bright at Mr. St. Ives as she does to young Tobias over there. And Tobias isn't a London swell, only a poor young fisherman from the village who works for you."

"But is it Gracie St. Ives has come courting?" Pascoe persisted. "He's smooth as silk this morning, because there's no distraction. But have you seen his eyes when Amber comes into the room?"

Tremellyn didn't answer. He'd seen Amber's eyes, and that was enough to discomfort him.

Pascoe knew. "Were I you, Tremellyn, I'd try to find out more about the fellow."

"You expect me to hire a Bow Street man to come investigate him?" Tremellyn said harshly. "So far as I can see there's no need yet."

"But there may be," Pascoe persisted.

"That's as may be."

"Were I you, I'd ask more questions myself."

"But you aren't me, Pascoe," Tremellyn said curtly. "Thank you for your advice. But I told you, I can steer my own craft."

Pascoe nodded. "Well, I can see I've reached the end of your patience, and my time. I'll be going. I'll be seeing you tomorrow night. I hope Amber will be here by then."

"She'll be here," Tremellyn said.

Pascoe left, reminding the other guests that it was time to go, too. They began to leave. Amyas said good-bye to his host and to Grace. He stood on the front step and watched the gigs and horses pull away. The rain had let up, and the sun was sifting through tattered clouds.

By the time Amyas folded his oilskin and tucked it in back of his saddle, he'd taken so much time doing it that he was the last to leave. All the other visitors had gone from sight by the time he reached the end of the drive. He'd planned it that way. But when he reached the gatehouse, he only stopped and sat looking at it.

Because, of course, he realized, she had to know Pascoe had been there. She'd told him about the view. The gatehouse overlooked the sea as well as the whole road and everyone who passed it: That was why it had been built there in the first place. The view of the sea might be lessened because of the weather, but not that of the road. And so now all he had to wonder was if it had been Pascoe Piper she'd been avoiding, or himself. If it had been him, then why that should make him feel so bad, when it was only for the best?

Grace Tremellyn was a very peaceful girl. There was no saying Amber would marry Piper. What if she met someone else, from somewhere else? She might even leave this charming little village, and he'd seldom see her if he stayed on . . .

It wasn't time to fold his hand. The future was still in play. Amyas kneed his horse and rode on. Tomorrow evening would be interesting.

Chapter 8

~~~⟡⟡~~~

There was no florist in the village. But Mrs. Bray, who lived down the road from the inn, was happy to sell Amyas nosegays from her garden He immediately selected a spray of pink roses for Grace. After wandering the garden, he chose three yellow roses for Amber, and sent the flowers to them both by way of Mrs. Bray's young son.

He'd dressed for the Tremellyn dinner party as he would for an evening in London, out of respect for Tremellyn, because to do less might be to insult him. But he hoped that he wouldn't stand out like a sore thumb. That thought made Amyas grimace and glance down at his hands. He wore thin tan kid gloves and supposed he'd have to explain them at dinner, if anyone asked. They might not. The people here were polite, and this village was far from London. They might only think dining with gloves on was the latest affectation of Town gentlemen.

Amyas shrugged. He never relaxed his guard, so he was prepared for whatever would happen at the Tremellyn dinner party. And it was, after all, only a dinner at a would-be gentleman's home by the sea, in a tiny, remote hamlet far from his reality. That was why he liked it so much.

It was a clear, calm, mild evening, the long summer day slowly fading away. Amyas could hear the distant susurration of the surf as he rode down the coast road, and he took in great breaths of clean, salty air. Tonight no smoke curled from the gatehouse's chimney. He smiled. Tonight Amber couldn't escape. He doubted she wanted to. This was likely one of the biggest events of the year here. The drive in front of Tremellyn's house was filled with carriages and gigs.

A boy took Amyas's horse, and Amyas went to the front door. He heard voices and laughter; the windows of the house were filled with light, just as they might be on the night of a grand party in London. He gave his hat to a maid and was shown to the parlor. He smiled. It was nothing like London.

It was an intimate gathering, by London standards, but it crowded Tremellyn's parlor. The guests were local residents, and though their clothing was doubtless their finest, it wouldn't have been deemed fit for servants to wear on their days out in London. The vicar and a man Amyas supposed to be the baron whom Tremellyn had mentioned wore rusty finery; the other men looked as uncomfortable as working-men who seldom wore good clothes could. Except for Captain Pascoe Piper: He wore a presentable jacket and breeches, and was all in black but for his white linen, and had even tied a credible neckcloth.

The women's gowns were either outdated or not the colors Amyas had seen ladies wearing this season in London. Grace's two girlfriends wore standard white; they looked as boring and proper as any young women newly out in society. Not Grace. Her white gown set off her ebony hair, and the circlet of blue flowers wound through that shining hair made her look fresh and charming.

Amyas glanced toward the center of the room, and finally saw Amber. Then he couldn't look away. Though she had no access to the great modistes of London, she'd surely consulted fashion plates. But it wasn't her gown that made him stare. The gown was simple enough, a slender column of russet with a filmy yellow overskirt, looking far less like a column on that generously curved body. Her coloring was spectacular, her figure no less so, and her smile was warm, wide, and confident. She wore her fantastic hair upswept, with what he'd swear were his yellow roses in it. It was hard for Amyas to see more because the men talking to her blocked his view. But he could hear her rich, infectious laughter.

He wondered why he'd ever felt sorry for her. She was mistress here in Tremellyn's house, obviously admired and definitely a part of local society. And, to judge by the laughter, enjoying it very much.

"Good evening, St. Ives," Tremellyn said, greeting him. He was beaming. "Glad you could come. Quite a do, isn't it? Nine to dinner, and with the three of us already here, an even dozen. Had to invite young Tobias to get the males matched up with the females. Devil of a thing, society manners. Oh well, the girls like entertaining, and I don't mind. We haven't had so many guests in years. You can use it to your advantage. The baron and his lady entertain more than I do, and might know more about your name. Come along, I'll introduce you."

Amyas passed the hour before dinner in a blur of introductions. The old vicar was there with his ancient lady; the baron was a talkative middle-aged man, his baroness even more talkative. Grace and her friends chattered together, Pascoe Piper's poor young crewman Toby looking as out of his depth as one of the fish he'd normally haul up to Pascoe's deck.

Amyas bowed and smiled, and listened. No one knew anyone else with his name. But they were all eager to talk to him. He was relieved when the call to dinner came.

The Tremellyn dining room was just large enough for the company. Amyas was pleased to see he'd been seated near the head of the table, with Grace at his side, and Amber across from him. It was a seat for an honored guest. He was less than honored when he realized how hard it would be to pay attention to Grace.

This wasn't London; there wasn't a massive arrangement of flowers or an epergne that cut one side of the table off from the other. Not only would the conversation be general, he'd see Amber clearly. And even a glance at her teased him. Whenever she moved, her low-cut gown showed fascinating peeks at the valley between her breasts. When she laughed, he could hardly tear his gaze away.

Amyas knew he couldn't ignore her, no matter how tempting she looked and so was pleased when Pascoe was seated next to Amber. That freed him to devote attention to Grace. He was tired of his own indecision; he'd use tonight to decide whether to go on courting her—or rather, to really start. He'd been pleasant enough, but if he wanted her as his wife, he had to begin wooing in earnest. If not? Then he'd be on his way to St. Michael's Mount to see the sights, then back to London and whatever awaited him there. He was done with his quest to find any trace of the infant he'd been.

It had come to him in the night, after he'd endured the butcher again. His childhood nemesis returning so soon made it clear he was in conflict with himself. If he wanted to be rid of his childhood, he had to leave it behind, both the known and the unknown parts of it. It was time to give up childish fancies and get on with his life.

"We have two kinds of soup," Grace said.

Amyas looked blank. "Oh," he finally said, amused to be torn from his sad thoughts by matters of soup. "Which do you recommend?"

"They're both fine," she said seriously. "But one's a local specialty and the other is one we heard was all the rage in London."

He couldn't imagine a soup being the rage anywhere. But she was watching him, her brown eyes so wide and serious that he tried to look as though he was really considering the subject. She was such a pretty girl, he thought. Up close her skin was pure and smooth as an infant's. He had to repress an uneasy feeling. He didn't want to take a child to wife.

But she was a decade younger than he was, at least. Many men married women years younger; such a pairing wouldn't even be commented on . . . Except by Daffyd, Amyas thought. And his other brother of choice, Christian, and Christian's father, the earl. He could almost hear the jibes now. He could deal with them, if it came to that. They'd respect any choice he made.

The point was whether he liked the girl enough to try to spend his life with her. If so, then the object would be to see if he could make her feel the same, and now was as good a time as any to begin.

He considered her carefully now: pretty, charming, and very young. A pretty wife was very nice, charming meant she wouldn't be a shrew, and with any luck young would grow old. And attention to soups wasn't a bad thing in a wife, after all

"Which do you suggest?" he asked.

"Oh, the consomme is fine. But I prefer the chowder."

"Then so do I," he said.

She smiled.

Amyas heard laughter and looked across the table. Amber's laughter was clear and bright. She'd seemed cool to Pascoe Piper before, but he'd just said something to her that made her throw back her head and laugh heartily. Amyas noted her smooth white neck as she flung it back, the way that gesture made her breasts rise, and was shocked to discover his groin tightened. His stomach did, too, when he saw Pascoe also watching her.

Amyas turned back to Grace. "And so," he asked her, "what are those flowers in your hair?"

She blushed. "I wanted to wear your lovely roses, the way Amber did. I mean," she said carefully, "not her roses, of course, but the ones you sent to me. Thank you for them. But I chose speedwell from our garden. It's so very blue, and though your pink roses were beautiful, they didn't match the dress. I put them in a vase instead."

Soups and vases. Oh Lord, he thought, a lifetime of such conversation when the sound of that golden laughter made him want to leap across the table and join in? But, "The blue suits you," he said.

"A toast," Tremellyn proclaimed as he rose from his chair at the head of the table. "To good company."

There were cries of "Hear, hear!" The guests raised

their glasses and drank. Tremellyn sat, and more wine was poured.

Pascoe rose and raised his glass. *"Kernow bys vyken!"* he said.

The company stood amidst shouts of approval, as Tremellyn leaned toward Amyas and translated, "Cornwall Forever!"

"I'll drink to that," Amyas said, smiling as he did.

"So, St. Ives," Tremellyn said, as they seated themselves again. "Still exploring the neighborhood?"

But wine had been served long before dinner, and some of the guests had already had more than their share. Before Amyas could answer, the baron craned forward and put in his advice. "Exploring? You'd best be careful what you explore, Mr. St. Ives," he said in a slightly slurred voice. "Best avoid our steepest cliffs, and especially the caves beneath them. There are some folk hereabouts who wouldn't care for you creeping into secret caves where they . . . keep their tubs of butter cool."

He laughed at his own witticism, but several guests frowned, and even the vicar gave him a hard look.

"I limit my exploring to the outsides of things, my lord," Amyas said smoothly. "I'm from London, remember? We live much closer to each other there and have learned to keep our noses out of other folks' butter tubs, early on. That is, if we want to keep our noses."

There was laughter and relieved looks around the table.

"So, what do you do in London, Mr. St. Ives?" Pascoe asked, fixing him with a stare. "I mean, aside from obviously keeping your nose?"

Amber looked annoyed, and Grace upset. Their guest's nose was not a polite thing to mention, considering the shape it was in.

"I kept it, but barely, as you can see," Amyas said, with a smile.

The tension eased. But not from Pascoe's expression.

"That's how I learned to keep it out of other people's business, by the way," Amyas added. "As to what I do in London? I keep myself busy enough. On a typical day I ride in the park before breakfast. After it, I pay morning calls. Then I either spar with Gentleman Jackson, or fence with Mr. Angelo for a few hours. Then I have luncheon, and after that I visit my friends either at their homes or clubs. I go home to change clothes, then dine with friends. And then I go to the theater or the opera, or to the gaming clubs. Before I know it, it's time for bed."

Someone sighed heavily, that sigh laced with envy. It might have been young Tobias. It could have been the baron.

"Now, that's an enviable thing," Pascoe said, making it sound the opposite. "Very nice. Now me, my life's simpler, and harder work, but I love it. I sail my ship, and catch fish. And one day, I hope I'll have two ships, and catch even more fish."

"Hear, hear!" the baron said. "Nothing like a fellow with ambition."

"Yes, my life is pleasant," Amyas said. "But it's all play and that's not enough for a man. I'm traveling now, but I have ambitions, too. I'd like to settle down, someplace by the sea. I'd like to tend my estate, raise a family, too." He smiled at Tremellyn, then glanced at Grace.

Her cheeks grew pink as one of the roses he'd sent her, and she looked down at her lap.

Amyas smiled. And then, to spare her blushes, he glanced from Grace to Amber. He couldn't help doing so.

Her face was still, until she saw him looking at her. Then she gave all her attention to her glass of wine, studying it as though it held all the secrets in the world in its crimson depths.

"A nice ambition," Tremellyn said with approval. "Living by the sea means life's never dull. The air is good, the views don't end. The storms might be cause for some fretting, but like they say: If you don't sail in a squall or build on a seawall, you can live a good life here. I can honestly say I couldn't think of living anywhere else."

A chorus of agreement went around the table.

"I agree," the vicar's wife said, "and I come from Kent, you know. But I've lived here forty-five years, and don't regret an hour of it."

This time, there was actually applause.

"I was born here and hope I die here, on land, that is," Pascoe said, as everyone laughed. "Where is it that you come from, Mr. St. Ives?"

"Why, London, as I said," Amyas said.

"Your family, too?" Pascoe persisted, his eyes locked on Amyas's.

Amyas inclined his head, a slight smile on his lips. "I was raised there, and know no other real home. Unlike you lucky few, I'd be very happy to pull up my stakes and move on. As I've said, I'm searching for my mother's family, and suspect they may well come from somewhere around here. Wouldn't that be lucky for me?"

He raised his glass and looked at Grace. She smiled at him encouragingly.

"And your family has no country estate?" Pascoe asked, with mock puzzlement.

Amyas was spared answering as a maid appeared at his elbow, bearing a tureen of soup.

Pascoe's question was forgotten as the guests were served. And Amyas cursed himself for not remembering that a man from a good family would have a country estate. He was having his third spoonful of soup, trying to think of where to say his estate was, and why he didn't want to live there, when he noticed how quiet the room had gotten.

He looked up. The company was looking back at him. The gloves, he realized. It was the damned gloves. Gentlemen removed them when they ate and no one here for one minute believed otherwise, whether he was from London or the moon.

"Excuse me, please," he said, trying for a brave, manly expression as he put down his spoon and held up his hands. "I should have explained. I know very well it's not at all the thing to dine with gloves on, not even in London, with all its whims and fancies. But I'm so accustomed, as are my friends and acquaintances, that I forgot. How rude of me. You see, my nose isn't the only thing I had to learn to keep out of other people's affairs. I was taught to keep my hands to myself, too. Only I learned it the hard way. A childhood accident taught me, too well."

And since that was only the truth, he went on more confidently, pleased to see expressions of pity and embarrassment coming over the other guests' faces, "My hand is distasteful to see. So I keep my gloves on. But if you'd rather . . . ?"

"God, no, St. Ives!" Tremellyn cried. "We're the ones who should apologize. Why, don't we see such every day of our lives? This is a fishing village, man. People get hurt every day. My own leg looks like I was whipped by a hard master. But it was only from a line I got tangled in when I was learning the ropes . . . aye, literally. I have a gouge in my arm . . ." He tried to push up his sleeve. "Aye, well," he said, when his tight-fitting jacket wouldn't allow him to move it an inch, "another time. But you should see it, from a fish that fought back—and won! I dropped it like a hot iron, and it vanished into the sea with a bite of me. As for hands and worse? Why, if I'd a penny piece for every man missing an eye, or a foot, or scarred from being caught by hooks or a line, I'd . . ."

". . . be a very rich man." Amber finished for him.

"Please, Mr. Tremellyn," she said lightly. "Fascinating though it is, I don't think this is the place to be showing off scars. Because if we did, we'd never finish the soup and get on to the fish you did win a battle with."

The laughter was loud, and Tremellyn sat back with a fond smile for Amber. "You're right. Fine thing for a host to start stripping down at the dinner table! But, Mr. St. Ives, you can see you've no cause to apologize for anything. I'm the one who should. Forgive me, all," he said with a wave of his hand. "I got carried away."

"Like that bit the fish took?" the baron called, to relieved laughter all around.

"Exactly!" Tremellyn said, and sat back, smiling.

The soup was followed by fish.

"Aha!" the vicar said when the platter was brought out. "We are being served Tremellyn's revenge, are we?"

Many of the guests were laughing too hard to eat, so it was a while until the fowl was served, and it was met by as many jests. In fact, each dish throughout dinner was discussed as it was served. Unlike dinners in London, the company shared one conversation instead of having several intimate ones. Amyas was relieved and entertained. That was noticed.

"I suppose you find us simple compared to Londoners, St. Ives," Pascoe said during a lull in the conversation.

Amyas looked up.

"You seem amused enough," Pascoe explained.

"I am, and gladly so," Amyas said. "I don't find anyone simple, it's merely that I'm having a good time. This is like sitting with one big merry family. Of course, I can't be sure of that, since I never had one."

"So it was just you and your father?" Pascoe asked, his eyes intent.

Amyas realized his mistake too late. The vicar saved him.

"Oh, but I don't believe a big family is any guarantee of a merry dinner," the old man said. "When I was young all families were big ones. My own had twelve in it, and let me assure you that half the time the squabbling equaled the merriment."

"So true!" the baroness said. "I come from a family of seven, and we children had to eat in the nursery. Too often for our poor nurse's sake, both the words and the food flew!"

The guests compared notes on their own families, even Tobias, Pascoe's crewman, shyly telling about the five children that crowded his parents' cottage. Amyas knew he'd have to explain more one day, and that day would be soon, if Pascoe Piper had anything to say about it. He wondered why, since Pascoe clearly wanted Amber. Surely the fellow knew he was courting Grace?

When the last dishes were removed, Tremellyn rose from the table.

"In London I suppose they ask the gents to stay for port while the ladies go gossip among themselves," he told Amyas. "But here we're afraid of what the ladies might say about us if we let them go off alone."

"And rightly so!" the baroness cried, as the girls giggled.

"And besides, we like to hear them sing more than we like to drink," Tremellyn went on.

"And that," the baron said, "is a lot."

"So," Tremellyn said. "Since the bottles can come with us, shall we all adjourn, as they say?"

The company went into the parlor. Grace sat down at the piano, Amber stood by her side. They made a pretty picture, Amyas thought. Grace looked like a sweet, sincere young maiden of good family. And by her side stood Amber, all russet and gold, dazzling in her fiery beauty, looking like the woman a man saw when he sat dreaming by his fireside, gazing into the heart of a fire.

Amyas stood by the hearth and studied them. He didn't have to force himself to look only at Grace, because Amber stood beside her. For the first time since he'd met them he could stare all he liked at Amber, and no one would know. In fact, Tremellyn was looking fondly at Grace when he saw Amyas's intent expression. He turned and tipped a wink at Amyas, along with a smile of approval.

The two women whispered together for a moment.

"Mr. St. Ives," Grace said shyly, "since you come from the farthest away, the first song will be for you. Please, anyone who knows the tune, sing with us."

She began to play, and she and Amber to sing, in clear sweet voices.

"You and I and Amyas, Amyas you and I, to the green wood must we go. Alas, you and I, my life, and Amyas."

Grace stole glances at Amyas as she sang. And so, he noticed, did Amber. It only made sense, it was his song, and they wanted to see his reaction. Amyas for once forgot his hungers, plans, and schemes. He felt not only touched and honored, but part of something he'd never known he missed, and wished with all his heart he could preserve.

Some of the guests joined in on the refrain, Toby in a surprisingly good tenor, Tremellyn putting in his ringing bass, the baroness carrying a soprano line as Grace's friends sang soft harmony.

A silent Pascoe only sat frowning at Amyas. And Amyas, against all odds and all his expectations, couldn't sing a note because he was too moved to speak.

When Amber got to her room that night, she found Grace already there, sitting in the middle of her bed, brushing out her long black hair.

"Dishes done, house cleaned, everyone gone to bed," Amber said on a yawn. "Time to sleep."

"Not before talking!" Grace said. "What do you think of him?"

There was no question of who "him" was. "I told you before," Amber said as she pulled the ribbon from her hair.

"No, you really haven't."

"Oh, please," Amber said, turning away. "What else have we talked about since he set foot in town?"

"You've agreed that he's attractive, and elegant and amusing, but you haven't told me what you think of him—for me."

Amber pulled her gown over her head. "I think," she said, in a muffled voice, "that's your decision, not mine. We've talked about that, too. You know what folly it is to say anything about a suitor. If I said one word crosswise, and you married him, you'd remember it and resent me to the end of your days. Not that I would!" she added quickly.

She walked to the pitcher and basin on her dressing table, poured out water, cupped her hands, and washed her face. "But if I said I liked him," she said through her fingers, "it would be just as terrible if you married him and discovered that you didn't. I'd be blamed either way."

"Do you?" Grace asked softly.

"Do I what?" Amber said as she toweled her face dry.

"Like him. I mean, for yourself?"

It was quiet in the room for a moment. Then Amber laughed. "It hardly matters. He's taken with you. We're Snow White and Rose Red, remember? Different as red and white can be. Few men like both of us equally, except for Squire Blandings and Mr. McGillicuddy."

She'd named two famous local lechers, who

weren't welcome in the Tremellyn house, and waited for Grace's laughter. It didn't come.

"Because if you liked him," Grace said slowly, "I wouldn't. I wouldn't even think of it. I mean, that would be worse than your not liking him, I think."

"So it would," Amber agreed softly. She put down the towel, bent her head so that her hair tumbled over her face. She separated her hair into three portions and kept her head down as she started making her night braid before she spoke again.

"Grace, if you like him, take him. I don't see why not. He's charming, smart, and surely, rich. But is he kind? Easy to anger or easygoing? Does he have friends? What sort of people are they? It isn't like picking a puppy. He will control your life. Before you decide anything, you must know more about him."

"I know that!" Grace said in surprise. "My goodness! I'm not a baby anymore. Be sure I'd find out much more if I were really interested. But I haven't decided anything, and there's so much to decide." She laughed, but Amber thought her laughter sounded a little uneasy. "I just wanted to make sure you didn't mind me walking out with him."

"I don't," Amber said. She picked up her head, glad she'd been able to keep her face from her sister, as well as her opinions. But she was sick at heart, realizing it wouldn't be the last time she'd have to do it.

Chapter 9

Amyas woke to a morning such as he'd never known. He washed, dressed, and left the inn to go for a walk through the village before breakfast. Everywhere he went, people greeted him. An old seaman touched his cap, a young woman tipped him a smile, an old woman rearranged her wrinkles in a grin: Everywhere, he was given a good morning.

The streets were narrow and tilted; neat little cottages sat close to those cobbled streets, and they tended to tilt, too. The sea glistened in the distance at the end of half the streets in town. There were flowers blooming in all the dooryards. The only dirt was underneath the flowers, because every doorstep was scrubbed clean.

The children were fully clothed, and their clothing

was mended, and even the thin ones looked fed. There were no rats as big as cats, or cats as lean as the day before death. No dogs with their ribs showing as they snarled over the garbage. No garbage either, no street peddlers crying wares that were little better than garbage. He heard only "good mornings" and the sound of the gulls overhead. Most wonderful of all, no one avoided his eyes.

Amyas remembered growing up in a world where eye contact might be deadly. A world roamed by packs of wolfish children scouring ragged streets for their dinners, running for their lives, or chasing someone to make them give up theirs. He remembered prisons so vile he longed for the freedom of those cruel streets again and a land where most of the people were prisoners.

Here, there was no crime that he could see. He supposed there was; this wasn't heaven, after all, only a small English village by the sea. He imagined the crime must be of a different sort than he knew. People probably stole here, but with skewed accounts and in short weights and measures, and not in order to eat. They might cheat, but not at cards or dice games in the streets. They likely gambled, but not for a living, and not on how long it took a dog to kill twenty rats, or twenty dogs to kill one bear, or one gamecock to kill another. He knew the people here had lusts, because they were human. He was sure they didn't satisfy their appetites in the alleys between their houses, or by force, anywhere they could find a victim.

He doubted the people here killed each other. At least, not often and probably not for survival itself, or as a job.

Amyas strolled down a street and came to the seawall. He stood there a while, just looking out at the sun on the glittering water. It was quiet, except for the sound of the gulls and the water slapping at the stones on the shore. It was peace, as he'd seldom known it.

All the boats were out to sea, so the strand was deserted, and yet he felt entirely safe, and knew he would even if he stood there at midnight.

By the time Amyas went back to the inn, he was totally in love. He had his breakfast and dressed himself to go courting, so that he'd always be welcomed and would never have to leave here again.

"Tell us more about the Antipodes," Grace said eagerly.

Amyas flashed her a warm smile. It was an overcast afternoon, the growing dampness making the scent of honeysuckle heavy in the air. They were sitting in the Tremellyn back garden, chatting without really saying much. He thought it was time to try. "Tell me more about yourself, first," he countered.

"Bah," she said, wrinkling her nose. "There's nothing more to tell about me. I don't even have a mystery to my name, like Amber does. I've lived here forever and don't do anything exciting. I don't even dream of traveling, the way Amber does."

Amber, Amber, Amber, he thought wearily, looking

to where Amber sat nearby, shelling peas for dinner, and listening. Listening was her job, as chaperone. But she did just as much talking as Grace, because Grace kept asking her to.

He was heartily sick of it. This would be so much easier for him if he could speak to Grace alone. Maybe he could actually get an idea from her, an opinion of her own. Because not only did she always talk about Amber, she quoted her, looked at her for approval, played for her laughter, referred every scrap of conversation to her. How would the girl cope without her adopted sister nearby? Or maybe she wouldn't? Amyas hid a smile at a sudden very improbable, and deliciously salacious, vision of his wedding night if he won the Tremellyn girl.

He killed his smile and dutifully asked the question that he had to. "And where do you dream of going, Amber?"

She looked up at him. He saw sudden hurt in her eyes, and realized he always called Grace, "Miss Tremellyn." He couldn't call Amber that, of course, it wasn't her name. But he might have said, "Miss Amber." By not according her the dignity of something in front of her name, he was treating her like a servant, delegating her to a lower status. He supposed he'd meant to. He couldn't court her; he had to keep reminding himself why.

She looked lovely today, even in a simple flowered gown with an apron over it. But she'd look lovely in anything, and the damnedest thing was that her glowing looks cast Grace's cool moonlight beauty into the shade. It was like comparing the sun to the moon, he thought bitterly. It was just his bad luck that he preferred the sun, and that Amber No Name fascinated him far beyond her looks.

Amber didn't answer him right away. She stared at him for a long cold moment. "Where do I want to go," she finally asked slowly, "apart from away from here?"

"Here, specifically?" he asked, his eyes narrowing, angry at her being there, as well as at himself for making her feel small. "Now? This moment, in this garden, do you mean?"

Grace sat wide-eyed looking from one of them to the other, like a child watching her elders having a quarrel.

"Why, yes," Amber said curtly. "Because if you believe playing the duenna is any fun, let me tell you it isn't. No, Grace, don't interrupt. I know I'm supposed to watch over you when he comes calling, but there's no point anymore. He's called on you for a week, and I doubt he's going to do anything especially evil today."

Amyas raised an eyebrow. She'd referred to him as "he," which was just as insulting in its way as his neglecting the "Miss" on her name. He was impressed.

"So, go." Amber waved her hand as though she was shooing a pair of puppies away. "Walk and talk without me at your side. I don't believe you're up to no good, Mr. St. Ives. At least, any no good that Grace couldn't scream for help to thwart. It's stupid for me to sit like a lump just so you two can talk. I have better things to do. But here I must stay listening to your inan . . . intimate conversation. Which isn't that intimate, nor can it be with me here."

She stood up, the bowl of peas in her hand. "I think it would be perfectly all right if you two went for a walk, by yourselves. In fact, I think you should."

Grace looked shocked. "But Papa . . ."

"Mr. Tremellyn was young once himself," Amber said firmly. "I'm sure he'll understand."

"I understand everything," Hugo Tremellyn said as he came out the door and into the garden. "What is it that I understand today?"

He was smiling. Pascoe Piper, walking behind him, was not.

Neither was Amber. She sat again, but her face was flushed, and her voice, though calm, was clipped. "I was just telling Grace that she could certainly go for a stroll with Mr. St. Ives without me always trailing after them. I have things to do, yet here I've been sitting with them all afternoon, just for propriety's sake. My goodness, Mr. Tremellyn, it's the nineteenth century, after all. Forget about London manners! I don't think girls are watched that closely even in Arabia."

Tremellyn laughed. He lightly caught the end of Amber's uplifted nose between two crooked fingers, as he had when she'd been a child and he'd pretended to snip off her nose. "Nose out of joint, is it?" He chuckled. "I never meant to make you Gracie's ball and chain. You don't have to play gooseberry anymore, girl. No matter how he feels about our Gracie, St. Ives wouldn't go so far as to forget himself with her. He knows she's young and inexperienced, and he's a civilized chap. Aren't you, St. Ives?"

"I hope so," Amyas said stiffly, feeling like a fool. It was one thing to be courting a young girl he didn't feel anything but a vague liking for, another to be painted as a dying swan of a suitor.

"You were here when I got here an hour ago," Pascoe said. "Are you staying? Has something been decided I don't know about?"

"Oh, no!" Grace said as Amyas pulled out his watch, and said, "I didn't realize the time."

"I did," Amber snapped, as she stood "Excuse me, gentlemen. I have things to do."

"I'll help you," Grace said, and after looking from one man to the other, she fled, following Amber as she marched into the house.

"I'll be going, too," Pascoe said. He glanced at Tremellyn. "Were I you, Tremellyn, I'd think about what I said again, I would."

"Aye," Tremellyn said gruffly. "I will."

In a matter of moments, only he and Amyas were left standing in the garden. Amyas bowed. "I hope I haven't offended," he said. "I certainly didn't intend to."

Tremellyn waved a hand. "You didn't. Pascoe's got himself into an uproar for nothing. He fancies Amber and thinks he has a rival in you, is all it is."

"And does she fancy him?" Amyas said before he could think better of it.

Tremellyn looked at him sharply. "I don't know. You know how it is with females. Or do you?" He shook his head, and patted his pockets until he produced his pipe and a worn leather pouch. "There's the problem," he said on a long sigh. "Ach, but Pascoe bent my ear; it's not easy being the father of a girl. This is hard for me, but I think he's right about one thing. You and me, St. Ives. Or should I say, 'You and I, Amyas'?" he asked on a chuckle, before his face grew sober again. "I think it's time we talked. Oh, don't get nervous. I'm not saying I think you've overstepped or taken any liberties. And I'm not asking your intentions, neither."

He poured tobacco from his pouch into the bowl of his pipe, tamped it down with a finger, patted his pockets again, then stopped and looked keenly at Amyas. "But Pascoe reminded me you've been here for a few weeks now. He claims you run tame here, and I suppose you do. He also says we really don't know Jack Squat about you, and I suppose he's right. So. How about coming for dinner tonight? Then after dinner, how about coming into my study, where we'll be safe from the girls? We'll share a glass, and maybe have a talk? That is, if you intend to stay on in the village. Otherwise, I'll not trouble you."

Amyas nodded. It was certainly within Tremellyn's rights to know the man he'd been entertaining and what his plans and prospects were, as well as what his full history was. The only thing he had to do, Amyas realized, was decide how much of the truth he should or could tell—and how much he had to tell. It would mean he had to come to a decision.

"Of course," Amyas said. "I agree. It's time."

The rain blew in after dinner on the wings of a thunderstorm and settled on for the night after the thunder rattled off to sea.

Amber and Grace sat in the parlor, before a blazing fire. It didn't take the damp from Amber's soul.

"Well, that was a pleasant dinner," Grace said happily.

"Yes. We were just like one big happy family," Amber said. "Which I suppose we'll be."

Grace looked up from her embroidery loop. "Don't say that! I haven't made up my mind. In fact, I'm not even sure Mr. St. Ives is courting me. I just meant it was a pleasant dinner. I loved the stories he told about the talking birds, didn't you?"

Amber nodded. "I loved them the last time I heard them, too. He does tend to tell the same stories."

"Well, but I asked him to," Grace said.

Amber looked at her keenly. "Will you have him if he asks, Gracie?"

Grace blinked. "Why, there's no saying that he'll ask."

"Oh, come now," Amber said roughly. "Give over. He's visited almost every day since he got here, and he's practically lived here all week. Now he's locked in your father's study with him. What do you think he's doing? Discussing the price of pilchards and asking about mackerel?"

Grace went pale. "I never thought . . . They're just getting to know each other."

"Oh please, Gracie, do grow up. The man's mad for you. He's asking for your hand."

"Pascoe comes to talk with Papa all the time in private," Grace flashed back at her, "and we know he's not asking for your hand."

"We also know they talk about what's being caught on Pascoe's boat, and it's not mackerel but merlot," Amber said, grateful that no one knew what Pascoe had already asked her.

"And yet," Grace said triumphantly, "Pascoe does nothing but look at you all the time."

"Yes. Because that's all I let him do. I don't want him, and so I don't want to lead him on. I don't flirt with Pascoe, just the opposite. But you've been all dimples and giggles with St. Ives, haven't you?"

Grace looked stricken. "But so were you."

"Oh no, I have not been."

Grace dropped her gaze and fell silent.

"Haven't you been wanting this?" Amber looked at her curiously. "Don't you want him?"

Grace didn't look up.

Amber frowned. "Gracie? This isn't like you. What is it? Why not tell me the truth?"

Grace put down her embroidery. "Because," she said with curious dignity, "although we're close, and

I do love you, Amber, I won't be with you always. I'm grown up now. I'll make my own life one day soon, as you will make yours. I'll go my own way in time, too. So I have to make my own decisions, especially about something as important as marriage. And if that means keeping secrets, that's just what has to be."

Gracie rose. "And now I think I'll go to bed. I didn't realize he'd be asking for my hand tonight, and if he is, I'm not ready to give any answers. I mean, I'll be going to my own bed. So I'll see you in the morning, Amber. Good night."

Amber sat stunned for several minutes after Grace left her. Then the clock on the mantel struck its tinny chimes, and she glanced up at it and grew pale. She didn't want to be found alone there when the two men came out, smiling. She was as sure of what St. Ives was asking as she was of what Tremellyn's answer would be. It needed only Grace's consent, and though she was behaving oddly, Amber put that down to prenuptial nerves. Who would turn down a man like St. Ives?

There was no more denying it. She lived for every day that she saw him. It wasn't just his looks, though they thrilled her. And it was in spite of his secrets, which fascinated her. It was because of his jests, his humor, his rich, slow voice, his slow, curling smile. Those half-lidded knowing eyes—eyes that avoided hers when she looked back at him when she caught him watching her.

She wasn't a fool. She knew what desire was; she'd

been wanted before, and she'd swear the man wanted her. But she knew as sure as the sun would rise that he wanted to marry Grace. It didn't mean he was evil or cunning, or even that he'd ever betray Grace. It just meant that he desired her. He'd tried to hide it, but she was sure he knew she knew. Why else should his attitude toward her sometimes border on rudeness? He tried to keep his distance. It must be as awkward for him as it was for her.

But there it was, and, whatever it was, Amber also knew it meant that her life would be hellish from now on, because she wanted him, too. How many years could she bear it? And what could she do but bear it?

She would see him greet Gracie at the altar. She'd see him give Grace his first husband's kiss. From then on, they'd exchange those slow, smiling glances that lovers always did, remembering what they'd done in the night, planning what they'd do again. He'd carve the roasts Grace would serve at her dinner, and he'd hold the sons and daughters Gracie would give him.

He'd always be there, always watching her, Amber thought, and even if he stopped doing that, she'd always remember that he had wanted her body, and that she hadn't been able to offer him anything else he wanted.

She loved Grace too much to tolerate the envy she'd feel. She had too much respect for herself to allow it. What a fruitless, stupid, pointless thing to covet Gracie's husband. It would be an obsession that would prevent her happiness in every way.

Amber held her head in her hands. It was beginning already; she rarely let herself dwell on what Grace had that she did not. What point would there be to it? But this marriage would surely poison their friendship and shatter their pretense of sisterhood—but only if she saw it every day.

She had to leave this house, and the village. She didn't know where she'd go, but go she would. That would take planning. But she also had to leave the house now. She couldn't stay to see his face.

She stood up and went to the hall, grabbed a cloak from the rack, and whistled. Old Ness slowly rose from his basket by the fire and wagged his stump of a tail. He gave her a guilty look, then sank down again, curling up tighter, nose beneath his tail. He didn't need a walk and didn't like the rain.

Neither did Amber. But she couldn't stay here now. She opened the door, bent her head against the slanting rain, and ran out into the night.

Chapter 10

❧❧

The fire in the hearth in Tremellyn's study crackled pleasantly. Rain slashed at the windowpanes, the sound muffled by the thick draperies drawn over them. Tremellyn lifted the bottle he held so Amyas could see the label. It was an old one, and in French. Amyas nodded and smiled, and watched his host pour him a glass of antique port the color of old blood. Amyas took it with thanks and sat back in his deep chair again. Tremellyn poured a glass for himself, then took a matching chair on the other side of the hearth and settled in with a sigh.

Amyas looked around the comfortable room. He felt at peace. This was how a gentleman of means should live. Not with running servants at his constant beck and call, and not in a room filled with expensive, fragile nothings on display. But in a strong old house filled with warmth and comforts. It was how he wanted to live one day.

Tremellyn smiled at his guest. "Well, then, St. Ives. I suppose this talk was inevitable. I knew it was coming one day but confess I'm still surprised to be having it. By God! The years flew. They grow up so fast. Everyone told me so, but I didn't believe it. Still, here it is, and here you are. I wish I knew how to start."

"I can't help you there," Amyas said. "I've never done this either."

Both men chuckled.

"Well, I'll start," Tremellyn said. "You've been calling here every day since we met, walking out with my girls, sending them flowers, setting them laughing with your quips and jests. You're practically part of my parlor by now. So, since you're a single gent, and they're unmarried women, you must know certain rules apply from here to London town. Am I to assume you're interested in one of them?"

Amyas smiled. "Certainly not both, sir!"

Tremellyn gave him a searching look. "Aye. That's only prudent. But which one, I wonder?"

Amyas sat up straight. "I've tried to be subtle, but have I been that dense?"

"You've walked with my Gracie," Tremellyn said, watching him closely. "Talked with her often enough, too. But you've talked to our Amber as well. And," he said, raising a hand before Amyas could speak, "God knows you've looked at Amber often enough, too."

"Who wouldn't?" Amyas said. "She's spectacular, isn't she? But I haven't been courting her, Tremellyn. I've never asked her out alone, nor have I singled her out for special attention."

"So why not tell me why you haven't? Because she's a foundling? Are you that toplofty? Would your family object? She may have no name, but I tell you right now," he said gruffly, "I'll dower her, maybe not as well as my own daughter, but well enough."

Amyas blinked. "Lord, no. I don't need the money, and my family will accept any bride I take." He passed a hand over his mouth. "I never thought I'd have to tell you why I *didn't* want her. How could I? She's lovely, as I said. But my preference is for Grace." He stopped, hoping he wouldn't have to explain why. The one reason, the real reason, the only reason, was one he was ashamed of, although he had a suspicion that an old-fashioned man like Tremellyn would understand it very well. "I never pretended otherwise. Surely you don't really think I did?"

"Nay. But what I think and what I see are often different things. And what our friend Pascoe Piper tells me is something else. He says you've eyes for Amber, no matter what your lips say."

"Does he? That makes sense. He's got eyes for nothing but her, and probably sees competition around every corner. She makes it worse, because so far as I can see, she can't see him at all." He laughed. "That's a lot of blindness, got the makings of a night of fine French farce." His expression turned serious.

"But I am courting your daughter, Tremellyn. I don't know how a fellow goes about doing that here. But in London, he asks her father permission to pay his addresses. Consider yourself asked."

"I do," Tremellyn said. "But before I give you an answer, here in this part of the world, a father needs to know something about a man who wants to be his son-in-law. Oh, I know you're clever well enough. And well breeched. I'll have a look at your finances, on paper, before you tie the knot, but that's standard stuff. I'm talking about you now, not your funds. You're friend to an earl, you say. You're looking for your mother's lost family. But what about the rest of it?"

He leaned forward. "Dammit, St. Ives, I really don't know one more damned thing about you. You come from London. Where in London? If you don't know your mother's family, what about your father's? Where do they live? Where did you go to school? Who are your friends? You've traveled. Exactly where, and why? Speaking of that, what else have you done with your life? Who are you, Amyas St. Ives?"

Amyas kept his face impassive, though his mind was working furiously. The man asked every question he had a right to. The biggest question was whether Amyas could answer any of them. Because to answer one truthfully would be to tell all. To continue to lie would forge a chain of deception that would eventually crumble. No one knew better than he that the best of schemes had only a short life. Truth could last a lifetime; lies needed constant care. Anyway, he realized—had realized during sleepless hours nights ago—he would and could not ask his brothers to keep lying for him. Nor did he want to lie to his wife and eventual children.

Time was up.

Tremellyn liked him. Grace seemed to as well. And why not? He had a lot to offer her, everything, in fact, except for a name. He did have money, friends, and connections. While he probably wouldn't be welcome in highest society or allowed to marry a wellborn woman, he was admitted everywhere in London. And for all that he liked Hugo Tremellyn, the plain truth was that the man was only a moderately wealthy commoner who'd never left this little village and had gotten his money from fish.

A self-made man himself, Tremellyn might well respect the way Amyas had raised himself from nothing. That would be a very fine thing.

Amyas decided. He might as well tell the truth now, if only because lies couldn't serve him anymore. "Well, now Tremellyn," he said, leaning forward, "it's like this . . ."

The fire in the gatehouse's hearth burned clean and hot. It cracked and sizzled, dispelling the damp and taking the chill off the stone floors and walls. But nothing could lighten the darkness in Amber's heart. She sat at the table in her sanctuary, but though the room was snug and cozy even in the storm, she wasn't content. She didn't know if she ever could be again. He'd ruined that for her.

Or maybe it was only she herself who had done it; she didn't know anymore. She'd never formed such an infatuation. She wasn't even sure it was that. One thing she did know: She didn't know where she'd ever meet such a man again.

Amyas St. Ives was intelligent and humorous, and better than handsome, so very attractive. Looks would fade, but it was a man's spirit that made him attractive. He was aware of the world, but not too wrapped up in it; he listened and had something to contribute to a conversation, though his eyes held volumes of other conversation that couldn't be put into words. Worldly, neat, well-spoken . . . where did such men come from? Where did he come from . . . ?

London, she thought suddenly, raising her head. Maybe other such men lived there. Maybe she was impressed with him because she'd never met such a fellow before. But all her "befores" had been in this little village where she'd been found. She'd never traveled much farther away.

But London town! There might be other such gentlemen, with such manners, wit, and charm and . . .

Amber put her chin down on her folded arms on the tabletop again, and stared vacantly at the walls. Because if there were other men remotely like him, they, too, would be delighted to court, then marry a foundling with no station in life. Of course. When pigs, and fish, flew.

She thought hard. She had to. She could mope and grieve later. Now, she had to act. After all, Mr. Tremellyn said that he'd only found her all those years ago because she'd been walking along the shore, wailing loud enough to wake the dead. If she'd sat still and suffered silently then, if she'd curled herself into a sad little knot on the sand, she might not even be here today. If she'd given up then, she'd probably have been carried away by the tide, instead of by a good and generous man. She couldn't give up now either.

Amber sat up. She ran a knuckle under her nose, reached into her pocket and dragged out a handkerchief, blew her nose and blotted the tears from her eyes. Then she concentrated, looking for a solution.

If she only had relatives she could go to . . . She scowled. Folly to wish it again. This was no time for fantasy. If she only had friends . . . She did. They all lived here. No! *Emily!* she thought, sitting up straighter. Of course! There it was, right under her nose.

Her old friend Emily lived in London now. Emily had been orphaned young and brought up by an aunt. The only two orphans in town, they had formed a bond because of it. Emily was a tall, lantern-jawed girl, not very pretty, but clever. She'd gone to London to be a governess, and they still corresponded.

Amber smiled. She'd write and ask Emily what employment opportunities there were in London. Surely she could get a post somewhere. She was educated and could take care of children, too.

And speaking of London . . . Charlotte Knight had

a cousin in London who had married a haberdasher, didn't she? Amber smiled with expectation. Yes, Magway, that was the name. They were decent and hardworking, and best of all, near her own age, and so more likely to be sympathetic. The Magways didn't travel in exalted circles, so they might know of a place for her. She could certainly sell things from behind a counter. Two opportunities then, and she'd found them right off.

It gave her hope. But it didn't make her any happier.

Amber looked around the gatehouse. She loved this place, this village, the sea, and the people who lived here. She especially loved Grace and Mr. Tremellyn. Her life here had been a good one. She'd always wanted to travel, she hadn't expected to do it by running away. But it was only sanity to leave a potential disaster in order to prevent it.

Amber rose from the table to get paper and pen. She often came here to write letters. By the time she'd finished these two she could go home again—if they were all sleeping. But if she still saw lights in the windows of the house when she was done, she'd sleep here. They wouldn't worry, she'd done it before. If she wasn't going home of a night, she left a lamp in a window of the gatehouse, and they'd know she just needed some time to herself. She thought about Grace and St. Ives, and the celebrations she would have to endure, hestitated, then lit a lantern, and placed it in the window. Now she had all the time in the night to compose herself.

She'd struggled through a letter to Emily, crumpling two sheets of paper before she got it right. She was starting the one to Charlotte Knight's cousin Mrs. Magway, when she heard the sound at the door.

She froze, then glanced at the clock. No one ever disturbed her here at such an hour. She was suddenly afraid. Not of intruders, but that it might be Grace, too filled with happiness to hold it to herself for another moment. It wasn't every day that a girl got engaged. If Grace had come out in the night in the rain to tell her, there'd be no escape, after all. She'd have to share in the laughter and the joy.

Amber rose slowly and put down her pen. She saw how her hand shook and hid it by clutching both hands together. She'd have to pretend delight for Grace, maybe even offer St. Ives her cheek so he could give her a brother-in-law's kiss. Then she could weep, and hope they took it for emotion because she was so moved by Grace's joy.

The knock came again. Amber went to the door, and cracked it open. She hoped the smile on her face looked real and not like the grimace of pain that it was.

She looked out.

"Miss Amber?" Amyas said woodenly. "I've come to say good-bye."

"What?" she said.

He stood in the doorway, blocking out the night. The rain pelted down. She saw him through a sheet of it; he was drenched, his greatcoat dripping. He wore no hat, his hair was sodden, water coursed down his face. He didn't seem to notice.

"I'm leaving," he said, and something in the way he said it made her look harder.

His eyes were opened wide, and reflected the firelight behind her. He seemed stunned.

"Are you hurt?" she asked, wondering if he'd fallen from his horse.

"Hurt? No. But I must go. Tremellyn threw me out," he added.

"What?" She stared and then, shocked, she said, "Come in. It's pouring."

He didn't seem to notice. She literally had to reach out and pull on his sleeve to get him to cross her threshold. Once inside, he looked around. The bright light and warmth seemed to reach him, because only then did he look down at her. "I doubt he'll be happy I'm here," he said. "But it would be a poor thing to ride off in the night and never let you know why. I couldn't be sure Tremellyn would tell you . . . no. I was sure he would. So I thought I should, too."

"Surely you should tell Grace?" she said, trying to collect her thoughts. "Or have you already?"

"No. But it doesn't matter."

"Doesn't matter? But you were going to ask for her hand tonight, weren't you?"

He nodded.

"So of course, it matters," she said.

He gave her a long look, his eyes finally focusing on her. "You know better than that," he said. "I'd swear you do."

"Why did he throw you out?" she asked, suddenly wary of him.

"Because I told him the truth about myself."

"I see," she said. She didn't. But he was obviously in pain. "Did he hit you? Did Mr. Tremellyn strike you?" she asked, when he didn't seem to understand.

His wide mouth crooked. "Hit me? You mean physically? God, no. Only with words."

"What the devil happened?" she exclaimed.

"I told him the truth," he said again. He ran a hand over his soaking hair and seemed surprised to see his gloved hand, dripping wet. He shuddered.

"Mr. St. Ives," she said patiently, "what is the matter?"

He looked up from his hand, his blue eyes wide, clear and suddenly lucid. "He found out who I really am, and he wants no part of me," he said. "So I'll be leaving this place in the morning, and never coming back. I wanted to say good-bye to you, especially to you. I think I wanted to talk to you because you may be the only person who can understand what I'm saying. You may be the only one to know the depth of my stupidity. See, I really didn't think it would matter to him, here, in this place."

"Take off your coat," she said. As he began to remove it, she added, "Wait. Where's your horse?"

"My horse? Oh. I rode down toward the sea when I left Tremellyn, and sat there on the horse, I suppose.

•

That's when I remembered, and came back to say good-bye to you. I left the horse tied right outside."

"Poor beast," she said, reaching for her coat on a peg on the wall. "There's a shed round back—actually around front, on the other side of the gatehouse. You can't see it from the house. I'll take him there."

"No," he said. "I will." He opened the door and disappeared into the teeming rain.

She stood where he'd left her, wondering if she'd imagined it all. But there was a puddle of rain on the floor. She'd tossed a cloth over it when the door opened wide again.

"He's secured," Amyas said. He shucked off his coat and held it on the doorstep. "This is too wet to be inside," he said. "So am I."

"But I won't stand and talk to you in the rain," she said. "I'm getting wet as it is. Close the door. Leave your greatcoat on that peg there near the entry. It will drip on the flagstones, that's what they're there for. Come in, come to the fire. You're drenched through. Wait, I'll get you toweling. You need to dry off before you can dry more."

She brought him towels, and he blotted the water from his face and hair, then, dutifully, like a child, followed her to the fire and sat in the rocking chair she offered him there.

He had dressed for his visit to Tremellyn. It made her feel even worse for him, because though his mood was strange and his face white with shock, his fine clothes were utterly ruined. He wore a fitted jacket, white linen, dark breeches, and half boots. But the rain had defeated them. His neckcloth was damp and crushed, his boots mud-streaked. She realized he still wore his gloves. They had been tan, but were now black, from the rain.

"You can take off your gloves," she started to say.

He raised his hand and let it fall on the side of the chair. "No," he said simply.

"You must have been outside a long time," she said. "I have brandy in the cupboard. That will take the chill off you."

"No," he said. "Don't entertain me. I shouldn't even be here, you shouldn't be talking to me. I only came back to explain it to you, because now that it's over, I find I feel the most guilty about you."

"Why me?"

"Because my crime, apart from not telling the truth about it, is the same as yours, Miss Amber. Not all of it," he muttered. "The fact that I was a convict, I suppose, matters, too."

She stood very still, and only cast a quick sidewise glance to see how many steps she was from her door. "I suppose it would," she said calmly and as patiently as she could, trying to keep her voice low and level. "Why don't you tell me about it?"

He laughed.

She edged a step closer to the door.

"I will, and gladly," he went on. "And you don't have to worry. I'm not mad, or dangerous, at least, not anymore. But the truth is that I was a foundling,

Amber. And I also was a convict. I swear I don't know which Mr. Tremellyn thinks the greater crime. He asked me to tell him about my origins. I decided to tell him all. When I did, I was ordered out. I'm not welcome here anymore; I've been told to never come here again."

She sank to the other chair in the room, and stared at him.

He nodded. "There it is. Do you want to hear the rest? Or would you prefer I left? I don't know the protocol. If a man throws you out of his house, does he also want you gone from his grounds? I'll go, and no hard feelings, if you'd like." He shook his head as though trying to clear it. "I don't even know why I'm here, not really. I was probably out of my mind to come here at all. But the words Tremellyn used were like a plank across my face and scrambled my brains, I think." He smiled at her. "I know, I've had that happen. Believe me, what he said felt the same and rattled my head just as much."

He stood up in one lithe movement, and in spite of herself, Amber shrank back. But he only looked around, as though he'd just woken up in a strange place. "What was I thinking of? I'll go now, Miss Amber. I apologize for troubling you."

"You'll go," she said sternly, gathering all her courage and standing to face him. "But not before you tell me what this is all about. You can't just come here and say such things, then turn and walk out, leaving me to always wonder what it was you had to say. If you promise to leave when I ask you to, I'd rather you stay and tell me what happened tonight."

He sat again. "All right," he said. "What happened was that I was a fool. Nothing new in that, for me. What is new is that I so completely fooled myself."

"Tell me, please," she said.

She realized she was afraid. Not because of anything he might do, but because whatever he had to say would be shocking. And she was more afraid for him than for herself.

Chapter 11

*C*onvict? Amyas could still hear the way Tremellyn's voice had cracked on the word, how he'd risen from his chair, his face growing red.

"He didn't believe me," Amyas said now, as he sat by the hearth in the gatehouse, telling Amber what Tremellyn had said.

Amber didn't believe him either, and waited for the end of the joke. But his face remained grave and wan as he went on.

"He thought it was a jest," Amyas said softly. "And in poor taste. That made him angry, understandably. Because there I was, a fellow about to ask for his daughter's hand, and yet I begin by making a stupid jest. He said it was clear I had no children, because it

175

was an insensitive way to go about the business. And he said it did me no credit in his eyes.

"I told him that I wasn't joking," Amyas related in a flat, exhausted voice. "I was a convict, sent to the Antipodes for my crimes."

Amber's eyes widened.

"It's only truth," he said with a shrug of one shoulder. "I was. I also told him I was only eleven or twelve years old—I'm never sure which—when it happened. And that the crime that sent me to prison was a mistake. You see, I filched a pound note instead of the shillings I usually picked from pockets. That made it a hanging offense, so I was lucky only to be thrown into Newgate and sent into exile.

"Telling Tremellyn that didn't help my cause," Amyas said with a bitter smile. "His mouth actually fell open. Then, when he got his wits back, he wanted to know where my parents had been, and how they could have let it happen. He wanted to know why they hadn't just paid the magistrate and taken me home, as people of good family did in such cases."

"Why didn't they?" Amber blurted.

He smiled at her wearily. "Because I had no parents. I told Tremellyn that, too. No father or mother, no aunts that I talked about; no family at all. I invented them. My first memories are of the Foundling Hospital in London. I escaped from there before they could send me to the workhouse. That's what happens to boys they can't apprentice. I was too tall, too thin, and too defiant for the hard masters, and was told I looked too clever for the lazy ones. So I left and worked on my own, in the streets. You see before you an entirely self-made man.

"I *am* wealthy," Amyas said, with sudden energy. "I *do* have influential friends. I did serve His Majesty during the war, gathering information. That's all true. It's also true that if I'd had family when I was a boy, they'd have been able to buy me out of trouble. I didn't, so I had to live through it, and I did."

He looked at Amber as though finally really seeing her. "I'm not evil, or bad in the bone. I haven't done a criminal thing since. Then I was starving and stole to stay alive. That's all behind me now, of course. And so I told Tremellyn, too."

Amber's eyes were huge, her breath stilled as she tried to take in what he was saying. Amyas sat by her fireside, his clothes slowly drying, a glass of brandy in his hand. He seemed calm, too calm.

Amyas paused in his story, trying to marshal his thoughts and edit what he'd heard. Telling Amber what had happened helped him put it in perspective, but there were things he couldn't tell her.

He wouldn't repeat some of the names Tremellyn had called him. Not only because he wouldn't dirty her ears with them, but also because they were names that would wound her. Too many of them could apply to her, too. Because, to his shock, Tremellyn hadn't just been outraged because he discovered the man he'd welcomed into his house and allowed to court his daughter had been a convict. He was equally furious because he'd been nameless.

"Bastard!" Tremellyn had said, his face contorted with fury.

"That's as may be," Amyas had answered, rising to his feet. "There's no way to know. Look, Tremellyn, I was wrong not to tell you I'd been in prison. Don't you think I know that? But you'd never have spoken to me if you'd known, would you? I could have kept lying, you'd never have known. But I'm being honest now. I don't want any more lies between us. Think, man: What crime was I in for, after all? Pinching a pound note. I was only a hungry lad. That's the law of the land, but as you said, as you know, a boy from a good family can do worse and suffer less for it. I paid many times over. And I have a written pardon from His Majesty.

"There are men right here on this coast, friends of yours, who steal ten times as much every day," Amyas murmured to Amber now, as he had then, when he'd tried to explain to Tremellyn. "They steal when they ferry wines and perfumes and such back from France, without paying a cent in tax. They did it during the war, too. It's a crime, a big one. Yet not only do they stay out of prison, everyone here calls them friend—if they don't call them 'father' or 'brother.' All I did was take a pound note, and I was sent to Hell and back."

"And what did he say to that?" Amber asked breathlessly.

He gave her a sad, crooked smile. "Nothing I can repeat."

"Lord! What a mess," Amber said, rising and going to the fire, taking a poker and jabbing at the logs. "Maybe if you give it time," she said. "That's a shocking thing for anyone to take in all at once. You really ought to have told us before."

He raised an eyebrow. "Really? And you think his reaction would have been different a week ago, do you?"

She shook her head, and looked down. "No, I suppose not." She sighed. "Oh, my." She poked the fire, thought a while, then spoke, slowly, and to the leaping fire. "Maybe if he thinks about it a while. Mr. Tremellyn's a fair man. Your news just startled him. Here he was thinking you were highly connected." She shot him a glance. "We all did. A criminal past is the last thing we'd have suspected. But Gracie is a good and fair girl. You'll have to give her time to get over the surprise, too."

He gave her a curious look. "You think she's so smitten with me that hearing my news will break her heart?"

Amber looked away from his gaze. She put the poker back on its rack and shook her head. "No, but that's not saying she wouldn't have considered your suit."

He laughed, startling her. "Yes," he said. "Exactly." He swallowed down the jot of brandy she'd poured him. "God," he breathed. "I must have been mad. I

was in way over my head here. Seduced by the life
and the look of the place and . . . Look, Miss Amber,
the truth, and we both know it, is that I courted a girl
who didn't care for me much more than I did for her.
So I didn't hurt her, I'm sure of it. But I wooed her under false pretenses, and that is wrong. I admit it, and
take responsibility. Don't waste pity on me. I deserve
whatever Tremellyn said. Except maybe . . ."

He didn't finish what he was about to say. No sense
telling her he didn't mind Tremellyn's fury when he
heard about his criminal past. He'd half expected it,
and had thought that given time, Tremellyn would
come round on that score. But he'd been deeply
shocked that the greater fury was reserved for the
fact that he was a no one, a foundling, nameless and
unclaimed. "Filth," "garbage" and "dregs of London's gutters," were only some of the names Tremellyn had called him in his rage.

"Did you think that just because we live in the
countryside we don't have pride?" Tremellyn had finally asked, raising his head high. "Or dignity?
Honor? I ain't a nobleman, but mine's as old and
good a name as any lord's in the kingdom. My ancestors founded this village. They fished the seas and
tilled the land, they manned the navies, they fought
in wars. My people are England's bone and blood."

Tremellyn's voice had grown calmer, but colder,
and his face set hard as he'd spoken to Amyas. "We're
not filth, not scum, like the men you know, like what
you come from. No, the men in my family take re-

sponsibility for what they do, and always have. If a Tremellyn ever got a female with child, and I'm not saying it never happened, because we're only mortal, he gave her his name, believe me. We don't have care-for-nothings, or their bastards, castoffs and castaways."

"Castaways?" Amyas had asked. "Do you put Amber into the same category?"

Tremellyn had shot him a furious look. "No. Of course not! And I wouldn't let such as you have her, neither. She deserves better. It wasn't her fault whatever ship brought her foundered and broke up. And besides, she'll take her husband's name. Her children will be honored, if he is. I don't know why I'm bothering to tell you this, St. Ives—if that's even your name. I suppose you wouldn't know, would you? And I don't care. But I'm done talking. No daughter of mine will ever marry a bastard. I'm sorry you even sullied her with your company."

Tremellyn had reached into his desk drawer and pulled out a pistol. "I'll ask you to get out now, before I really lose my temper. You're younger than I, but I don't think you can best me hand to hand, even so. It don't matter. I wouldn't dirty my hands on a piece of filth like you. I have a gun, and I will use it to rid my house of vermin. Get out!"

"And so," Amyas said now, picking his words carefully, "he asked me to leave and not come back."

He took a long, steadying breath. "What a nodcock I was to be surprised. So," he said, slapping his hands down on his knees, and standing up, "what do you think of all this? I mean the fact that I was a convict and am no one? Do you want me to go right now? I aim to. But I wanted to say good-bye and apologize in person, so that you'd know what happened. Tremellyn was so mad, God knows what he'd tell you."

"He's a good man," Amber said. "I think he'd tell us everything. But what did you mean, that you courted a woman you didn't care for? You didn't really want Grace?"

He looked at her and smiled. She felt her heart clench. His hair had dried to its usual burnished gold color, his eyes to their usual sleepy awareness; his mouth had relaxed from the thin hard line he'd held it to. But he was still pale, and looked infinitely weary. It made him even more attractive to her.

"Amber, Amber," he said softly. "I lied to you by not being honest. I ask your pardon for it. But since we're not likely to meet again, at least please be as honest with me now. You know damned well that I didn't want Grace for any reasons of the heart."

She bit her lip.

"Excuse me," he said, dipping his head in a brief bow, "I meant to say . . . you know deucedly well.'"

"No," she said, "that's all right."

"No," he echoed, on a bitter smile, "that's not. Don't give me license now because you know where I come from. I have learned how to speak to a well-bred woman. I wanted Grace for my wife because she seemed good, biddable, and sweet. But mostly because she came from Tremellyn's house, with all its attendant charms. You can't know how valuable that made her to me. I wanted the friends and family, the name and respect that I saw Tremellyn has here. He was right about one thing, we nameless are like some kind of leech creatures, always looking for something solid to attach ourselves to so we can suck out substance for ourselves and our lives."

Amber put her arms around herself as though she felt a sudden chill. "Is that what you think I've done?"

His eyes flew wide. "No! Forgive me. I never meant you. You're part of the Tremellyn household, an important part."

She stayed very still. He saw her thinking, the emotions playing across her lovely face as swiftly as the shadow and light from the leaping firelight. Then she nodded. "Well, then, since it's true that we'll probably never meet again . . ." She spoke so softly he had to lean forward to hear her above the sound of the rain on the windows and the snapping fire in the hearth. "May I ask you a question, too?"

"Any," he said quickly. "Feel free, lass. We're already like two people who are parted, never to meet again. I'll be gone in moments, and never trouble you again. So you can say anything to me. Don't worry; I know the way of it. We used to talk like that in the old days, when I was a boy in Newgate, and in the Hulks, and on the way to Botany Bay. See, prisoners never know when their time will come. Some do, of course: the ones with a date with the hangman. The rest of us always knew our end could come at any time. So ask me anything, I'll tell you everything."

"If you didn't care for Gracie," she said in a rush, "why didn't you court me? I'm the elder, after all. And I know . . . you looked at me."

She refused to look at him as she waited for his answer.

His voice came slow and sad, and caressing. "Who wouldn't look at you? You're very beautiful."

"I didn't want a compliment. I thought you'd give me an answer. You said you would."

"So I did," he said. He spoke, reluctantly. "All right, then. Why didn't I court you? One reason was because you look so much like me. We foundlings have to be careful how we love, in case we wind up like that old Greek king. I rather like having both eyes, you see."

She looked at him in surprise. "What? Oh. King Oedipus? But I'm not old enough to be your mother, and . . . oh. You think you really come from here? And since we both have mysterious origins, that we might be related?" She considered it.

"You have fair hair and skin, and blue eyes," he added.

Her blue eyes lit up with humor. Her mouth crooked upward too. "Oh my," she said in a stifled voice. "You think your parents . . ." She pressed her lips together, but couldn't keep doing it. She gurgled with laughter. "Oh no, you don't mean *your* parents. I guess you mean you think *our* parents were that thoughtless? Dropping you off in London, then what? Five, six years later, nipping back to Cornwall to leave *me* on a beach? Oh my! Once might have been a tragedy, but twice? That's more than careless. And leaving their offspring in so many places? That certainly was provoking, not to say rude of them." She put her hand over her mouth, but couldn't keep in the giggles. "You are serious?"

He was startled. But then his lips bowed upward, too. "I was. You saying it out loud does make it sound improbable. I suppose it is, but when I first thought about it, it seemed plausible . . . but then, I may have wanted it to."

"Why?" she asked.

He frowned, and hesitated. "You know why, I think," he said. "Unless you're like me in mind as well as appearance, in that you can blind yourself to what you don't want to see."

She frowned back at him.

Then he saw the realization of what he meant slowly take hold. All laughter left her face.

"Oh," she said. "You wanted Mr. Tremellyn's daughter, not his charity case. I see. That makes sense."

"No," he said. "It doesn't. It only made sense to a man who wanted to be something he could never be. Damme for a fool," he murmured, "My brother—that is to say—the man I call my brother, was right. I have money now, and a smattering of education. I can mimic the way the nobs speak and act, if I want to.

But I should never have forgotten who and what I really am, or tried to pretend it wouldn't matter. I'm double the fool for trying to hide that, especially from myself. God, no wonder Tremellyn looked shocked. It must have been bizarre. There in his house sat a nameless product of the London gutters, *and* a convict, blithely expecting to be welcomed to the family."

He took her hand. "Amber, I'm not such a vain, silly ass as to think you'd have wanted me. But if my not courting you, when I couldn't take my eyes off you, made you think for one minute that I didn't want you, I'm sorrier than you can know. Had Tremellyn accepted me, I'd have been in worse trouble. I see that now. He did me a good turn, after all. I didn't want Grace. I wanted to be a man like Tremellyn. And what a damned stupid way I thought of doing it!"

He noticed that her hand felt icy cold in his, even through his gloves, so he put his other hand over it, and looked down at her. "I was in love with respectability, with belonging and family. You were, you are, one of the most glorious females I've ever clapped eyes on. I told myself the stupidest faradiddles I could imagine to keep away from you. I actually convinced myself I was afraid you might be my sister. But you've got too many brains for that," he added with a rueful smile. "It was all because I wanted to be Tremellyn's son-in-law. I wanted to buy a house by the sea and live here forever, and forget the sneaking little thief I was; the convict I was; the empty man I turned out to be.

"You tell Grace how lucky she was. But now I've got my wits back, I really don't think she'd have had me. Her eyes were always on that young sailor. You know? I think your Grace was using me as I was trying to use her."

He smiled his old easy smile, but it had a mocking edge. "What a pantomime we must have been! Me, staring at you whenever I thought no one was looking. Grace always looking at the sailor lad out of the corner of her eye. Pascoe Piper watching you like a hawk and snarling at me whenever our paths crossed! Was anyone watching the way we behaved? Not even a canny old trader like Tremellyn, I think. He saw what he wanted to, too. Well, I'm sorry to have lost his friendship, and sorriest to have upset you in any way.

"So I'll say good-bye now, and thank you for your friendship, and again apologize for what a dunce I was, and what a coward, too. I should have told Tremellyn from the start. That way we'd never have met, and I'd have no reason to apologize to you now."

All trace of shock was gone from his eyes, replaced by regret. Those eyes were clear, and blue, and full of pain. His voice had been rough with contempt for himself as he'd confessed. He had finished. But he didn't leave. He continued to stare down at her, caught by the sympathy he saw in her eyes. Then slowly, he bent his head, never leaving off looking in her eyes, giving her time to step away from him.

She didn't.

He came so close she let her eyelashes flutter down, because she couldn't keep her eyes focused on him. That was what she told herself as she waited for his kiss.

But nothing happened. When her eyes flew open again she saw surprise in his. He dropped her hands, and stepped back.

"I'm making it worse," he muttered angrily, "staying here with you, alone. God, I do it, and I know it, and I keep doing it." His hands were fists at his sides. "I really must be as bad as Tremellyn thinks. I'm sorry."

He turned to leave.

She couldn't let him go like this, hating himself, blaming himself. He was what he was. But none of it was a crime, or at least, one he hadn't paid for. "Wait!" she said. "You never said what I was doing."

He turned back with a puzzled frown.

"You said you were looking at me, and Grace at young Toby, and Pascoe at you. But what about me?" Her mouth twisted. "If you were watching me, you must have seen who I was looking at."

"Yes," he said. "That makes me feel worse, because it reminds me of what a fool I was."

"You were right to ignore me," she said. "And there's nothing wrong with a man trying to improve himself. That's what everyone does. Marrying Grace *would* have established you here. Or at least, as much as anyone not born here can ever be. But me? I have nothing but whatever Mr. Tremellyn decides to give me, and everyone knows it. Why should you have ever considered me for a wife? And what else could you have considered me for?"

She shook her head. "You know that answer as well as I do: nothing at all. And a fellow can only keep company with a respectable woman if he has respectable plans for her. Most of us here have known each other all our lives. But even here a man can't spend time alone with a single female without being thought to be trying for marriage. There are no such things as friendships among young unmarried people of any quality. You couldn't court me, and whatever you once were, you're certainly gentleman enough not to have thought of me as anything else."

He reached her in one long stride, and gripped her hands again, his eyes blazing with anger. "No. I'm not, I was not, and I can't be a gentleman, understand? I wanted you every way you can imagine, and a lot more you can't, because you're a lady even if you weren't born one. I just knew what I couldn't get away with." His lips curled. "We old lags are very good at judging risk. So I'm even less of a gentleman than you thought, and you're well rid of me."

It was the right thing to say, and it made him feel both better and worse, but he couldn't seem to let go of her hands.

She stood very still, and then closed her hands over his.

Chapter 12

⟋⟍

•

Amber heard the rain slapping against the windows and sizzling down the flue and knew the storm had set in and would last all night.

"What are you going to do now?" she asked Amyas. "Where will you go from here? Will you keep looking for your mother's family? Oh, I suppose you really weren't, were you? So, are you going to keep searching for a respectable wife? I suppose it's none of my business, but I'd like to know so I can put an end to this story. Or at least, our part in it. Because, as you say, we'll never meet again, and I know I'll always wonder about what happened to you."

"I owe you that, at least," he murmured.

"You owe me nothing," she protested. "But I confess I'd like to be able to tell Grace what became of you. And I think that when Mr. Tremellyn calms down, he'd want to know, too."

His nearness was making her nervous, but she couldn't bear to send him out into the rain again, to let him go, once and for all. "I tell you what," she said on a sudden inspiration. "I'll put on the kettle. We can have some tea, and talk. Then when you do leave, at least people will have your side of the story."

And there'll be a line left open, she thought, a road back for you, or us, so that one day . . .

She bustled over to the hearth, took down the old iron kettle, and slung it on a hook over the hearth, poked up the fire, and turned to speak to him again. He hadn't moved. He still stood by the door.

"Please sit down," she said. "Unless, of course, you want to leave us as soon as you can." She paused and knotted her hands together. "I wouldn't blame you, actually."

The silence ticked on. Then he smiled, and shook his head. "What *would* you blame me for? You're too good. You should be as angry at me as Tremellyn was."

"Maybe," she said, her head to the side as she considered it. "But the only thing you actually did to me was to not have anything to do with me. And I don't have an angelic temperament, you can ask anyone. It's just that you didn't get me angry. I care for Gracie, but as you said, I suppose you really never disappointed her. I didn't see her staring at Tobias, though. Still, you may be right. But as for me? How can I be angry? You were only trying to better yourself."

"I couldn't have done better than you," he said quietly.

She looked down. She couldn't look at him too long when he was this close. He dominated the little house; she hated to imagine how empty it would feel when he left. He'd been soaked to the skin and dried by the fire, and still looked wonderful.

His butter-colored hair looked shaggy and mussed, but that only made it more attractive. She wondered if the fire had shrunk his clothes, then realized they couldn't be tighter than the fashionable ideal. A gentleman's clothing was supposed to make him look like a classical statue. Amyas's clothes now made her notice just how wide his shoulders were, how trim his waist and flat his stomach, how long and well muscled his legs, even the one he favored.

He looked so appealing that he hurt her eyes. But with all that he was, she was very aware that he was a man who could lie blithely, and beautifully, and might have neither morals nor conscience.

She believed in plain speaking, and so lifted her head and forced herself to look him in the eye. "You could have done a great deal better than me, Mr. St. Ives, and we both know it. You may have been a convict, and you may suffer from having no family, but you still have a great deal to offer, and I think you know that, too. You wouldn't be so shocked by Mr.

Tremellyn's reaction if you didn't. As for me, you can't pretend you know me much better than I do you."

"But I do know you," he said. "How could I not? I spent as much time in your company as in Grace's. You're devoted to your family, that's obvious. You have a sense of humor and moral standards. Even when you were trying to ignore me while you sat and watched over Grace and me, I could see your lips quirking when I said something amusing. After a while, I said those things for you. Grace often didn't appreciate them.

"You have a well-informed mind," he went on. "I always saw you reading. In fact, though you've never left this place except through the pages of your books, you know something of the world; I've heard you talk about it. But you don't know hunger or debasement firsthand. You don't even really know shame, except in your birth, because you've never done anything to be ashamed of. I have. I know all the cruelty and evil you don't. And so you're nothing like any woman I ever met before."

"Can't you tell the truth at all?" she demanded angrily. "That's a lie. You've met Grace."

"I told you I'm done with lies," he said. "Grace is a very good girl. You're a woman."

"Oh," she said.

"The women I've known," he went on, "weren't respectable ones, at least, not as the world saw them. Some married the wrong man and had to follow his path. Some couldn't marry and had to give up their morals in exchange for food long before they were old enough to marry." He frowned. "Not stuff I should be telling you. But what I want to say is that didn't make all of them evil. Most had morals, but only ones they could afford."

He smiled reminiscently. "It isn't just poor females you're superior to. I've known rich as well as high-born women with no morals. I suppose they felt they could afford not to have them. The rich can afford anything they want, and the well-bred think they can. Amber . . . I mean, Miss . . ." He paused. "What the devil *is* your last name?"

"I don't have one," she said simply. "I'm listed in the church register as what I am: 'Infant Girl Found.' Rather a mouthful, so it's just as well that Mr. Tremellyn said I didn't need a last name because I'll get one when I marry. What would I do with a last name anyway? I own nothing. I sign my letters 'Amber' and letters addressed to 'Amber' at Tremellyn House reach me. Everyone knows who I am," she said, feeling tears prickling at her eyes. "Why should they know more than I do?"

"Don't," he said. "I never meant to make you cry."

"Well, I'm not,' she said, with tears rolling down her cheeks. "This is just stupid stuff."

He opened his arms. She stumbled into his embrace and laid her head against his chest. She told herself she did it so he wouldn't see her cry. But as she lay against him, feeling his hard chest beneath her cheek, hearing his beating heart in her ear, experiencing the sensation of his big hand stroking her hair, it occurred to her that she'd never been held by a man before. Not by Mr. Tremellyn, of course, not even when she'd been a child. And the few boys she'd kissed hadn't held her long, or if they had, it hadn't felt like this. She was surrounded by the scent of a warm, clean male, spiced by firewood, faint bay rum, and rain. She felt warm, protected, and stimulated, all at once. It was glorious.

She didn't want to move away.

She knew she had to.

"Well," she said on a shuddering breath, "I've made a fool of myself, haven't I?"

He couldn't answer right away. He held her, wishing that he could remove his glove so he could feel the texture of the silky curls under his fingers. He could feel her warm body very well though, every curving inch pressed so close to him. Her breasts were flat against his chest. That was the only thing flat about them, he thought, glad he could still call up humor, because he didn't want to embarrass himself.

By God! he thought, but she had delicious contours. He wished he could run his other hand along them. But he had to play the role of comforter now, for her, not himself. Although, he thought, his treacherous body beginning to respond to hers, he could certainly comfort himself as well. . . .

He had to put that thought out of his mind so he could subdue his body. There was nothing more for him here, certainly not this warm, yielding, charming young woman. He had nothing to give her but himself, and that only for the night. She definitely didn't need that.

Think of someone other than yourself, you selfish swine, he told himself, and said, "No. You're not a fool. You've had a hard time of it through no fault of your own. I'm sorry if I made it worse."

Amber sighed. His voice was a rich rumble beneath her ear. It was lovely being sympathized with. She was always so strong, for Gracie, and so competent, for Mr. Tremellyn. For once, here was a strong man talking over all her guilt and saying she shouldn't regret her resentments, and so absolving her of them. It was grand.

She murmured her response in a little voice she hardly recognized. "You didn't make it worse," she said. "I am what I am, and there's the end of it. It could be worse. A lot of people blame love children for the sins of their parents. I don't know if I am one, so at least I was spared that."

He chuckled. "You're right. It's true for me, too. I could have been the rightful son of a foreign prince, you know, stolen away by his enemies. They could have been running from my father's army and gone to London. Once there, one day, they thought they heard pursuers, so they put me down for a minute and ran, to get away. They got pretty far, but they were killed, and so no one ever knew where I'd been left."

She raised her head and looked up at him with

wonder. "You thought of that, too? I used to think I could be a princess, or at least the daughter of some important foreigner. Since I was found on the beach, I thought that he and his wife might have escaped from the Bastille, or Napoleon, and were making the run across the Channel when their ship went onto the rocks. I liked to imagine they sacrificed themselves to save me."

They smiled at each other.

His eyes were so bright and blue and filled with warmth, humor, and understanding that she couldn't look away.

Her lips were so damned plump and pink, he thought. And then she had to go and part them, and he was lost.

He lowered his head. She raised hers.

The first touch of his lips ignited a spark, making her feel the way she did when she'd crossed the good carpet in the parlor, then touched the metal door latch. Then he pulled her closer and opened his lips against hers, and she felt so much more she couldn't think what it felt like, she could only drown in the intoxicating depth of it.

She put her hands on his shoulders and clung to him, learning what to do with her tongue from what he did with his, feeling the heat and sweetness of his mouth, learning the strength of his body from the way he restrained himself as he held her.

Their clothing was as thin as fashion demanded, so his excitement was as easy for her to feel as hers was for him. She pulled back from him a fraction, shocked at the extent of his response.

He was done with kindness, and tired of need. He cupped the back of her head with one hand, and her backside with the other, and dragged her back for another kiss.

She went, willingly. It was so good not to have to make decisions anymore. And she had to taste more of him.

He wasn't thinking at all now. Her mouth tasted as delicious as it had looked. Her body was pliant and curved, and he had to know more of it. He bent, eased an arm under her knees, and stood again, sweeping her up in his arms. She murmured something; it didn't matter what. It wasn't "No," and that was enough encouragement for him. He wasn't hearing much but the blood beating in his ears anyway. It was only a few strides to the big bed in the corner of the room, and he took them quickly, and tumbled down on the bed with her, never letting her out of his arms, never lifting his mouth from hers.

He raised himself from her only so he could raise her skirts. Then he pulled the neckline of her gown down to meet the hem of her skirt, at her waist. He lowered his eyes to her beautiful breasts and lowered his mouth to them. They'd peaked against his chest; he finally had to feel them, with his lips.

Now he heard what she was murmuring. She was saying, "Oh, oh my, oh!"

He held one beautifully contoured breast in his

hand and raised his mouth from it so he could admire it. He blew a breath across the dimpled nub of it to watch it tighten to a smaller dark crimson bud. The sight of his big, gloved hand against that delicate white skin gave him a pinch of regret, made him feel a twinge of guilt at doing something wrong. And so he lowered his mouth to her nipple so he could sip pure desire in order to forget.

She sighed, and threw her head back, her eyes closed tight. He kissed her until his senses swam, then he drew his mouth down along her outflung neck and down to her breasts again. He was burning now, his excitement rising as his body was, almost unendurably. But he knew what pleasure could come later from endurance now and kept on teasing her, tasting her, showing her how much delight there was in his touch. He knew she wasn't as experienced as most women he'd had, but she learned quickly and followed his lead in everything.

She surged against him, her breathing so ragged he knew he could go on, had to go further. He cupped her and kissed her, never leaving her long, but sometimes leaning back in order to get glimpses of her to fuel his desire. He admired the soft swell of her stomach, the gentle curve of her hips, the curling golden thatch that covered her sex. But eventually he had to pause in order to strip off one glove, at least, so he could touch her tender nether petals and not hurt her by doing so. And he had to feel the slippery smoothness of her flesh so he could be sure she was ready for him. He wouldn't go on until he was sure of it. That way, too, he could bring her to her highest peak before he brought them both to it together.

It only took a moment. He raised himself from her to tug off his tight left glove. It was a moment too long. The rain had shrunken the leather, and it was dry now, and tighter than he knew. He struggled to pull his glove off.

And so she felt his absence. She opened her eyes.

She gasped, and sat bolt upright. Her hands flew to her breasts to cover them, her legs, which he'd moved so that they'd been so sweetly splayed apart against him, clapped together as she drew up her knees and curled up tightly.

Even so, he knew women. Even now, he knew that if he put his arms around her and murmured assurances as he eased her back on the bed, he might win her back again. But her moment of awakening woke him. He saw her shame at her nakedness as clearly as he saw his own excitement.

Amyas closed his eyes and took a deep breath. The blood pounded in his ears and throbbed in his swollen sex. He was actually in pain, but he welcomed it, because he realized he deserved it. A few minutes more and he wouldn't have been able to leave her again, conscience be damned. Another minute or two, and he'd have had her—and all the problems that would bring.

He'd have to stay with her then; he would have to marry her. Amyas was many things, and he admitted them all, but he was never a cad, and not a man who hurt women if he could help it. He wouldn't marry her. He couldn't seduce and leave her.

He had to leave her, and soon, no matter that he could make love to her and it would feel fine. What were a few minutes of pleasure against a lifetime of regret?

It was hard for him to talk, difficult to think. But he had to pull himself together. "Oof," he groaned, and turned aside to hide his evident state of arousal, turning his head to look at the fire so that she could dress herself again. He ran a hand through his hair. Her hands had completely disheveled it.

"I'm sorry," he finally said to the empty air. "I didn't mean for it to go that far." He tried to laugh. "I suppose there's your reason men and women, even moral ones, shouldn't be alone together. I should have known better. Forgive me. At least, we stopped in time."

She didn't answer. That made a new, cold fear grip him. Not because he was in any danger of forgetting himself now, but because he didn't want to entertain the notion that occurred to him. Had she *wanted* to seduce him? Had he been three kinds of a fool: to be tempted, to succumb, then not to know he'd been set up to do it?

"Amber?" he said, risking a look at her.

She'd pulled up her gown and pushed down her skirt, so she looked decent again. But she was still disheveled, and that along with her kiss-swollen lips and pinkened face, and those sweetly strewn curls about her shoulders, made him want to take her back into his arms.

"Yes," she said in a small tight voice, "it was a very bad idea. I don't know that I can ever look at you again."

He realized with sorrow and horror that she was about to cry, and it killed his desire entirely.

She saw his expression change and frantically flapped a hand at him. "Don't touch me! I'm just weeping a little. It's a thing I do, and it means nothing. I'm very strong; it's my one weakness. But I can stop it if you give me a minute. But for God's sake, Mr. St. Ives, don't touch me again!"

He didn't know he could feel worse. He'd been wrong. This gentle, lovely woman had just almost given herself to him, and she still called him "Mr. St. Ives."

"You're too trusting," he said roughly. "You should have thrown me out the minute you knew what I was, just like Tremellyn did."

She looked down at the bedcover and didn't answer him. That wasn't like her. He almost preferred she'd weep, though he hated to hear a woman crying.

"Amber?" he asked. "Are you all right?"

She shook her head so that her tumbled hair covered her eyes. "No," she said.

Chapter 13

He hadn't taken off one item of clothing. That was the first thing Amber realized when her swimming senses sharpened, and she snapped out of the sensual daze she'd fallen into under Amyas's hands. There'd she'd been, as near to naked as makes no matter, in his arms. Not only in his arms, but laid out under him like a bedsheet, and yet all the while he'd been dressed as fine as a man ready to go visiting. He'd even kept his gloves on. Nor had he forced her to do a thing. But oh, the things she'd done. She was speechless with shame.

But he'd been so golden, warm, and sweet, the taste of him was like wild honey and wine, he'd been fragrant and clean and strong, his kisses dizzied her and made her senses sizzle. Even now, knowing what she knew about her shocking response to him and all the danger in it, she could scarcely look at him without feeling a fresh surge of desire. She didn't know what to think of herself, much less what to say to him.

Still, he'd asked her a question and she had to answer, though she found it hard to speak. "You never undressed," she whispered.

She'd felt his skin glowing under his thin shirt, though. She'd felt the muscles shifting in his back under her hands, felt the tension in his body and the rising of his sex against her body. But all along he'd been as well dressed as a gentleman could be.

"All you took off was your glove," she added sadly, looking at the big bare hand that rested on the bed, between them. There was nothing wrong with it, she noted, except maybe it was a bit paler than most men's hands, probably because he always wore his gloves. It was a large, shapely, masculine-looking hand, with a broad palm, long fingers and well-kept nails. He'd spoken about a childhood injury. Did he never tell the truth?

He glanced down at his hand. "Oh," he said. "No, this one's fine."

He read her expression and smiled as sadly as she had. "But I'd look foolish wearing only one glove. Here, see." He raised his other hand and began pulling the glove off it. "It's not pretty," he said, "but I don't think you'll believe me if I don't show you."

He tugged off the glove and held up his right hand. She shrank back.

"Yes," he said, and began to put the glove on again.

"No!" she blurted, "You don't have to cover it up for me. I was upset because it was such a cruel sight, but it doesn't frighten me."

"Revolts you more like, I'd think," he commented, looking at his hand ruefully.

He had only two complete fingers on it, the thumb and forefinger. The last three fingers had been severed cleanly and neatly, but at an angle from the last toward the first: the third finger at the second knuckle, the ring finger above the first knuckle, the little finger had only a stub left.

He waggled his fingers and contemplated the sight. "They all work, but it's ugly, isn't it?" he asked. "I ran into an angry butcher when I was eight. Literally. He was trying to chop off my hand for stealing a sausage from him, but I gave him the slip just in time. See, if you relax, the person who holds you relaxes, too, even if only a second. That's all you need. It helps if you've been really frightened, I suppose. The sweat makes your hand wet. So then all you have to do is wait for the right second, then twist and turn and pull and run. I did. A little late for the fingers, but I kept the hand. I reckon a few fingers is a small price to pay for it."

"He wanted to chop off your hand for taking a sausage?" she exclaimed in horror.

"Well, a sausage that day. The day before it was an end of a ham, and the day before that another cut of meat. I was taking from his store every day, so it was inevitable. He wasn't planning the worst, so it was lucky for me, believe it or not, because I think he'd just as gladly have taken off my head. You probably understood how he felt," he said, giving her a tilted smile.

His voice was light, urbane, and amused, as though they were chatting in a salon amidst a crowd of people. She realized he was doing it to calm her. But they were alone in the night, sitting on a bed where they'd just almost made love, and it was bizarre. Still, she did forget her shame and embarrassment as she listened.

"I was living on my own then," he went on. "I'd just run away from the Foundling Hospital. It wasn't a bad place; they fed me and taught me my letters and my prayers, and some manners, too. It was the only home I'd ever known, and they didn't beat you unless you really needed it. But I didn't want to go to the workhouse, which was the only thing they had in store for me. I heard it would be harder to escape once I had a master, so I ran. I didn't want any fate I had no say in." He shrugged. "They taught me too much, I suppose.

"But they didn't teach me how to live on my own in the streets. I went hungry for days. There are too many boys without homes in London; the competition for food is fierce. I found scraps in the alley behind that butcher shop, and it drew me the same as it did the rats. In fact, it was a rat that I saw slipping into the butcher's wall that gave me the idea. I found the hole behind a trash pile, hidden from most eyes, and I realized it could be made big enough for a boy. I decided I could use it if I didn't find enough food during the day. Then I discovered I could curl up and sleep in that little space and be safer from the rats and the other boys, plus pinch my meals every night.

"I found a way to burrow in, and I lived in a hole in the wall in the alley behind his shop for a week. I thought I was clever. But I wasn't clever enough to avoid being found, because I didn't know that a thief should only strike once and never return. So the butcher nabbed me.

"After I got away from him, I was lucky enough to meet up with a boy in the street who saw my face and the blood on my hand, and asked me about it. I'd wrapped a stocking round my hand, but couldn't hide the damage. Tell the truth, I was afraid to unwrap it because I didn't want to see how much was gone," Amyas added, nothing in his expression but rueful regret, though Amber sat listening, appalled, her shame forgotten.

"He helped me," Amyas said simply, "and introduced me to the gang of lads he lived with. We stayed together, Daffy—I mean, Daffyd, and I. In fact we were sent to Newgate and went to New South Wales together, and still call ourselves brothers. He taught me kindness, his gang taught me survival. I learned how to steal much more effectively. I practiced the arts of the swipe and the drop, the nab, and the push and run: all the kid lays that a boy could master."

He saw Amber's puzzled expression. "I mean, I learned all kinds of clever ways to distract men and pick their pockets, as well as how to slide in their windows when they were sleeping or out for the day, or night. They taught me how to cut purses and run, and which streets to run down after I did. That's important. Some lead to avenues where a man can outrun you, but some to alleys where grown men can't fit."

He shrugged. "I learned many useful and illegal arts. They filled my belly, if not my purse, because I had to share my pickings, and never took too much for fear they'd catch me with it. Too much swag means the noose, you see. Of course, my work got me to prison a few times, too, but so long as I never swiped anything extravagant, I was safe enough. I got a few beatings and had some dangerous moments, but always came out knowing more. I even learned how to pass myself off as a toff's son, if I had to, because I was good at accents." His voice changed to such a rich and plummy accent as he said that, that Amber smiled.

But then his voice and expression changed again, becoming wooden, as he added, "Then one day I picked that pound note from a pocket by accident, and was nabbed while I still had it."

He gazed at his maimed hand reflectively. "A fellow can pick a pocket very nicely with two fingers, you know, so long as they can pinch together," he said, demonstrating. "And if a maimed boy gets caught, he can claim he didn't do it, of course, because how could he? Then he can get sympathy, which sometimes gets him coins, too. But that won't save him if he's caught with the goods and has no one to defend him.

"Be that as it may," he said briskly, "I don't need sympathy or the extra coins now. And so I find a bit of padding in the proper places, and . . ." He drew on his glove again and held up what looked like a whole hand. "*Voilà!* as the Frenchies say. I have a normal hand again." He grinned. "At least, one I can work with. I can eat and ride, and dance with the ladies, and no one ever has to know what I'm hiding, unless I want to make love . . ."

His smile faded. "Amber," he said softly, "again, I'm sorry. You offered me sympathy. I tried to get much more."

She blinked. His terrible story had made her forget her own terrible actions. She remembered soon enough.

"I behaved badly," she said. "In fact, I thank you for stopping when you did. I'd have been ruined." She held up her head, her face pale as she confessed, "I'm deeply ashamed, and want you to know that I've never done anything like that before. I know some people say that whenever they do something wrong, but in my case, it's true. You could ask anyone . . . I suppose you couldn't, and I wish you wouldn't, but it's true."

He put his gloved hand over hers. His voice was sad and deep as the sympathy in his eyes. "It wasn't altogether your fault. I know what I'm about in a bed, you see, and I soon realized you didn't. Not that you weren't delightful," he said quickly. "No, better than that, you were so delicious, you were . . . oh." He saw her avert her face again. "I forgot. That's not a compliment to a decent woman, is it? You have to forgive me again. As I said, I don't know many other decent ones."

"But you must have thought I was like them," she said in a thickened voice, "I mean, like the indecent ones you knew. After all, you saw me here on my own, alone in the gatehouse. Then I invited you in, even though it was night. I kissed you, allowed you to take me to bed . . ." She looked up at him, her eyes misted; she was obviously fighting back tears. "I couldn't have acted more the wanton.

"It may be in the blood after all," she said miserably. "My mother may well have been no better than she should have been. I've often wondered if I wasn't on the beach that day Mr. Tremellyn found me, not because of a shipwreck, but rather because my mother abandoned me there. She might have been passing through the area and simply had enough of me, and didn't care about me anymore, and so just left me there and went on her way, like a turtle laying her eggs on the shore." He heard her swallow before she went on. "That would account for my behavior tonight, because a decent woman wouldn't have allowed any of it."

He wondered if it was his conscience or his heart

that hurt more. "Amber," he said sincerely, "I may not know many decent women, but I know quite a few who once were, and let me tell you, that's just not true. I don't want to give myself airs, and I promise you I wasn't always the first to lead a lady down dark paths, but if a fellow knows what he's about, and *especially* if she doesn't, she may find herself following him into the most interesting places. Don't blame yourself. Only the thinnest line separates a decent man from an indecent one, and that goes for females, too. Desire isn't just for bad men and women. Those of us from the gutters know that, even if real ladies and gentlemen don't.

"As for you being left on the shore," he said, "I don't think so. First off, you don't look the least like a turtle." He waited for her smile, and seeing none, went on more seriously. "Listen. I'm an expert on unwanted brats. I've met more foundlings than you have. I can tell you that they're commonly left on doorsteps of hospitals and churches, or at the front doors of rich men's town houses or the back steps of busy shops. Unluckier ones are left on trash piles, or in dark alleys. I never heard of any being abandoned on a beach. Unless, of course," he said with a smile, "you're a mermaid's daughter. Can you swim really well?"

She started to nod, then, realizing the joke, she smiled, too. It was such a wan smile it pained him.

"So," he said, "I'd think your mother was on a ship that broke up in the storm, just as Tremellyn said."

She seemed to consider his words, leaving him time to plan how he could decently leave her. As on fire as he'd been to make love to her, he now was twice as eager to go. She made him feel terrible, and not just because of the unsatisfied ache in his loins. She was lovely, kind, bright, and good. And he'd tried to seduce her, knowing he had no plans for her outside the bed they sat on. He felt as low, dirty, and depraved as he supposed he was.

He'd tried to change that. He'd wanted to do everything right this time. He'd been ready to marry Grace Tremellyn, live with her as honestly and decently as a man could even though he didn't love her especially, and settle down here as a person of importance, respected and loved. Instead, he'd told the truth and been tossed out on his ear for it. And how had he dealt with that? By hurting this lovely woman, and in some as yet unknowable way, maybe hurting himself even more. He didn't know if he could feel worse about himself and didn't want to stay around to discover if he could.

Poor Amber No Name, he thought, watching her. She'd glowed so bright he thought he could warm himself with her, and now she looked lost, vulnerable, and even more desirable in her sorrow. He wanted to take her in his arms and comfort her, and himself. But that way lay disaster.

He had to find a way to turn her anger outward, at him, where it belonged. He realized he only had to tell her the truth.

"You had no experience with men like me," he said, "or men at all. At least, not in bed. Don't you think I knew that? Don't you think I used that?"

She stared at him.

"Amber," he said, "I'm a criminal. A bona fide certified and indemnified criminal. I was a convict, for God's sake! A man who learned to cheat his fellow man—and woman—in dozens of ways, and perfected those ways in His Majesty's best and worst prisons. I don't have to do it anymore, but the lessons linger. So stop blaming yourself. In a way you could say that it's my business to do as I did."

"But you stopped . . ." She paused, and swallowed hard again. He looked so concerned, so compelling, that she wondered where she'd gotten the strength of will to make him stop making love to her. She looked away from his eyes, because it was too easy to become lost in their blue depths, "You were honorable enough to stop making love to me the minute I wanted you to stop."

He could only nod.

He wished he could stop this right now. He wanted to tell her not to worry. He wanted to just reach out and touch that smooth cheek, move close and place a light kiss on those beautiful lips and make her an offer of marriage. Anything to get her smiling again, to get her back in his arms and make his own hurting stop. But he knew what he wanted even more.

Tremellyn's daughter was lost to him. That was nothing. But Tremellyn's respect was gone, too. The man would never treat him as an equal again, nor would anyone in this village, even if he married Tremellyn's ward and built the finest house in the district to raise his family in. He'd always be the outsider and the villain. He'd had enough of that in his lifetime. He had to find another village, another woman, another life to adopt. He had to leave here, and now.

"Consider yourself lucky," he told Amber. "If I'd made love to you, I would have offered for you after. I have some conscience. And you, being moral as you are, regardless of any doubts you had about me, would doubtless have felt you had to accept. But I wouldn't be good for you. I have friends and funds, but I don't have a place in this world. You know what that means. You've suffered from it enough, haven't you? It means always having to feel inferior to inferior people who just had the luck to have parents who gave them a name and a place. I made up 'St. Ives.' You need a real name."

And though he wouldn't say it, he wanted to marry a woman with a name he could use to forget that he was no one with no name.

He stood in one swift movement.

She slipped off the bed and came to her feet as well.

He looked down at her. She'd tidied herself, but her hair was still down and framed her face. It was all he could do to keep his hands by his sides. But the gloves he wore were like a reminder of all the artificial surfaces he'd had to keep up, and for once, he was glad of them. Because if he touched her again, he knew he would be lost.

"I'll go now," he said, "as I should have an hour ago. One day, you'll look back and be glad I had honor in this, at least. No one will ever know what happened here but you and me, at least not from me. Tremellyn never need know, or Grace, unless you want them to. I won't speak about it, but I'll always remember the kind and good woman who offered me solace, never realizing that she ought never have offered that to a bad man. Thank you, Amber. And please, if you do nothing else, forgive me."

He bent and brushed a kiss against her cheek. It almost undid all his resolution. Then he straightened and, without looking at her again or giving her a chance to speak, strode to the door. He threw it open and went out before he could change his mind.

The rain still pelted down, and he was drenched in an instant. But nevertheless he made a dash for where he'd stabled his horse, to the side of the gatehouse. He'd get soaked to the skin riding to the inn, and knew it. But running now was absolutely necessary. He had to get away.

Amyas got on his horse and rode it into the storm. He never looked back, though he could think of nothing but the woman he'd left behind.

After he left, Amber sat by the gatehouse window looking into the darkness, until it became light. Even then, she didn't want to go home. She was no longer sure she deserved to be there. Because the truth she'd admitted during her long vigil through the night was that she'd never felt so much like herself, or so where she belonged, as she had in the arms of a liar and a cheat and convicted criminal, a man who didn't even want her. And because to her confusion, shame, and constant sorrow, whatever she'd said, she hadn't told him something he'd probably guessed. She would have given herself to him if he'd only asked again.

Chapter 14

Amber went home as the morning sun came up. She went because there was nowhere else to go. As she walked toward Tremellyn House, she tried to decide how to react to the news of Amyas St. Ives's deception when she heard about it from Grace and Mr. Tremellyn. She decided to take it as it came. She'd worried too much through the night to deal with it now. She raised her head to the sun and took a deep breath. The storm had cleared the air, and it smelled sweet and wild and fresh. The sunlight sparkled everywhere; the light off the sea glittered like a turning glass. It was a morning that fit her perfectly; she, too, had survived a passionate storm and had to get on with a new day.

She wished she could blame Amyas St. Ives for how

she felt, but couldn't. She more than anyone could understand his powerful drive for respectability and tranquillity after his fitful and stormy life. And after all, he hadn't hurt her more than she'd let him.

Still, she felt numbed and empty. Her heart was broken, she supposed. It shocked her only because she hadn't realized how very much she cared about the man until he'd touched her. Now he'd gone, taking every last shred of hope with him. In leaving her he'd not only rejected her, but also confirmed her worst fears about her future. She had nothing but what was given to her and little more to hope for. Amber took a deep breath and walked faster. She'd be all right.

She'd oooh and ahhh with Grace and cluck her tongue at Mr. Tremellyn's story of his encounter with St. Ives. And then she'd go on, because there was nothing else she could do, even though she felt smaller and less sure of herself than she'd ever done.

Amber reached Tremellyn's back door and steeled herself. She let herself in and hung her coat on a hook by the back door. Then she went into the kitchen, and stopped, amazed.

Cook was there, of course, but so were Grace and her father. They were sitting at the kitchen table, having their breakfasts. But Grace usually slept for another hour, and Mr. Tremellyn was usually up and gone by dawn so he could see his ships off, and so seldom took his breakfast with them. Most startling of all, when they looked up and saw Amber, they both gave her wide and welcoming smiles.

"Good morning!" Grace said, her face shining like the morning, "And it's a beautiful one, isn't it?"

"You were a clever puss to stay in the gatehouse last night," Tremellyn told Amber. "The rain and the wind were fierce. Did you sleep well?"

"Not very," she said. "The sound of the storm was so loud. But you two look very merry. What happened last night?"

Grace exchanged a sparkling look with her father. "You tell her," she said.

"Aye, I would," he said, "but I think you should."

"Oh, very well," Grace said, hopping a little in her seat. She fairly bounced with glee. "Amber! Just think! I'm going to be married."

It was a good thing Amber stood by the sink. She gaped at Grace, and then fell back. The sink was all that kept her upright. "*Married?*" she gasped.

Had he come back to Tremellyn House last night after all? She couldn't have seen that from the gatehouse, not in all that rain. Had he made some excuse, talked himself round them, gotten back their esteem? How had he done it? But then, remembering him: how he'd looked last night, how he'd sounded, how he'd felt in her arms, she realized it was a miracle he hadn't done it right away.

But to go from her arms to Grace's? She shivered. That was vulgar, disgusting, unforgivable. Not that it would matter if she forgave him, she supposed. She'd have to leave this place now, certainly. She couldn't live with that knowledge, always knowing what he'd done, what she'd done with him, what he could do again, if she let him.

"Oh my!" Grace exclaimed. "Are you all right, Ambie? I didn't think you'd take it this way."

"I—I'm just surprised," Amber said. "That's all. I wasn't sure Mr. Tremellyn would give him permission. I mean, so soon."

"Why shouldn't he?" Grace asked, now looking anxiously at her father. "And why do you think it's too soon?"

Amber swung her gaze to Mr. Tremellyn, too. Had he not told Grace what St. Ives had confessed to him?

"Gracie." Tremellyn chuckled. "You forget she's been gone all night and half the morning. She doesn't know anything that happened. She thinks you're talking about that bas . . . blackguard, St. Ives. Aye, Amber, your guess is good. I did refuse that villain permission to court my daughter, when he asked it of me. Turns out the fellow was a liar, no more or less than a criminal. He'd been a convict! Would you believe it? And he had the ballocks . . . the brass to court my Grace! I sent him straight on his way, you can be sure. I told him to leave and banned him from this house. He was lucky I didn't shoot him.

"But not an hour after he'd left, and good riddance, when up rides young Tobias—aye, in that pouring rain. He comes in shedding water like a landed fish, and stands in my study telling me he's there to make sure I know Grace has someone who'd give his life for her. Aye, that's what he said, and he'd his fists cocked when he said it, too. He'd made up his mind, he said, and marshaled his resources, rehearsed his speech, and couldn't wait another minute to declare himself. See, he'd marked how particular St. Ives's attentions were getting and was afraid I'd allow St. Ives to court the love of his life, says he." He grinned as he added, "Insolent puppy."

"Hush, Papa," Grace said, with a giggle. "It was just that he was so upset. If that wicked St. Ives did nothing else, he finally gave my Toby the courage to speak up for me. He knew St. Ives was coming here last night and guessed his purpose. But you see, he and I . . ." She paused, her cheeks turned charmingly pink. "We've been seeing each other, when we could, without much fuss, for we neither of us knew how it was going with the other. That's why I didn't say anything to you about it, Amber. But I wished he would speak up. Then when Mr. St. Ives came and started to woo me, Toby realized it was time to declare himself. I couldn't be happier! I do love my Toby so!"

"Aye, well," Tremellyn said, sitting back and tucking his thumbs in his fob pockets, "I won't pretend I was delighted, at first. Grace could have any man she wanted, and the lad's just a boy with nothing but plans in his head, and less in his pockets. But he's a good lad, say all, and a good worker, says Pascoe Piper. And he tells me he wants his own boat someday. No, two! And most important, he's daft about my girl."

He smiled fondly. "So, it appears, she is about him, too. But I didn't know that then. I just gave him permission to pay his addresses, for only a fool would say no, since however she felt, she'd want him even more if I didn't. That's the nature of females. And not knowing how she felt, I didn't want to risk a wedding in the spring that would make gossip for the next twenty years. I want my girl to marry, *then* get me my grandsons. We Tremellyns have to set a standard here in St. Edgyth."

Grace smiled. "So, we're marrying in the spring, right after Easter. That's almost the year that Papa wants us to wait, but I don't think I could wait a day longer." She blushed, and added, "Neither can Toby, he says."

"Toby says a great deal now," Amber murmured. She danced over to Grace and gave her a hug and a kiss. "That's wonderful. Tell me what I can do to help prepare for the wedding and I will."

"I know that," Grace said comfortably.

"But—what about St. Ives?" Amber asked. "Are you upset about what happened?" She faced Tremellyn and looked at him steadily. "I know. He came to the gatehouse to say good-bye before he left." Useless to lie, she thought. She wasn't a good liar, anyway. Telling the truth was so much easier. She didn't have to tell the whole truth, though.

"What?" Tremellyn demanded, leaping to his feet.

"He went to see you? The dirty bastard! How dare he? I told him to leave!"

"Papa!" Grace said. "Your language, sir!"

"Pardon me that," Tremellyn growled, "but I'll break his neck."

"There's no reason to be angry," Amber said. "He only stopped to say good-bye, and rode on." That was, after all, partially true. She waited, breath held.

"Well, I'll just stop by the inn on my way to work and make sure he's gone for good!" he said.

Amber relaxed. The sun was well up. If St. Ives was leaving as he said, he'd be long gone by now.

"We were taken in," Tremellyn said. "My fault, for taking a fellow at face value after hearing his fair speech and seeing his good clothes, never knowing they hid a thoroughgoing rascal. A *convict*, no less!" he muttered. "But you know, Gracie? You've cause to be grateful to him, I think. For I'm not all that sure I'd have so hastily allowed Tobias's suit if I hadn't been so fed up with men whose smart appearances cover their villainy. Not that Tobias is ill-mannered or ragged, but he's just a country lad. And you could have anyone."

"I'm only a country girl," Grace said happily. "And I don't want anyone else."

"But mind, you have a year—or almost that—to decide for certain," he father said. "An engagement isn't a wedding, you can slip out of it if it don't suit, so take your time before you get spliced for good and all. Speaking of time, I must get to work. My ships have all sailed, or at least, they better have done; but I've accounts to go over and tallies to run. I'll see you at dinner."

He paused to drop a kiss on Grace's forehead, then turned and frowned at Amber "And you get to bed, my girl. You've got circles under your eyes like a badger's and look as though you sat up all through the night. You'll sleep better in your own bed. See you both at dinner, then."

"Can Toby come to dinner tonight?" Grace asked, as he went to the door. "Please?"

He smiled. "Aye, he may. Best I get used to him, eh?"

"I am so lucky!" Grace caroled after her father had left. "Oh, Amber, I do so love Toby. He's smart, but so shy you wouldn't know it, but you'll soon see. And isn't he handsome, though?"

"So you weren't unhappy about finding out about St. Ives?" Amber asked, unable to believe that the man had meant so little to her.

Grace laughed. "Oh no, not really. To tell the truth, he frightened me. He was so very attractive, and clever. Whatever he really was, he was always a gentleman with me, but I never knew how to talk to him."

"Fine feathers don't make fine birds," Cook mumbled darkly from her corner of the kitchen. "And him a jailbird at that! Fooled me, too," she muttered before she remembered it wasn't her place and started to collect their breakfast dishes.

Grace took Amber's arm and walked out of the room with her. "I don't care that he was so bad. What does it matter to me? But you know?" she asked Amber. "He really wasn't that bad, when you come right down to it, was he? He only wanted to marry me. He left without fuss when Papa turned him away. I wonder what he went to jail for?"

"Stealing," Amber said softly. "He said he'd been a thief." And he still was, she thought sadly. He'd taken her self-respect, and her heart.

"We plan to live nearby," Grace said happily, as they went up the stairs. "Toby and me," she explained, when Amber stopped in her tracks and stared at her. "But not with his mother, though she's a dear. We'll take the old Williams cottage, because it shouldn't be too expensive for Toby. Papa is already making noises about building us a new house. I think Toby is too proud to let him do that—though I wouldn't mind. Still, I suppose if a child comes soon, even Toby won't mind such a gesture. What do you think?"

"I think you're right," Amber said without thinking, as she made her numbed legs carry her up the stairs again.

She hadn't realized that Grace would leave when she married. That was foolish of her, and she wondered why she'd never contemplated it. It was only natural, after all. But it would change her life drastically. As she was neither daughter of the house nor blood relation, she'd have to go, too. It didn't matter that Mr. Tremellyn had known her since she was a toddler and that she was like a daughter to him. A grown maiden woman, especially a nameless one, certainly couldn't stay on here unchaperoned with him. After all, he wasn't her father, and he was a widower, and so a bachelor, and not yet in his dotage.

There was no way around it. Society had rules, and this was a small village. Amber didn't expect Mr. Tremellyn to go looking for some other homeless female to live with him just so that a foundling he'd taken in to be companion to his daughter could stay on. Nor would she want him to go to the expense and effort. It wasn't fair. And she also knew that if she stayed under such circumstances she'd feel compelled to free him of the obligation of her welfare by finding herself a husband. That, as she already knew too well, wasn't possible in St. Edgyth.

So, Amber thought sadly, sweet Gracie, all unknowing, took all again. She'd have a husband and a home. And Amber, her gift from the sea, would have neither, nor any real chance at either, perhaps ever again.

Oblivious to such problems, Grace prattled on, giddy in her newfound joy, supremely unaware that it would change her pretend sister's world forever.

"Got a surprise," Tremellyn called from the doorway when he came in that evening. "An unexpected guest. Mmm, lucky for him, too," he said, as he lifted his nose and took in a deep breath. "Turkey! And roast? There's a feast cooking, my friend," he told the man standing next to him. "Take off your coat, have a seat."

Tremellyn's deep voice carried throughout the house. Amber heard what he said and handed the plate she was holding to Cook. She swept a hand over her hair to make sure it was in place and whipped off her apron. It couldn't be him, could it? But maybe he hadn't left town after all. Amyas was silver-tongued, and if Gracie was already safely matched, maybe he'd managed to talk Mr. Tremellyn round again. She hurried to the parlor and stopped short when she saw his guest.

"Good evening, Pascoe," she said, all the foolish excitement draining from her.

He eyed her curiously. "Give you good evening, lass. If my coming tonight is trouble, I'll make it another time."

"No trouble," Amber forced herself to say brightly. "I'll just set another place. Don't worry; I was thinking of how to stretch the table, not about who sits at it. I think we'll just have to dine in style tonight instead of eating at the kitchen table."

"Well, why not?" Tremellyn said expansively. "It's a celebration, isn't it? Where's that daughter of mine?"

"She and her Toby are out walking in the garden," Amber said.

"That seems safe enough," he said. "Pascoe here says the lad's so excited about being allowed to court her that he's a danger to himself on the boat."

"Aye," Pascoe said. "Almost hooked a mate and netted his captain this morning. I think the boy needs to take a few days to cool his head, before his crewmates do it for him—in the sea."

As they laughed, Amber took the moment to excuse herself to prepare dinner.

"The girl's a wonder," Pascoe said, watching her as she left the room. "Cooks for you, too, does she?"

"No, won't let her. Helps Cook, though." Tremellyn said as he went to pour Pascoe a brandy.

"And supervises the housemaids, shops, and keeps a clean house for you. How are you going to get on without her?"

Tremellyn stopped, his hand on the bottle. "Why should I?"

"Well, can you imagine the talk if she stays on here alone with you after Grace is wed? Unless, of course," Pascoe said slyly, watching him, "you want to have to be telling everyone you can't and you don't, you couldn't and you won't."

Tremellyn frowned at him in puzzlement.

"Well, you may think of her as your daughter, Tremellyn, but we all know she isn't. Old as you are, you haven't got one foot in the grave yet, or if you do, there's another part of you that's easily risen. Or so at least, Widow Bray's been known to say." Pascoe grinned.

"Oh." Tremellyn turned and poured out a glass. He was smiling again when he turned back and handed it to Pascoe. "Hadn't thought of that. Well, it's a problem we'll face when the time comes. Who knows? Spring's a long way off. Young Tobias may fall in love with a fish, or my Gracie may find a new love by then. They're young, and the young are up to anything."

"Aye," Pascoe said thoughtfully. "And maybe by then, Amber will have found a home for herself, too."

Tremellyn look at him sharply.

Pascoe shrugged. "Well, why not? I thought she might take off with that St. Ives, from the way she looked at him sometimes. But I should have known she's too canny for a shifty piece of work like him. She's young and good-looking, and good around the house, as you know. Why shouldn't she find a husband for herself?"

"She hasn't yet," Tremellyn said mildly. "And God knows, she's had her chances. I let everyone know I'd dower her."

"A dower and a name are two different things, Tremellyn. Especially around here. Not every man has the money and freedom to decide on his wife for himself. Like I do."

"Ah. Now that's curious," Tremellyn said, looking into his glass, "And here I thought your mother was in good health."

Pascoe's smile was thin. "She is. But I'm not a man to marry to suit his mother."

"You serving me notice, Pascoe?" Tremellyn asked.

"You want to start courting? You're free to woo her, but I'd advise you to know her mind before you ask for the terms of her dowry."

"I will," Pascoe said. "And be damned to her dowry, Tremellyn."

"Ah," Tremellyn said.

"Dinner is served," Amber said from the hallway. She looked at the two men curiously. "Is everything all right?"

"Couldn't be better," Tremellyn said.

Dinner could have been better, Amber thought. Not that there was anything wrong with the food. Everyone complimented her on it. But Grace and Tobias were too busy eyeing each other, smiling, and sighing, to notice what was on their plates. Pascoe seemed preoccupied, and even Tremellyn's appetite was off. She herself couldn't eat. She was so filled with confusion and sorrow she felt a bite of food would choke her.

The talk was all about Grace and Tobias, at first. But since all Grace could do was giggle, and Tobias was so awed at dining at the same table with his employer and his future father-in-law, he didn't say much. Pascoe was always short-spoken, and tonight was no different. Tremellyn seemed peculiarly thoughtful. Then they started talking about Amyas St. Ives, and the conversation flowed through soup and fowl, fish and roast, and on to dessert.

Amber learned nothing new. She knew more about

the man than any of them did. And though the others wondered how they hadn't seen the rot in him, or pretended they'd had hints of it, and damned him and promised to trounce him thoroughly should they ever so much as catch sight of him again, she didn't say a word.

By the time they all rose from the table, Amber's mood was as sad as it had been in the morning, made worse by the fact that she had to pretend such joy for Grace. She felt strained to her limit and couldn't wait to escape to her bed, even though she was afraid nothing but doubt and sorrow awaited her through the long hours of the night ahead.

Grace and Tobias went to sit in the parlor. Tremellyn said he'd join them but first he needed a different pipe since his own wasn't drawing well, and he went into his study to get one. That left Pascoe in the hall, standing next to Amber.

"Come out for a walk with me," he said urgently.

"Now?" she asked in surprise. "A walk? But it's night."

He nodded. "Dark, but not dead of night. Can you think of any other way I can talk to you apart?" he asked bluntly. "I've got something to say to you. And I've got Tremellyn's permission to say it."

She shivered. She'd feared this moment for some time now. But it was impossible to turn a man down before he asked, rude and cowardly if she did. He stood staring at her, that brutally handsome face intent. She had to hear him out before she rejected him.

There was nothing wrong with Pascoe Piper except for the fact that he didn't understand her, wanted her for all the wrong reasons, wasn't aware of her hopes or dreams, and didn't seem interested in them either. And, of course, that he wasn't Amyas St. Ives.

But he'd never knowingly insulted her, and at least deserved his say.

"I'll get a wrap, we'll go into the garden, round back," she said.

Chapter 15

Pascoe wore simple, neat clothes this evening: a clean shirt tied at the neck with a knotted handkerchief and dark trousers with a dark jacket over them. Neither fashionable nor a workman's kit, but what he would wear after work, to visit friends. Still, his clothing was immaculate. Amber silently congratulated his mother. The man made his livelihood on the sea and fished half of the time he was on it. The women must have literally beaten his clothing on rocks to clean them.

She stole a glance up at him as they walked. The moonlight flattered him, softening the harsh contours of his face, making him look mysterious, not pitiless. She doubted he was cruel, but his face didn't entirely lie. He was a man of strong opinions that weren't easily changed. She didn't know why he wanted her so badly, and hoped he'd tell her so she could tell him why he was mistaken in her. She wasn't for him. It pained her, because though she couldn't accept him, she still wasn't exactly sure why.

They stopped a short way from the house. He turned and looked at her. "You know what I want to ask," he said. "Grace is getting married, you can't stay on with Tremellyn. Why not marry me?"

Amber put a hand on her heart. Her smile was genuinely amused. She tossed her head. "Gracious me,' she said. "You flatter me too much, Mr. Piper."

He scowled. "You know damned well what a tempting piece you are. And I know you're too sensible to fall for a heap of slush, or I'd pour it on. I'm not a flowery-spoken man, but I'm not a fool, either. Listen. I have money and will have more. I'm not bad to look at, and no woman has ever complained of me. I can give you a fine house. And I won't work you hard. My mother likes running the house, so you can have time to yourself, for your books and suchlike," he added, with a dismissive gesture.

That last was clever of him, Amber thought. She wished he hadn't remembered to mention her love of books because that would make her refusal more difficult. Then she remembered he was, as he said, not a fool.

"And," he added, "I can give you a good name. No one will ever talk about you being no one from nowhere again, believe me."

She couldn't stop herself in time. She winced.

"What is it?" he asked.

She sighed. "Your name would be a fine gift, Pascoe. But it's a gift you'd never forget, one you'd always expect me to be grateful for."

"Aye?" he said. "And so? What man wouldn't?"

Her eyes opened wide. Slowly, she nodded. "That's true," she said softly.

"Look," he said. "I won't keep coming back to where I'm not wanted, so if you don't want me, say so, and we'll be done with it. I offer you marriage, a good home, and children. I run a tidy ship, but I'm not a harsh master. Be fair with me, and I'll be fair with you. Well, what say you?"

She hesitated, but only so she could carefully compose her rejection. He was right about himself, at least. Pascoe Piper wasn't a bad man, but he had enormous pride. She didn't want to hurt his feelings.

"Ah!" he said suddenly, his lips parting in a smile that showed his white teeth. "I am a fool in one way, I suppose. I don't go in for fancy speeches, but only a fool would ask a woman to marry him without giving her a taste of the goods. Come here, Amber, and let me show you what life would be like with me."

He reached for her, giving her time to evade him if she chose.

And because she was still feeling bereft, and because she sincerely wondered, and because she felt so alone and afraid, she went into his arms.

Pascoe's hard mouth was not harsh against hers.

His lips were surprisingly soft. He touched the seam of his lips with his tongue, and she parted her own, slightly. His mouth was hot, but she felt no response to his questing tongue, only a sense of wrongness and unease. His body was warm and well muscled, his arms were strong though he held her lightly, and she could sense as well as feel the passion rising in him as they kissed. He smelled of seawater and hard soap, and it wasn't unpleasant. But though he pulled her closer and she could feel his breathing quicken, Amber felt nothing but a growing sense of despair and shame.

She stepped back from him. He dropped his hands.

"Shy?" he asked. "Or disappointed?"

"Neither. Pascoe, I wish I could say yes. But I'm not the right woman for you."

"Another way of saying I'm not the right man for you?" he asked expressionlessly.

"No, not exactly." She shook her head. "Pascoe,'" she said on sudden inspiration, "we've known each other for years now. Tell me, why aren't we friends?"

He looked surprised. "You're saying we're enemies?"

"No, of couse not. But we aren't close friends. We never have been. Why not?"

"I don't know . . . maybe because it's a damned fool notion." He grinned. "I'm a fisherman, lass. I also do the odd bit of to-ing and fro-ing along the other coast with richer merchandise when I can, which is easier than hauling fish, but I'm a grown man who works with his hands, on the water. How could we be friends? You're a woman."

"Ah," she said with enormous relief to have found the obstacle at last, at least in her own mind. "Well, there it is. You see, I want to marry someone I could be friends with, and as you said, you've never even entertained the notion."

He stared.

She shook her head. "Oh, I'm a strange creature, Pascoe, and I know it. But that's my dream, and I won't become a wife or make a good one for any man, without at least thinking that my husband and I could be friends as well as lovers."

Remembering his pride, she added quickly, "As to that, there's nothing wrong with your kisses, as you must know, quite the contrary. But I don't think you expect your wife to be a lover either. Not in the way I hear men think of such, the way some women dream about. There's nothing wrong with what you want, just that it's different from my expectations. You want a woman to be a wife and mother, and give reasonable . . . comfort in the marriage bed." She dropped her gaze and felt her face heating up, but persisted, "But being a lover is different. Isn't it?"

And what of Amyas? she wondered even as she said it. Could he have been a friend, and a lover? A lover, certainly. But a friend? Yes, they were that, already, though they'd never meet again. There had been that instant communication between them, that need for each other's company, that absolute pleasure in it. Unlike Pascoe, she had been a fool, but she knew that for certain she'd lost a friend as well as a potential lover in Amyas St. Ives.

"Books have filled your head with those odd notions, haven't they?" Pascoe asked quizzically. "Because I don't think there's any man around here that has. Except for that St. Ives, and he was watched every minute, so he couldn't have done more. But aye, being a lover is different. Because for all I like a good time in bed, as would any man, I don't want my wife to be a wanton, nor would any decent man. As for her being a friend, too? I tell you truly, lass, I don't know if I could be your friend. I have no women friends, nor know any fellow that does. I don't like foolish chatter, and don't care about clothes, or knitting, or gossip, or babes, unless they'd be my own, or other such female matters. So I can't offer you that, nor will I lie to you about it.

"No, I don't believe we could be friends, so since that's what you're looking for, I'll say good night now. I wish you well," he said, drawing himself up. "It won't be easy for you, being the village spinster, and it's a damned waste of a good woman, to my way of thinking. But I'm no liar, and I won't start now. If you change your mind, you know where I live. Give you a good night. *Bedheugh why lowenak.* Happiness to you."

He started to walk away, toward the stable and his horse. But he paused. "Oh, and say a good night to

Tremellyn, will you?" And then, whistling an old sea chantey, he strolled away.

Amber would never know whether that saunter and whistled tune was easy or hard for him to do. But she knew it was what a man like Pascoe had to do, and respected him for it. And if it were possible, she disliked herself even more for possibly hurting him. She shouldn't have kissed him; she shouldn't in any way have encouraged him. Worse, she'd only done it to compare his kisses with Amyas's, and that was very wrong, because she'd known from the start whom she wanted to make love to.

Or had she been looking for a husband, no matter what? If so, if only for a few moments, she'd been about to give herself in order to make her life easier. That, and not Pascoe's kiss, dismayed her, and made her life now seem almost unendurable.

She waited until she heard Pascoe's horse canter off into the night, then she went back into the house.

Grace and Tobias were in the parlor sitting close to each other and talking in low voices. Tremellyn was in a chair by the hearth, trying not to look as uncomfortable at being chaperone as he probably felt. He greeted Amber with a relieved smile. Then that smile faded.

"Where's Pascoe?" he asked, looking behind her.

"Gone home," she said casually as she could. "He said to give you a good night."

"Ah," he said. "I see." He looked at the newly engaged couple. They looked back at him expectantly. "I've a few things to talk to Amber about," he announced as he rose from his chair. "But I'll be back in a moment," he added, lowering his brows.

Grace giggled. Tobias looked nervous.

"Come into my study," Tremellyn told Amber.

She followed him down the hall to his study and sat in the chair she always used when they went over the accounts each month. He closed the door and went to his desk. But instead of sitting behind it, as he always did, he poked up the tiny fire he had in the grate, and then stood before it, looking at it steadily, a frown on his face.

He stood there, strong and stolid, a middle-aged man with a thick body and thinning hair, wearing his second-best jacket, as familiar to Amber as her own face in the mirror.

"He asked for your hand, did he?" he asked her.

"Yes," she said sadly.

"And you refused him?" he asked, turning to look at her at last.

She nodded.

"Did he get angry?"

"I think so, he said his good night in Cornish," she said, then hastily added, "but if he was, he hid it well. All he did was leave."

"Mind if I ask why you turned him down?" he asked. "He's quite a catch, is Pascoe Piper. From an old family, a hard worker, handsome, well enough off, and on the way to doing even better for himself.

Truthfully, I'd hopes he had his eye on Grace. He's a little brusque, but he'll mellow in time."

"I think he will," Amber said. "But even so, he's not for me. I have foolish notions, he thinks. He may be right."

She looked up at him and smiled, a little unsteadily. Mr. Tremellyn was the closest thing she had to a real father. He'd always acted as such, and she loved him very much. He wasn't affectionate, and never demonstrative, and had been distant, though generous to her all her life. He'd never let her down, and she thought he understood her as few people did. He'd never been a confidant, or precisely a friend, but he'd always protected her. She couldn't tell him what hurt her now, but she might be able to tell him enough, she thought, to get her through the night.

"I want to be in love with the man I marry," she told him earnestly, her eyes begging him to understand her. "Not wildly, madly, giddily in love, maybe, the way Gracie is for her Toby. But with all my heart, nonetheless. So I can't, or rather won't marry any man just to be comfortable. You see, I realized, as Pascoe did, that I can't stay on here once Grace marries and leaves."

"That's true," he said. "So, if you won't marry for comfort, you will for love, is that it?"

She nodded.

"A nice notion," he said thoughtfully. "And have you ever met such a fellow?"

She nodded again.

"Ah. I see. So, is there any man you know that you do want?" he asked softly.

"Yes," she confessed, "but I can't marry him." She had to look down, because she felt emotional, much-hated tears welling in her eyes.

"Ah," he said, and fell still.

She tried to compose herself, and wondered if she dared tell him everything, after all.

"Amber?" he asked in such a strange voice that she had to look up at him. His eyes gleamed; his face was ruddy with suppressed emotion. "I never thought I could ever say this to you," he began, and stopped, as though all his dawning smiles were making it hard for him to continue to speak. "Say instead that I never expected to be able to say this to you. But it seems I can, at last, if only because you seem to want me to." He grinned widely, took a deep breath, and exhaled.

Amber became rigid. She concentrated, reviewing what she'd just said. She saw Tremellyn's sudden exhilaration and realized the implication she hadn't meant. She froze and hoped against hope she was wrong, and that he wasn't going to say what she suddenly was terrified he might.

"My dear," he said. "When I found you, all those years ago, I took you in out of pity. But I confess I'd probably never have done it if I hadn't just lost my dear wife. I wish you'd known her. She was a good woman, an excellent wife, and would have been a fine mother. I let you stay because I thought you'd be a companion for my newborn daughter. Maybe, in a way, I was taking in another female because I'd just lost one dear to me. I never guessed how capricious Fate can be, or that you'd become just as dear in time."

"Mr. Tremellyn," Amber said quickly, not sure where his thoughts were going, and unwilling to let them go further, "I don't think you understand."

"Oh, but I do," he said. "I know how painful unrequited love can be, how unbearable a desire is that you feel can never be fulfilled. Who better? I know that too well, my dear. I'm old enough to be your father," he said ruefully, "and well I know it, too. I see it every morning in my mirror, after all, and am always surprised, because my heart's still young and will keep on beating for some time, or so I hope. Or rather, so you've given me hope that it will do.

"What I mean to say, Amber, is that I never gave you a last name—maybe because I foresaw this day. No matter. I offer you one now. Mine. If you marry me, we can go on here as we have been, but in an even closer and more intimate way. I'm offering you marriage, Amber."

She opened her mouth to speak, but couldn't think of words to say.

He smiled even more widely. "Oh, I know there will be those who will mock me for it. But no one mocks a Tremellyn out loud. Not around here. Gracie will be surprised, but delighted, too, I think, in time. I'd never have made this offer before she decided to marry and leave us, but it's just as well. Because now if one day she has a new brother or sister, it won't trouble her as it might have then. She'll be having her own brood soon enough. She did us a good turn. I doubt I'd have told you any of this, though I might have wanted to, if she hadn't made it necessary. But I gave you every chance to find someone else.

"It's true that when Grace marries, you won't be able to stay on here with me. You would, as my wife. That's what I'm offering, Amber, at last. Now you can be a Tremellyn in truth."

Amber stood. Tremellyn moved toward her. She put up a hand to stop him. He paused, and seeing her ashen face, frowned.

She prayed for the right words, words to explain without hurting him. "I thank you for the honor that you do me," she said, "and I do love you, Mr. Tremellyn."

He moved toward her again. She took a step back, and kept her hand up as she quickly went on, "I love you. But as a father, which is what you've always been to me. And I think that if you search your heart, you'll see that you've always felt that I've been like a daughter to you, too, and anything else would feel as wrong as it would be wrong for you as well as for me." She struggled for words that could heal, so that they could both remember this night without shame.

She looked at him steadily and sadly, and spoke half the truth that she knew. "It's so like you, Mr. Tremellyn, to offer to sacrifice yourself for me. I appreciate it, and it's only one of the reasons why I love you. It's true I'll have to go when Gracie marries, but all children must leave the nest one day. And when I do go we both know there'll be many good women eager to take my place, as there've always been through all these years. So I thank you from the bottom of my heart for your charity toward me. You've always sheltered me. But now it's time for me to find my own place in the world."

He stayed still.

She stood quietly, hoping she'd said enough and not too much.

At last, he smiled again. But it was a sad, knowing smile. "You're welcome, Amber," he said. "I've always had your best interests at heart."

A great breath of relief escaped her. She raised her head. "And now, I think," she said, "I should go. We can't leave Gracie and Tobias together alone this long."

He nodded. "Yes."

She went to the door, and had her hand on the knob when he spoke again.

"Amber?" he asked. "Since we'll both try to forget this night, or at least never speak of it again, tell me. Who is the man you would have, if you could?"

She dropped her gaze. He deserved all her honesty now. "Amyas St. Ives. I know," she added to his look of surprise. "He's a man with a terrible past, but with all of that, he wasn't a bad man. We'll never meet again, though."

"My pride be damned, girl!" he said angrily. "I've acted as your father, and I can continue to. Tell me, did he give me reason to go after him and force him to make an honest woman of you?"

"Oh, no." she said. "I promise you, he left me with honor, and with my honor intact." She looked at him steadily. "But it was he who made that decision. So you see, he was not, after all, as bad as you thought. But maybe I was worse than you, or I, imagined."

"I see," he said softly. He thought for a moment, and added, "I give you a good night, Amber."

"A good night to you, Mr. Tremellyn" she said.

She went to the parlor and sat so still and quietly that it wasn't long before Tobias grew nervous and left. Her stillness was so rare and Grace so involved with her own happiness, that Amber was able to say good night to her, too, and leave soon after.

Amber went up to her room and sat at her desk. She took paper and pen and wrote letters until the lamp burned low and flickered too much for her to continue. Then she took the sheaf of papers and leafed through them. She'd written another letter to her friend Emily in London, asking if she knew of any positions there for her.

She'd written to Charlotte Knight's cousin Mrs. Magway, asking the same thing. And she'd penned three letters to employment agencies in London. In the morning, she would get their addresses from the London paper that Mr. Tremellyn subscribed to, then walk to the village to send them on.

Then, as the last of the lamplight flickered, she thought of Amyas. He was never far from her mind. But now she remembered one of the ways he said he'd searched for his family. She picked up her pen. Then she put it down, remembering that had just been another of his lies.

Still, the lie, like all his lies, was too tempting to resist.

She took another sheet of paper and wrote an advertisement to send to the newspaper. It was one last attempt to find a name before she had to invent one to wear out into the world.

> *Any information regarding an infant girl of about two years of age, found alone on the shore near St. Edgyth, in Cornwall, after a shipwreck with all hands lost, in the spring of the year 1798, will be appreciated. The infant was wearing a blue smock, and had blond hair . . .*

Amber smiled for the first time in a long time as she wrote. It seemed foundlings had one thing that other people didn't. They had hope that never died, even if all their other dreams did.

Because whatever the advertisement brought her, it wouldn't change her plans. She'd go to London and find herself a future, and maybe find herself, too. She had to. She'd burned all her bridges behind her.

Chapter 16

$\curlyvee$

Amyas looked at the half-naked woman on his lap. For the first time since she'd landed herself there, he took a good look. He craned his neck back and stared down at her. She smiled up at him. She was young, and even prettier than she'd seemed from across the room, blond as morning, everywhere a man could see. And he could see almost everywhere. She had a remarkably firm body. He was sure of that because she was wearing more scent than clothing.

She noted his careful inspection and took a deep breath so he could see how high those firm breasts could rise.

"And what would you like, sir?" she asked as coyly as if she was a maiden showing him a peek at her ankles instead of a full view of everything she had except for her ankles.

"To thank you," he said. He slipped his arms under her, picked her up, and rose from the chair in one smooth movement.

The dark-haired young gentleman sitting nearby looked up at him with a slight smile.

The girl giggled, until Amyas set her down on her feet as quickly as he'd picked her up. He put a finger on the tip of her nose and smiled down at her confusion. "Thank you," he said, "but I've got other plans for tonight. But here's something I think you'll find even better to keep you company," he added, handing her some banknotes.

"Daffy," he said to the dark-haired young man, "I'm going. Will I see you in the morning?"

"No," Daffyd said, as he, too, stood up. "You'll see me now, unless you'd rather walk alone?"

"Come along then," Amyas said, and strode out of the richly furnished salon toward the door.

"My good sirs!" a stout, well-dressed woman cried, rushing over to Amyas after he requested his hat and cloak from a footman. "How have we failed you?"

"You haven't," Amyas said. "My mood has. You have the best whorehouse I've seen in London, Daisy, but I'm not in the market tonight."

Her smile faded, and she scowled at him. "Here!" she said, angrily poking him in the ribs with one finger. "Mind your manners, luv. It ain't no whorehouse, it's a house of convenience, and I'll thank you to remember that. And I'm not 'Daisy' no more. It's 'Missus Dalyrimple,' and don't forget it.

"Ah," she said, instantly relenting, giving his arm a light swat with one beringed hand, "you never mind me, Amyas. I don't know what gets into me—it ain't trade though," she said, giggling like the young woman he'd just left had done. "I don't have to work for my supper no more. That's what does it, I think. I'm too used to being respectable these days. But if I forget them what helped me in the old days, where would I be, eh? You done me too many good turns for me to mind anything you do—or don't do. So you don't want to make faces with any of my girls? That don't surprise me. You never had to pay for it in the old days. But didn't you know? For you, lad, it's free, and always will be. Any of my girls is yours for the asking. I don't forget favors."

"Nor I," he said. "We're halfway round the world now, Mrs. Dallyrump, my old duck." He tipped her a wide grin. "But I hope we still count each other as friends. So I won't lie to you. I have a lot on my mind right now, and though wine helped some, women won't. And I can't carry a tune. So the old wine, women, and song cure won't work for me tonight. I'm off to sulk it off. You take care of yourself, and thanks for the offer."

"You leaving, too?" she squeaked, looking at Daffyd as he collected his high beaver hat from a maid.

"Yes, I'm going with him," Daffyd said.

"Yeah, you always was, Daffy," the madam said on

a sigh. "You, that handsome lad, Christian, and Amyas. We used to call you the unholy trinity. Remember? Wish I had a brother."

"You told us you had six!" Daffyd said, turning to stare at her.

"I did, but they was drunken louts," she said dismissively. "I mean a *real* brother, like you and Amyas is."

"Oh that," Daffyd said. "Well, the best brothers are those you chose for yourself. Good night, Daisy."

"Dallyrump, that's a good one," she murmured, and chuckled, then gave the footman trying not to grin a hard look. "Take care, lads," she told Amyas and Daffyd. "Lord, but even though you bring back the old days, you do brighten a person's night."

Amyas and Daffyd left the elegant brothel and stood on the pavement, looking into the mild, dark London night. "Where to?" Daffyd asked.

"I wish I knew," Amyas said softly. He didn't know where he could go to escape himself, and he'd tried, every day and night since he'd returned to London.

Daffyd fidgeted. "There's always a game for good stakes at Whites'. I know a bloke or two there. But there's one for higher, in a lower place, to the east. Mack Dougherty runs a hazard parlor that's said to be honest."

"No," Amyas said. "We gambled the other night, remember? All I can do is win."

"And that makes you sad? Better get you to a good doctor then."

Amyas shook his head. "Money always makes me

happy. But remembering the old saw about 'lucky at cards, unlucky at love' took the pleasure from it. Could be true."

"You loved her?" Daffyd asked, surprised. "The wench in Cornwall? But you hardly knew the girl, you said."

"Don't be daft," Amyas flashed back at him. "How could I love her? How well can a man get to know a female he doesn't live with? Especially a respectable one? You can't keep company with them for a half hour alone without first promising to keep them for life. You can't sit and talk for hours, like you can with a whore, if you choose. What sense does that make? You're supposed to make up your mind on what female you're going to spend your life with based on how she talks about the weather or pours you tea?"

Amyas clutched his walking stick hard, knotting his gloved hands in his frustration. "I don't know how a man's supposed to get on here in England, at least, among the respectable people. And I've had my fill of the other kind."

"You thinking of going home? To Port Jackson?" Daffyd asked.

"I said I had my fill of the other kind," Amyas said bitterly. "And anyway, where's home? When we were in the Antipodes all we could think of was coming back here. Now I'm here, and this isn't it either. I came back to set up respectably and live the good life. And what happens? I don't have to go to old Dallyrump's brothel, I can rut wherever I will among the wild and sporting class. But respectable folk only have to hear what I was, and they slam the door in my face. I could marry any girl back there at Daisy's house, or any like her, in a second. But I can't get a 'good one' because I was so bad."

"She turned you down?" Daffyd asked carefully. He didn't know who "she" was, but wanted to. He'd been trying to get Amyas to tell him what happened in Cornwall since he'd gotten back, weeks ago. All he'd heard was that Amyas hadn't found his family, had met a woman, but not his future wife, and didn't want to talk about it. But now, in the middle of the sidewalk in the middle of the night, Amyas was talking.

Daffyd listened as closely as he could, prodding gently. When Amyas was in a touchy mood like this, anything could happen. He wasn't a violent man. But he was a private one. He could take it into his head to stride off and disappear for days if Daffyd wasn't careful. That wouldn't do him any good. He was clearly suffering, and Daffyd wanted to help.

In that spirit, he'd gone with him to gaming Hells and brothels, taverns, boxing parlors, horse races, and livestock sales. They'd never stayed any place long enough to sport, and Amyas increasingly looked as though he longed to spoil sport. They'd taken long walks, gone riding and driving round London's parks. They'd sparred and fenced and attended the theater and the opera, and as many balls, parties, routs, and masquerades both high and low, as Daffyd could find. Amyas's mood just seemed to worsen; he didn't take his usual enjoyment in anything.

Daffyd suspected Amyas's problem was related to a woman, which in itself was strange. Amyas never had problems with women, except, maybe, for being able to rid himself of them, because he was soft-hearted where females were concerned. But Amyas had just said this mysterious female was respectable. That, Daffyd thought, might make the difference. He wasn't sure, because he wouldn't know about them.

"No, she didn't throw me out. Her father did," Amyas said. "Their father did," he corrected himself, making Daffyd wonder how much he'd had to drink. "Threw me out of the house and threatened to shoot me like a dog if I came back. She took me in, out of sympathy, and I almost ruined her as thanks for her charity."

He fell still, a muscle moving in his tight-set jaw as he stared into the night.

"So," Daffyd ventured, "seems to me she wanted you. You don't want her?"

"I," Amyas said, grinding out each word, "Don't. Know."

"Why not?"

"I didn't know her well enough," Amyas said, to end the matter.

"Want to tell me more?" Daffyd hesitated. He knew his limits. He was a man with a lot of experience of the world, but little with the kind of people

Amyas called "respectable." He had known to a
nicety how to cheat and deceive them, and brilliantly.
But he knew next to nothing about how to live with
them in this new life.

Thinking hard, he remembered what a defrocked
priest he'd met in Newgate had once told him: that a
man often solved his own problems, just by talking
about them. He'd found that to be true. "So," he
asked Amyas, hoping he wouldn't take offense and
walk off alone into the night, "what about talking to
me and Christian? Like in the old days?"

"He's newly wed. He's got a wife. A fine woman.
No need for her to hear sordid stuff like this. And
even if he promises not to tell her," Amyas said
quickly, "I don't want to be the one to give him something he has to keep from her. That can poison a marriage."

Daffyd nodded. Now he had no idea of what to say.
He knew less about marriages than he did about respectable women. But he knew someone who did.
"Well, what about talking with Geoff—the earl—
then? He used to have words of wisdom in the old
days."

"We were boys. Now I'm a man. I should be able to
work this out for myself." Amyas said roughly, and
started walking, striding down the street, not looking
to see if Daffyd followed.

But, of course, Daffyd did. "So the thing is that
there's this female, who's respectable, who wanted
you but you don't know if you want her?"

Amyas didn't answer, but he nodded.

"Ah, well then," Daffyd said. "Best thing then is to go see her again and find out."

"I can't. I said her father threw me out. If I go back, I'd have to take her away with me, and right away. So the thing is I either leave her forever, or take her as a wife, forever."

"That's hard," Daffyd agreed. "Especially on short notice."

They walked in silence.

"Can you forget her?" Daffyd asked.

"Damned if I can," Amyas said. "I think of her all the time. That blond whore taking up room in my lap tonight was a fine-looking article. But when I looked at her, you know what I thought?"

"No," Daffyd said, fascinated.

"I thought that Amber was much more beautiful," Amyas said.

Daffyd made a note of the name and kept up his stride alongside Amyas as he marched through the streets.

"I also thought that she'd have to be half-dead from starving before she'd sell herself like that," Amyas said angrily. "Then I thought that she might do it even if she weren't, if her sister was starving. She'd sell herself in a minute if it could help someone she loved; but I bet even so she wouldn't be able to laugh like that while she was doing it, or show herself off so proudly to a man she didn't love. Then I thought of how sad being a whore must be for some females.

"Damnation, Daffy! I was offered prime goods, and all I could do was think of another woman. It didn't shrivel me. No," he said bitterly. "I couldn't rise in the first place. Thinking of her in the same situation made me dead from the waist down. Hell, from the neck up, too. That never happened before."

"That's a powerful thing," Daffyd said, repressing a shiver.

They kept on walking, not watching where they were going. But even as they coursed alone through districts known for nighttime trade, none of the legion of prostitutes approached them. The pair striding through the streets were dressed as gentlemen. But their faces didn't promise money or pleasure. Nor did any of the many men set on stealing take a step toward them either. However they were dressed, the two men looked able-bodied, and also as if they'd welcome a fight.

They walked through a better district, and whatever street they passed along, the Watch grew nervous and observed them narrowly.

"So," Daffyd finally said again, "if you can't forget her, and you can't go talk to her, why not write her a letter?"

Amyas stopped in his tracks, turned, and stared at him.

"That way you can let her know what you're thinking," Daffyd said. "Right? But you don't have to see her father, or take her with you neither. It would be like talking, only different. Maybe better, because it takes a long time to think of what to write down, what you get is more reasonably said. And since she wouldn't be sitting there, looking at you, your glands won't get in the way neither. And remember to put another name on it, so her old man don't know it's from you."

Amyas clapped him on the shoulder. "Daffyd! You are a genius."

Daffyd shrugged. "I do my best. Now, can we stop walking?"

Amyas sat at his desk, and took out another clean sheet of paper. He'd thrown away three so far, and hadn't even written a word. He'd think of all the things he wanted to say and put his pen to the paper and write, only to find he'd done nothing but make deep scratches because the ink had dried as he'd waited for inspiration.

He wanted to find a brilliant way to open his letter to her, a way that would intrigue her, stop her from seeing his signature at the bottom of the page and tearing the letter to bits before she read a word. Even more, he needed a way to explain himself to her.

He gripped his hair in both hands. How could he do that when he wasn't sure of how to explain himself to himself?

He told Daffy he didn't know her well enough. That had been a damned lie. There'd been a bond between them since the first time he'd clapped eyes on her. It only strengthened that night they'd been together. He'd looked forward to seeing her every day. It was there when they'd kissed, enhancing his love-making as it had never been before. It was there when he left and felt his heart starting to ache.

She knew him as well as he knew her, he'd swear it. He'd tried to resist her, but failed. It wasn't just her beauty and appeal. She understood his jests and caught his every comment; he didn't feel he was swimming against the tide when he spoke to her, as he had with pretty, vacuous little Grace and other women in his past. He lusted after Amber, of course. But he could also talk with her, and wanted to, as he'd never done with any of his flirts, mistresses, and chance-met partners.

He didn't know her? That was a joke. He knew she loved to read, walk, swim, and laugh. It was a wonder to know a woman who read so much. It made what she said so interesting that he sometimes forgot he was talking to a woman.

He remembered whenever he looked at her, though. And he couldn't stop doing that, even though he hadn't actually been in her company for a month. But he had seen her. He'd seen her face every day since he'd left her, and sometimes in reality, too. It gave his heart a jolt every time. And each time, when he realized his mistake, his heart felt colder. Soon he'd freeze to death, he thought.

Just last night at the theater, he'd been sitting in his high box when he'd seen a glimpse of bright hair beneath a dashing bonnet below in the audience. He'd dashed out of the box, down the corridor, and followed his vision down the stairs to find the woman. He had, and she'd been stunning. She'd smiled at him, then frowned to see his sudden scowl, because she wasn't Amber. He'd saluted her with a shrug and a bow of apology and slunk back to his box.

What had he thought? That Amber would come to London to seek him? Not in a thousand years. That she'd visit for sport? Not even if she desperately needed diversion, because her place was with Tremellyn and his daughter, and she'd never ask anything for herself. But if she felt as lost as he did? That gave Amyas pause. He put his pen down.

Then he almost laughed aloud. He shook his head to clear it. Was he entirely mad? If she was hurt, she'd swallow her pain and go on with her life as she'd always done, and as, damn him, he'd seen her do because of what he'd done to her. She'd stay with the Tremellyns whatever her private sorrow, and she'd keep her own counsel about it, too, because she was brave and loyal and faithful, and had a heart too big for her own good. She felt inferior because she never knew her parents, but she loved the man who had taken her in, and thought of his daughter as her sister because she longed for family. Oh, he knew a lot about her.

He'd lied to Daffy, for the first time since he'd met him.

He'd told him why he hadn't offered for Amber, but hadn't mentioned the only important reason. Daffyd had shared his triumphs and his woes since that painful day they'd met in an alley. But Daffyd didn't really understand how he felt about being nameless. How could he? Daffyd was the only person Amyas had ever heard of who had run *away* from the Gypsies, because he hated his father so much. But even so, he knew who he was and where he'd come from.

Amyas realized he hadn't told Daffyd the truth about Amber because he wanted him to respect her. It hadn't been a noble impulse. He hadn't told Daffy because he'd been afraid it would show him what a great fool and pompous ass his adopted brother was.

He'd wanted to marry up. He'd looked for a woman whose name would give him respect he wouldn't have to work for, the way he'd worked for everything all his life. And so when he'd finally found a woman who appealed to him heart, mind, and body, he'd rejected her, because she had no more name than he did.

Now he was afraid he knew that name: coward.

"Be damned to you!" Amyas cursed, rising from his desk.

"Sir?" his sleepy valet asked a few minutes later at the door to the study.

"I spoke aloud? Never mind," Amyas said. "Talking to myself. Go to sleep. Thank you," he added belatedly.

Then he sat down, dipped his pen in ink, and began to write as though inspired. He was. He wrote what he felt, without thinking, and he felt so much he couldn't contain it anymore.

My dear Amber,

I've been a fool, and a blind man, a coward and a climber, and I am sick of it, and myself. I don't know how such a fool dare ask a woman such as yourself to forgive him, take pity on him, and forget his transgressions, those made both before he met you and after. But this is what I'm doing now.

Amber, I do love you, and love you entirely. My only regret, and it is a mighty one, is that I may have hurt you, even for a moment, by my idiocy. I miss you very much. I need you even more. I don't want to think of spending the rest of my life without you.

Enough of me. What can I offer you, apart from my foolish self? As to that, I have funds aplenty. I have good and decent friends. I'm in good health, and of sound mind, usually. I've never raised my hand to a female or anyone smaller than I am. I'm done with crime, which I only took up because I knew no better and had no other way to live. I promise you that I will devote the rest of my life to making you happy. I can't promise that I will. But I will try.

I will be faithful, and I will try to learn how to be a good husband, but I have no family, except for those I chose to be family, and I have no name, except for the one I invented. Can you accept that? Although I have no real name, whatever I do have, I offer you. Will you marry me? I'll come to St. Edgyth after I post this letter, giving you time to read it and make up your mind. I hope your answer will be yes. Please say yes. If you do, you must be prepared to come with me immediately, since your adopted father has vowed to put a hole in me if I show my face. You need not worry. I can defend myself without hurting him. And I have decent friends you can stay with until our wedding day.

Please say yes when I come to call again.

Your humble servant,
Amyas St. Ives

The lamp was low when he was done. The ink on the page was dry by the time he had finished reading and rereading it. But when he had, Amyas shrugged on his jacket, picked up the letter, and strode to his door. A month since he'd laid eyes on her, and now it was hard to think about waiting even another minute to see her again.

The morning sun was coming up when he left his house and went round the back to the stable. He saddled his horse and rode down the alley to the street. There wasn't much traffic yet, the Quality was still sleeping—even the earliest recreational horsemen weren't out. Apart from the milkmaids, most servants and barrow peddlers were just rising from their beds. But Amyas knew that the first stage from the west would be arriving at the Bull and Mouth soon. If he hurried, he could have the letter in a packet for the return trip.

Amyas rode to the famously busy coaching station to the west of the city and got there even as the first dusty coach was unloading passengers, boxes, and bags. Other coaches were loading. Even at this hour the inn yard was crowded with travelers coming and going, as well as those there to greet or send them off.

A few questions and he had the name of the guard on the Flier, the next coach to go into Cornwall. He found the man and paid a handsome sum to entrust his letter to him.

Then, at last, seeing his letter go into the guard's leather pouch, Amyas was able to relax. He felt the tension drain from him. He lifted his face to the newly risen sun. It was done.

He turned to go, and froze in place. He thought he caught a glimpse of honey gold, and amber. He stared. He saw the back of a woman with the same color hair as Amber. She was getting into a hackney cab, and the coach door closed behind her. In that second, Amyas really believed he'd glimpsed Amber herself. He almost dashed over to to see if it was really her . . . *again*? His heart slowed to its usual beat.

Now that he'd written to her, it would be worse, he'd

think he was seeing her everywhere he went. He only wished it were that easy. It wouldn't be. With luck, and with patience, he'd see her again. With luck, and patience, and, he thought, maybe even a little prayer.

The thought of the look on Daffy's face should he tell him he was going to church occurred to him. A second later and the passengers and those greeting them at the Bull and Mouth began to give the tall honey-haired gentleman in their midst a wide berth. He was well dressed and respectable-looking except for morning stubble on his face. But the daft fellow was standing there, laughing uproariously, and he was all alone.

But not for long, Amyas thought, sobering. *Please, not for long.*

Chapter 17

Amber sat back in the hackney cab but held her hands tight on her purse. She'd gripped it like grim death since she'd left Cornwall, fearing highwaymen. When her coach finally stopped at the Bull and Mouth in London that morning, she'd clung to it ever tighter, fearing pickpockets. In the inn yard, waiting in line for a hackney cab, she clutched it close every time an older woman passed. She'd heard the stories about London, and the procurers who regularly deceived unwary females as they came to the city. So her hands ached now. But not so badly as her heart did.

She'd done it. She'd left her home for the first time, or perhaps more rightly, she thought sadly, for the second time. But she couldn't remember anything but Tremellyn house, and it had been wrenching to leave it.

"Are you sure?" Grace had asked yet again the night before she'd left. "Completely sure?"

"Completely," Amber had said. "Don't fret. You won't be lonely. You'll have Tobias, and he's a very good boy . . . man."

"I know." Grace had sighed. "But Papa will miss you, too."

"I know," Amber had said, sighing even more softly. "But look at it this way: Mrs. Ames, Mrs. Tiddle, and Miss Williams will be tickled. I ruled the roost here. And with you going soon, too, he'll be much more likely to pick another wife if he's alone, and each of them has hopes. Why, the only reason to worry about him is that they might bury him under a heap of pies and puddings and other gifts of food." She saw Grace smile, and went on, "Or they could suffocate him with attention, or run him ragged with sudden social calls. That could be dangerous to his health."

She waited until Grace had stopped giggling to speak more seriously. "You know, having us here all these years prevented his remarrying, and so our leaving may be the most loving thing we can do for him."

Grace hadn't looked convinced.

"Gracie," Amber had persisted, "you won't have any reason to be jealous even if he does remarry, because he loves you entirely and always will, and when you have a baby he'll be over the moon for it."

"But what about you?" Gracie wailed. "Gone to London? On your own? With no one to watch over you? He'll worry about you every minute; you're just like a daughter to him."

Amber nodded, not trusting herself to speak at once. Mr. Tremellyn's offer was something she'd never let Grace know. "Don't worry," she finally said, "we spoke. He knows children have to leave home one day, and he understands."

"Does he?" Gracie asked. "It's almost like he's been avoiding you since the day you said you were leaving."

"I hadn't noticed," Amber said, trusting she'd be forgiven for the lie. "He's just not a man who likes to show his emotions. Why, didn't he just call me into his study to talk with me an hour ago?"

He had, and if he couldn't show emotions, at least he had shown his concern.

"You don't have to leave," Tremellyn had told her. "I know you might feel . . . uncomfortable since our talk, but damme, Amber, you don't have to leave here because of anything I said. We can still get on together. I'll hire on a companion for you."

"What a bother and an expense!" Amber had said, trying to make her voice light. "And not necessary. I'll do very well. It's not because of anything you said. That only made me realize how much you care for me." This was a hard good-bye, but she'd struggled to make it softer for him, mixing truth with hope, trying to ignore the greater truths that made them both uncomfortable now.

"But I must make my way in the world," she'd gone on. "Don't worry about me, I won't be in any danger. You read Mrs. Magway's letter. She couldn't be kinder, and she and her husband are respectable. As is my old friend Emily, who is already employed in London. They'll all help me look for a decent position and won't let me take a wrong step. And that other letter I just got," she'd added, trying to keep the excitement from her voice, "that's a possibility, too, if a remote one. You said you'd let me know what the solicitor in London you wrote to said about it, remember?"

"And so I will," he said gravely. "But I wish . . . Well, your mind's made up. Know this, Amber: You can come home at any time, anytime at all."

"I know," she'd said, catching up his hand and pressing it for a moment, before, embarrassed and near tears, she let go. "I know that very well. Be sure I'll remember it. Thank you." She wished his offer of marriage had never been spoken, because not only was it sending her away, it was robbing her of the chance to hug him now, as she so wished to do.

But she still owed him more than she could ever repay, and it wasn't fair to make him feel guilty for his deepest wishes for her happiness and his own. So she'd wiped her eyes and tried a wavering smile. "I daresay there isn't a maiden lady or widow within ten miles who won't want to send me flowers for leaving. I doubt you'll be alone very long, Mr. Tremellyn."

"Aye, exactly why you shouldn't go!"

They'd laughed. For a moment, things seemed normal. Then realizing what had to be done, she'd dropped her gaze. "I have to see to finishing up my packing now."

"Be sure to take my lo . . . affection," he'd said gruffly. "And all my wishes for your success."

Pascoe Piper had come round in the morning to say good-bye, too. But that had been brief, and Amber had seen no regret in his eyes, only an expression that told her he thought she was committing a great folly.

And so now, her farewells made, and her course set, Amber rode through London to the house of Charlotte Knight's unknown cousin, Mrs. Magway. She wore a sober traveling costume. All the clothes in her case were similarly simple. A woman who was about to make her way in the world did not need fripperies. She'd bound up her hair because it was wild and bright, but she would let it down every night to remember how it could look if she were free again. She wondered if she ever would be.

She was terrified. Her heart had been beating so fast since she left home that she wondered if it would tire itself out and simply stop. But every time she wondered about that, something would happen to make it beat ever faster.

Still, Amber was determined. She would find a position. She would make her way in life. But she knew it was going to be a lonely one, because she'd had to leave the home she loved, because she couldn't love the man who had given her that home, at least not in the way that he wished. And because the only man she did want hadn't wanted her at all, precisely because she had nothing and was no one. She'd change that, or die in the attempt. And at the moment, as she saw more people outside the hackney's window than she had seen altogether in her entire life, she truly didn't know which it was that she would do.

She thought of the possibility of a good-paying position, and it calmed her a bit. Then, although she'd vowed not to indulge in fancies about it anymore, she again thought of the other letter she'd gotten, and the promise of hope it held out. It was surely only a dream, one that would soon fade away. But until it did she had something else to give her the courage she'd needed to leave her home and go on in search of a new one.

She didn't have to look at the letter anymore to read it. She could just close her eyes and see it.

In response to your inquiry of the seventh of September, as seen in the Times *of London, we have reason to believe that the infant girl found on the beach near St. Edgyth might be of interest to our clients. If the young person in question would apply, in person, to the law offices of Treadwell, Haverstraw and Fitch, in St. Michael's Road, London, she might find items of interest to her . . .*

If the solicitors Mr. Tremellyn wrote to said it was a reputable law firm, she'd go there and speak to them. "But even if they are sound," Mr. Tremellyn had cautioned her, "there's not likely much of value for you there. All these years, after all . . ." He'd let the sentence go unfinished.

She knew it. Anyone looking for a child more than eighteen years after she'd been lost was not someone who'd looked very hard in the first place. But what Mr. Tremellyn hadn't known was that anything, even if not of much value, could mean the earth to her. If she could learn her name! That would be enough. Then she'd be a person with a background. Then, perhaps even a man like Amyas would want her.

Amber opened her eyes. She refused to think about him. She smiled sadly. That was nonsense. He'd changed her life. She couldn't stop thinking about him; it was thinking about him that made marriage to anyone else seem impossible. The thought of him haunted her day and night. Just now, even in her terrifying first moments after setting foot in London, as she'd stood astounded and afraid, she'd looked up and across the crowded inn yard and thought she'd seen him standing there.

Tall, well dressed, with an arresting face, battered nose, and thick honey-colored hair, the man had looked exactly like Amyas St. Ives. On an astonished second glance, she saw that though the gentleman was well dressed, he wasn't well groomed: He wore no hat and needed a shave; he was wind-tossed and crumpled. Amyas had always looked fastidious. Nevertheless, he looked so much like Amyas that she caught her breath.

She didn't get a third glance at him. An enthusiastic family greeted a new arrival beside her, and she lost sight of him for a second in the swirling crowd of people around her. That was what she needed to regain her senses. What would Amyas be doing here?

Maybe he'd found out she was coming to London?

That sudden wild surmise died as she realized no one in St. Edgyth would have told him that. If he'd found out somehow, he'd know what coach she was on, and would have been standing with the others welcoming new arrivals. But what folly. Why would a wealthy, worldly fellow like Amyas be in a public coaching inn yard, near dawn?

When the people around Amber moved away, she looked down to her bags, picked them up, and didn't look up again until she reached the waiting hackney cab.

She just had to get used to thinking of him when she didn't want to and wait for it to stop. Surely, one day he would leave her heart and mind as certainly as she was leaving her past life behind. Amber looked out the window at London and waited for that new life to begin.

"Are you sure you don't want me to come in with you?" Mrs. Magway asked Amber.

They sat in the outer offices of Treadwell, Haverstraw and Fitch, waiting for Amber to be called in to speak about the curious letter she'd gotten in reply to her advertisement.

"Thank you," Amber said, "but I think it's better that I go in to speak with them alone. But thank you for coming with me. It would have been more difficult by myself."

Iris Magway nodded, setting the birds on her stylish bonnet bobbing as though they were still alive and pecking for seeds on the top of her smartly dressed hair. She was a tiny, lively little person, and Amber knew she was lucky to have her as hostess. She'd come to the Magways' house, in a charming neighborhood filled with neat little houses, and had been greeted like a long-lost friend. She'd been given a bedchamber and a lavish dinner, instead of being begrudged a scrap of food and the roof over her head, as she'd feared she might have been.

Since Mr. Magway worked in his shop from sunup to nightfall, her hostess was bored to flinders, she said, and she looked at Amber's arrival as a gift. Iris Magway's three small children were in the care of a nurse, leaving Iris time to do what she pleased during the day.

The problem was that she never found enough things to please her for very long. She painted limp landscapes, she did good works for the missionary foundation; she helped her husband in his shop whenever allowed, and ran her household in league with her cook and maid. But none of it seemed to satisfy her relentless energy or need for constant conversation.

Any worries Amber had that the man of the house

might prove a problem because of how he reacted to a homeless young woman under his roof were put to rest. Mr. Magway's only interest seemed to be in his shop, and he was too weary every evening to do more than talk about it; he was pleasant enough to Amber, but nothing more.

Iris Magway was neither well-read nor well educated, but she was merry and friendly, and hungry for company. She'd heard Amber's story from her cousin and found it romantic. Once she'd seen Amber, she decided the story would have some wonderful fairy story ending. Since the day after Amber had come to her house, her hostess had insisted on taking her out, driving and walking around London, showing her the sights.

In all, it was a great relief to Amber, except when Mrs. Magway took her through the better neighborhoods. Then Amber worried what she would do if she really saw Amyas and not just men who reminded her of him. But she never did.

The only problem was herself. Because even Iris Magway couldn't talk all the time, and when she was alone, Amber was lonely, for Grace and for Mr. Tremellyn.

Nights were hardest for her. Lying in bed, alone, knowing she was hundreds of miles from home, set her to aching. Lying there knowing she might only be a mile from Amyas was worse. She wondered where he was and what he was doing, and what he'd do if he knew she was so near. Realizing that he'd do nothing different made it even more painful because nothing had changed between them but the miles.

The other problem was that she hadn't been able to find a position in the weeks since she'd arrived. Either they weren't suitable, or she wasn't, or her hostess pointed out something wrong with them. She kept imploring Amber simply to stay on as her friend and companion. Amber knew that would be folly since she had no work but that of amusing her hostess. Still, she was so lonely and homesick she might have been happy to go on that way. The day she'd gone to see Emily, who was working as a governess for a family in the diplomatic service, brought her down to earth.

They took tea at a parlor in a quiet part of London on Emily's one-half day off that week. Amber was surprised to see how quiet and dull Emily had become. She seemed older, walked stiffly, and talked precisely, and only laughed once, when she told Amber why. "I speak to few people except for the children," she said. "And I'm not sure they are precisely 'people' yet. Helping them achieve that state is what I've been hired to do, and I often despair of it. But that's my lot in life. And what of yours?"

She heard Amber out. "She'll tire of you," Emily finally said, when Amber finished telling her about her life with Mrs. Magway. "Her sort always does. And then where will you be? Find a position, Amber. It may not be pleasant, it may even be difficult, but it will be your only chance at independence. And from what you've told me, that is all you'll ever have."

It was sound advice, but Amber hadn't asked to see Emily again.

Now, Iris Magway was all atwitter. Amber had showed her the mysterious letter, and now she'd find out what it was about. The law firm of Treadwell, Haverstraw and Fitch was not only respectable, Mr. Tremellyn had written, it was prestigious.

He'd also asked her if she wanted to come home yet.

So Amber made the appointment with Mr. Treadwell, put on her best gown, a simple green frock, refusing all of Iris's offers of something finer, although she did accept her offer of company on the trip.

Amber wore a plain dark pelisse over her gown and hoped she looked serious and sensible. But she'd borrowed a tiny hat from Iris, a fetching little concoction of felt and lace, and she wore her hair as a young woman of means would, drawn up and allowed to tumble in a swirl of red-gold curls in back. It was her one vanity. Because today, possibly for the last time, she'd present herself as a young lady and not just a young woman, as she tried to find out her history, possibly for the last time as well.

The law offices were dark, the walls and floors all highly polished ancient wood, accented by ancient heavy chairs. Amber gave her name to the young man at the desk and took a chair, as he directed. She sat and let Iris's prattle wash over her.

"No," she murmured once again, when Iris stopped for breath, "as I said, Iris, I don't believe it's a scheme to get money, because I have none. Nor are they trying to lure me into a life of shame, because they haven't seen me. Women lured into such lives are beauties. I'm not, and besides, I could be hideous, how could they have known? So I think it's just some mistake on their part. Of course, I hope not."

After what seemed like an hour, a tiny bell sounded at the young clerk's desk. He rose. "If you would come this way, Miss?" he asked Amber.

She took a deep breath and stood. "I'll be back in a moment," she told Iris and, head high, followed the clerk down the dark hall.

He opened a door, and bowed, indicating that Amber should enter. She blinked, because the room before her was so bright. But she walked in and faced the man who rose from behind an enormous mahogany desk. The windows behind him had their draperies pulled back, flooding the chamber with light. Amber inclined her head in a short nod. She wouldn't curtsey to a man she didn't know. She wasn't a servant yet.

"Miss Amber . . . ah. Yes, from your letter I see there is no last name, of course," the man said. "But you are the young woman who placed that advertisement in the *Times*?" He was very old, dressed in clothes that were fine, but out-of-date. But he spoke like a gentleman.

"Yes," she said.

"I am Jerome Treadwell." He glanced away from her to a gentleman that Amber just noticed, who was rising from a chair on his right. He stared hard at her. She stared back.

That man was middle-aged and dressed exquisitely. He drew in his breath so sharply that Amber could see his thin nostrils narrowing. His cold blue eyes also narrowed as they fixed on her. Then he nodded. "It is she, to the life," he said in a slightly foreign-accented voice. "It is she, returned."

"Not so fast, my friend," Mr. Treadwell said on a huff of a laugh. "There are questions to be asked and answered."

"Then get on with it," the other man said. "I would return as soon as I can. I'll take her, I think."

Amber blinked again, but this time, not because of the bright light. She drew herself up. "I have a great many questions," she said. "But no answers. That is precisely why I have come here. And I shall not go anywhere with anyone, until they are answered. And perhaps not even if they are."

"Ah, yes," the gentleman said, with a wry twist to his mouth. "Indeed. It is she, to the life."

"No mail?" Amyas asked his valet as he strode into the hall.

The man looked puzzled. "No, I gave it all to you not an hour past."

Amyas scowled. "Yes, I remember. Invitations and advertisements. Not what I'm waiting for."

"So now can we finally go?" Daffyd asked.

"Where?" Amyas muttered.

"To the races, to the moon; don't you hear a word I say?"

Amyas turned and strode back into his study, and flung himself into a chair. "Two weeks," he said, frowning. "Two weeks and no answer. I collared the guard on the Flier yesterday. I actually went down to the Bull and Mouth again, and found him. He swore on the graves of his ancestors that he delivered the letter."

"Maybe they didn't give it to her," Daffyd, commented, from where he stood leaning against the wall watching his adopted brother. Though Amyas hadn't said much about his trip to Cornwall, what he did say was enough to give rise to interesting speculations. Amyas hadn't found any trace of where his name came from. But he'd been distracted and restless since he'd returned, which made Daffyd wonder if he hadn't found something else. He guessed there was more to the woman Amyas said he'd met than he was willing to discuss.

"Why shouldn't they give the letter to her?" Amyas asked. "She rules the roost there. I doubt they inspect her mail before she reads it." He smiled slightly. "I know I wouldn't dare. No. She got it, all right."

"So she doesn't want anything to do with you," Daffyd said. "And that's that."

"No," Amyas snapped as he stood up. "It's not. That's not like her. She faces the world square and full on. That's what's so good about her. One of the things," he corrected himself as he left his study again.

"So, we're going?" Daffyd asked, following him.

"No," Amyas said as he headed toward the staircase. "I am. To St. Edgyth. To make sure. To speak to her and hear it from her lips. And then maybe it will be that's that. Not before."

"Never thought I'd see you go this far for any female," Daffyd said.

"I wouldn't. But I would for a wife."

"That Tremellyn chit you told me about, is it?" Daffyd asked, following him.

"No, the other," Amyas said as he mounted the stair.

"The one they found on the beach?" Daffyd asked, amazed. "Thought you said she had no name."

"She doesn't. She will. Mine. Or so I hope."

"By God!" Daffyd said. "She must be a powerfully fine female."

Amyas didn't answer; he was already too far up the stairs.

Chapter 18

Amyas knew the way. So this time the trip should have been shorter, but it felt like weeks since he'd left London instead of days by the time his horse trotted up the lane to Tremellyn House again. The sky was lowering, the breeze freshening. There was a storm on the way, the innkeeper where Amyas had left his bags said. He suggested Amyas wait until morning, when it would have blown itself out before he rode on. But he couldn't wait another hour, much less another day, and would have gone on in the teeth of a gale.

When Amyas reached the stone gatehouse, he paused and remembered how he'd passed the last rainy night he'd spent in St. Edgyth. Then he rode on. He had a pistol in his pocket and a knot in his stomach. He wasn't worried about Tremellyn. He knew the man despised him, but at least knew where he stood with him. What worried him was what Amber would say to him if she would say anything at all. She might refuse to see him, and he wouldn't blame her. She could have gotten his letter and read it. She might greet him with laughter, or tears, or a kiss. Or more likely, a slap and a slammed door.

He wouldn't accept that as a final answer until he spoke to her, but he wouldn't blame her.

He'd behaved badly, and he knew it now. Knew it then, too, but ignored it. It had taken him only a day away from Amber to discover the depth of his feeling for her. It was giving up his dream that had taken weeks. His new dream was brighter, but now harder to attain. He needed only her. He had to let her know he was prepared to make any kind of penance to win her.

He didn't think she'd torn up his letter, but was by no means as sure of that as he'd told Daffyd. It was entirely possible that she might refuse to talk to him. She might never trust him again. Again? He gave a cough of a laugh that made his horse's ears swivel back. It was bizarre that she'd trusted him in the first place. But she wasn't an experienced woman, and he'd won many of them in his time, too. The trick was intensity, the method was charm, the lure was sex, the prize, he thought with disgust, had always been himself. He worried. This separation might have woken her to reality; it had certainly done that for him.

That wasn't the only thing that worried him. In the weeks since he'd left, she might even have accepted Pascoe Piper. It was the sort of thing a rejected woman would do.

Amyas had thought of all these things as he rode all the miles to her.

He'd lived a hard life and endured more rejection and outright pain than most men. But physical pain was nothing to him anymore, and mental pain was a fact of his life. Still, he was in a state that had gone beyond anxious as he rode up to Tremellyn House.

He tied his horse to a tree, and went to the door.

The maid opened the door, looked at him, and her mouth fell open.

"I'd like to speak with Miss Amber," Amyas said.

She disappeared into the house, leaving him standing on the front step. Amyas braced himself.

It was Tremellyn who came to the door, his face set, his mouth tight.

"I know you said I shouldn't come back here," Amyas said. "But I must speak to Amber."

"You can't," Tremellyn said.

Amyas was prepared with more than the pistol he carried. He'd rehearsed this part too, on his long journey. "Just for a few minutes," he said. "That's all I ask. I know you've no reason to trust me. But the only lie I ever told was about my family. What I didn't tell was a great omission, granted. But it wasn't a lie. Come, if you were me, would you have done different? They used to brand criminals on the face in the old days. They don't anymore. They punish them but leave them unmarked so that if they live, they can go on to make a better life if they can. I was trying to do that. When you asked my intentions, I told you the truth. Tremellyn, be reasonable. I won't hurt her. You can stand right here and listen, but I must talk to her."

Tremellyn's smile wasn't pleasant. "Nicely said. But it's no use."

"She said she won't speak to me?"

"She's not here to say it. She's gone."

Amyas went pale. "Gone? She married Piper? So soon?"

Tremellyn frowned. "Pascoe? No. Never. He asked. She refused him. Then she left."

"But where did she go? She had no family . . ."

"So we thought," Tremellyn said. "We were wrong. She does. She did. She put an advertisement in the paper, and they found her."

Of all the things he'd imagined, this was one thing Amyas had never anticipated. He was, for the first time in a long while, at a loss.

Tremellyn studied him and seemed to come to a decision. "You hurt her, even I could see that. Don't know how, but I suspicion it. If I could do more than that, I'd put a hole in you where you stand. But she denied it, so you're safe. My Gracie hurt her, too, though she didn't mean to. Did you know that Grace accepted young Tobias the same night you left? I see you didn't. Nobody saw that coming. I don't know what happened between you and Amber that night, but I think it was more than what should have. When she came home the next morning she looked sick. When Gracie gave her the news that same morning, she looked sicker. And then . . ."

Tremellyn stopped what he was about to say, and went on, "And then, what does Amber do but decide she can't stay on here anymore." He scowled. "Well it's true that since she isn't really my daughter, she couldn't stay with me without a chaperone, but that wasn't all it was, or I'm a donkey. Anyway, she wrote to her friends in London and went there to look for a position."

"London?" Amyas asked, his eyes widening as he remembered that impossible vision he'd had in the inn yard those weeks past. "When?"

"Weeks ago. No matter. She's gone."

"Where in London is she?"

Tremellyn didn't answer.

Amyas tightened his jaw. "Look, Tremellyn, I have friends, high and low. I will find her. You might as well tell me where she is now."

"You won't find her in London." Tremellyn said with bitter pleasure. "I told you, she went back to her family. She's a Frenchie. Would you believe it? All these years and nobody knew. She couldn't say anything right when I found her, because she was saying it in French, or at least, a tyke's version of it. Who would have guessed? Not only that, but her folks are aristocrats, or near to it as makes no matter, now that the French killed off most of the important ones they had. Rich as they can stare, and kept their money because from what I gather they played both sides of the fence when Napoleon took over. Our Amber," he marveled, "a lost princess, or like one, after all."

Amyas stood stock-still, stunned, as if Tremellyn had struck him across the face.

"Her name is Genevieve, would you credit it?" Tremellyn asked, Amyas's shock as well as his own secret sorrow were making him as garrulous as if they were friends again. "She's got a sister, and a half brother. The family lives in a palace, imagine that. She had amber hair and white skin," he murmured, as though to himself. "And here I thought all Frenchies were dark."

"Are you sure they are her family? How can they prove it?" Amyas demanded, the thought of Amber's beauty making him think of dark plots to enslave a homeless beautiful woman.

Tremellyn looked scornful. "Don't you think I made sure? There's a scandal there. Her mother was eloping with a lover. She took her youngest with her, because Amber, I mean, Genevieve, was her spit and image and she loved her too much to leave her behind. They sailed to England, swinging around this way to avoid being caught by the husband, who was following. The lover was an Englishman, but no sailor. Their ship was nothing more than a pleasure boat fit only for a day's outing, with no crew but for the lover. A storm blew up, and they capsized at sea, miles from here. They found the remains of the lady, and the lover, but never the tyke. She must have been put in an even smaller boat, at the last minute, and the tide took her all the way here."

"Didn't the family search for her? Why didn't they scour the shore?"

"There was a war on, remember?" Tremellyn asked scornfully. "They'd have been blown out of the water, or put in prison if they showed their French noses on land. Besides, they found all the others floating, dead as day-old mackerel, almost right off. And babes don't last long in the water; if the fish don't get them, the tides tear them apart. I can understand why they didn't keep looking. It was a miracle the tide took her so far, carrying her all the way here and not dumping her out at sea. Instead, she came in with the tide, to our beach.

"She must have crawled out onto the beach after she landed, and toddled away, and the dory was taken out again on the next tide. What wreckage we found was only sticks of wood, likely from some other wreck. This is a rugged shore. I don't blame them for not searching more." He saw Amyas's expression, and added, "She doesn't blame me for not doing more either. I tried, and she knew it. I put notices in the papers, but the Frenchies couldn't get hold of ours during the wars, and weren't looking in English papers besides. So there you are. She's got her home, at last. And it's a fine rich one."

He looked at Amyas, and for a moment, his expression and his voice softened. "She don't need us, any of us, anymore."

Amyas was too dazed to speak much. "Thank you," was all he said, and turned to go. Then he spun around. "Her whole name, at least, that."

"Genevieve Dupres, daughter of Compte Henri Dupres. The bastard wrote and offered me money for the years she spent with me. I turned him down, of course. He didn't send a gift or ask what I wanted; he just asked my price, so be damned to him. Well, I suppose he doesn't like Englishmen. They have a house in Paris and a mansion by the sea. There's more coincidence, it's not far from the other Mount St. Michael. Going to visit her there?" he asked, with a thin, mocking smile.

"No," Amyas said dully. "Of course not."

Amyas wasn't surprised to see who was waiting for him when he got back from his slow ride to the inn. He saw the dark man at a table the moment he entered the taproom.

"She refused you?" Daffyd asked, his smile slipping after one look at Amyas's face.

"No," Amyas said, taking a chair, slumping in his seat, stretching his long legs out before him.

"I see. You came to your senses and realized the single life is better. Well, I'll drink to that," Daffyd said, raising his glass.

"How did you find me?" Amyas asked dully.

"Followed. Wasn't hard. We Gypsies are stealthy devils, remember?"

"Don't blame it on them," Amyas said, with a faint smile. "You're only half Gypsy, the other part's sneak."

"I'll drink to that, too," Daffyd said. He put down his glass and looked hard at his friend and adopted brother. "What is it?" he asked, suddenly serious. "I've seen you hurt before. This is a bad one, ain't it?"

Amyas shrugged one shoulder. "I got what I deserved. Never minded a thumping when I earned it, and I don't now. Listen close. This is a rich one. Here I come, going to offer the poor homeless girl my hand in marriage. Noble of me, right? She should have been thrilled. Well, what sane female wouldn't be? After all, there she was, a beautiful, smart, good-hearted young woman, going to be offered the chance to take a convicted criminal, a bastard, to boot, more than likely; a maimed and disfigured fellow, a liar as well as a thief, for a husband. And that—after he'd spent weeks deciding whether he'd have her."

"She refused you," Daffyd said flatly.

"No. She couldn't. She's gone. Went to London to find herself work, which is the best thing for a wench to do when she's left in the lurch. That's likely what my own dear mother did, after casting off her extra weight, that being me. But instead Amber found a new life: her family. Her real one, and guess what? Turns out that she's rich and titled! That's not only irony, that's a real fairy story ending," he said with a

twisted smile. "Aye, including escaping from the
clutches of the ogre. Which would be me. You're
right," he said, sitting up and signaling to the
innkeeper. "Let's drink to that."

"Want to tell me more?" Daffyd asked. He'd met
Amyas when he was suffering, the day he'd lost his
fingers. He'd seen him through the pain of loss of
many other things, many times more through the
years. He'd seen him lose his dignity after a hard
fight for it, he'd seen him lose people he'd loved, and
more often, had seen him almost lose his life. He'd
never seen him like this. Amyas always fought back,
with grace and determination, and humor, not this
terrible mocking self-loathing. Now he looked wild, a
little crazed, and wholly lost.

"It's simple enough," Amyas said. He quickly repeated what Tremellyn had told him, adding, "His
ward won the prize, and still the man looked
crushed. I wonder if it was only because he felt he lost
a daughter. Ah, what a sewer of a mind I have!" he
said with disgust.

"No," Daffyd said thoughtfully, "she wasn't his
daughter after all. But that don't matter. So, she's a
French heiress. Lucky you."

"Are you mad?" Amyas asked. "I'll never see her
again."

"You said she felt something for you."

"Almost felt something from me," Amyas muttered. He tugged at his hair with one gloved hand,
then held out the hand and looked at it. He scowled,

then smiled. "This damned glove saved her. Who would have thought this cursed hand could ever do anyone a good turn? But it kept her safe, and in a way, ensured her future. Because I would have asked her to marry me that night, if only because I'd have felt I'd had to do if I hadn't stopped . . ."

He shook his head and grimaced. "It wouldn't have done," he muttered to himself. "I'd always have felt my hand had been forced, and so would she. That's a joke, my hand saved her from being forced . . ."

He remembered he was talking to someone else, even though it was someone he trusted with all his secrets. But the secret of his night with Amber wasn't his to tell. "Anyway," he told Daffyd, abruptly changing the subject, "though I think I hurt her feelings, I did her a good turn. If I hadn't been such a fool, she'd never have written that advertisement, never have gone looking for a family, because she and I would have made one."

His eyes were bright, and clearly full of pain as he looked at Daffyd again. "Ah, Daffy, I've been so stupid, deluding myself about everything since I came back to England. Playing the fop and the gent, talking like a toff, lying to myself as much as everyone else. I'd never have lasted an hour in the old days if I'd been half so brainless. I came all the way here to find my name, just because someone told me it was a Cornish one, when any fool could have told me that was impossible."

"And did," Daffyd said, to make him smile.

Amyas didn't. "And looking for a highborn wife, so I could be one of the ones who belonged? I should've known better," he said in an achingly tight voice. "When I met her, I certainly should have. She's a very lucky woman, because she might have accepted me then. There wasn't anyone better on her horizon, and I was trying to cut a dash, to impress her adopted sister. I suppose I did."

"Oh," Daffyd said innocently, "she was a tart, was she?"

Amyas's gaze grew cold and sharp. "No, she was not. What gave you that idea?"

"Well, you're saying she'd have married any man to get a better life, just like the girls we used to know."

"No, I'm not. I only meant that she didn't have a wide choice, but I don't think it would have mattered to her. After I left, she got an offer, and a good one. I know the man. A hard fellow, but a knowing one. He captains his own boat; he's young enough, and not bad-looking. Between the wines he smuggles and the smelts he catches, he makes a good living, and could have given her a good life. She turned him down,"

"Really? So why do you say she'd have taken you?"

"Because she . . . Oh, I see," Amyas said wryly, looking at Daffyd with grudging admiration. "You're trying to get me to say she cared for me. Maybe. She may have done, at the time, and for the moment. She was sympathetic, and she is kind. No chance of that now. Not after I left her only because she wasn't wellborn, and certainly not since she found out she is and came into such good fortune."

"She's that sort of girl, then, is she? Unforgiving. Throwing a fellow over because she came into money, too. You're well shut of her then."

Amyas leaned forward. "Daffy, I see what you're trying to do. It won't wash. Why the devil should she want me now?"

Daffyd looked him in the eye. "Why the devil shouldn't she, if she's the woman you think she is? And she must be. Whatever you are, Amyas, my lad, you can read a man or a woman to the bone. It's what kept you alive all these years." He shook a forefinger at Amyas. "So if I was you, which I thank God I ain't, because I've got no taste for settling down, I'd at least go see for myself what she thinks now and hear it from her own lips. I wouldn't give up. And I tell you, my boy," he said, lapsing into their old way of speech to make his point, "if *you* was you right now, you wouldn't neither."

The innkeeper placed a mug of ale before Amyas, and he didn't seem to notice. Daffyd drained his glass and waited.

"No," Amyas finally said, "I admit I'm floored right now, but even if I were myself, I wouldn't bother her again."

"Because you don't want to admit you made a mistake?"

"You know me better than that. Because she's done better for herself, and I can't top what she has now.

And because, think on, there's no reason in Hell why she should ever believe me now."

Daffyd sat silent, and Amyas gave him a tight nod. "There it is, lad, and so let it be." He drank, at last.

"Still," Daffyd said slowly, "there she sits in France. Maybe in gravy, but still, in France." He looked at his fingernails. "The place is unsettled right now. There's rumors the Emperor is coming back."

"There'll be rumors of that when he's in his grave," Amyas said.

"But more war and more fighting may come. Would she be safe?"

"She's in clover, Daffy. The rich are always safe."

"Aye, tell that to the French nobs what got topped on the day they threw down the Bastille. You know they had heads rolling like croquet balls for years. Rich people's heads."

Amyas made a dismissive gesture. "If they survived this long, they probably paid off both sides and can keep on doing it."

"It's easy to get to France now," Daffyd persisted. "Like taking a rowboat on the lake in the park."

"When wasn't it?" Amays asked. "It was like a turnpike all through the war, customs men, Royal Navy or not."

"I only meant that I know you don't like sailing," Daffyd said.

Amyas sat up as though stung. "I do it when I must. You know I sailed halfway round the world twice, and round France a couple of times, too." He relaxed again, his smile thin. "Look you, Daffy, I know you want to see me happy, but this isn't the way to do it. I lost her, and that's that. If I showed up now, she'd laugh in my face, and I wouldn't blame her. I had my chance, or so at least I think I did, but I mishandled it. Only fitting for a fellow with my hands, isn't it? Yes, I'm drowning in self-pity, and the thing of it is, I think I need to drown in some fine brandy and ale as well, then forget it, and her."

"Can you do that?"

"By God," Amyas said, raising his hand and trying to catch the innkeeper's eye, "I intend to try."

Chapter 19

The comte looked up from his luncheon plate. "Your gown," he said, after Amber entered the *petit salon* and took a seat at the table.

"Yes?" she asked, nervously, fingering the skirt of her best frock.

"It is fitting for England, perhaps, but not here. I will have dressmakers attend you. My newfound daughter must dress the part."

"*Monsieur . . . Mon père,*" she said, stumbling over the French words he had directed her to use when addressing him. She didn't speak French, so the words sounded awkward on her tongue, but she suspected it would be difficult to say his name easily in any language. Even so, she was glad she didn't have to call him "Papa." He wasn't the sort of man she'd ever imagined as her father.

"Thank you," she said. "But I think it would be better to wait for further proof of who I am before you buy new clothes for me. After all, so far we have no real evidence that I am who you believe me to be."

"Indeed? I had no idea the shores of Cornwall were littered with amber-haired infants that year," he said, his smile genuinely amused for the first time since she'd met him.

The Comte Dupres smiled, but his smile seldom seemed to signify either happiness or amusement. Instead, it was as polished and emotionless as everything else about the man. She'd always thought the French were supposed to be passionate. But then, nothing Amber had learned about the world seemed to apply here, in the heart of the comte's elegant home.

The French people were said to be starving after all the years of war that had wracked their country. No one lacked for anything in this house. She'd thought the aristocracy of France had all been beheaded, or at least jailed or forced to flee. She'd even wept over some of the sadder stories she'd read. And yet the comte and his family had lived very well through the long years of war. He'd told her so on the journey from England.

"We had royalty visiting us before Napoleon came to power," he'd said with barely concealed smug pride. "And after. We often entertained the Emperor himself. *Plus ça change, plus c'est la même chose.* The more things change," he translated for her, "the more they remain the same. At least, so it is with the Dupres."

She felt like an empress herself when she'd arrived last night. She'd actually gasped at the size of the bedchamber she'd been shown to. A family could live there with ease, she thought, though few families she knew could afford the lace, silk, and satin that had been so lavishly applied just to her bed. The other furnishings were equally sumptuous. There were so many mirrors she saw herself dazed, coming and going, as she'd been taken on a quick tour of the house. It was the size of a palace and as elegantly furnished. There were at least three salons, a grand salon, and a grand ballroom. In fact, there were more rooms than she'd ever heard of a house having, with more servants to tend to them than she'd ever seen working in one house. They glided through the rooms, heads high, their uniforms finer than most of the clothes the people of St. Edgyth owned.

"Infants aren't usually found on our shore," Amber agreed, "but it does happen. Without witnesses and papers, I don't see how you can be so sure I really am your lost daughter."

He raised a thin eyebrow, put down his napkin, and rose from his seat. "Come with me," he said.

Amber followed him out of the room. One did not question a man like the comte. He led her, without another word, along a long, shining hallway and as a footman bowed and threw a door open, into a large salon.

"There," the comte said in bored tones, as he gestured to a picture on the wall above an enormous carved pink marble mantel. "She may have chosen to leave, but still she hangs there. She was my wife. To deny her would be stupid and give rise to even more talk. But look at her, then tell me there has been a mistake."

Amber looked at herself. Or at least, she gazed at a woman who might be she, if she had an antique ball gown, incredible jewels, a small lapdog, her hair dressed in an outrageously ornate style, and no laughter, ever, in her heart or eyes. The woman she saw might have looked beautiful if a gifted artist had painted her. Even as it was, she was striking. But she was also as cold as the paint that created her image. It was hard to tell if it was the woman, or the artist, who had made the image look so lifeless.

"Not very good, is it?" the comte asked dryly. "It will have to do. I have no other portrait of her. The artist was the fellow she ran away with. He was no better a sailor than he was an artist, as it turned out. But now, do you see?"

She nodded. "I do," she said softly.

"Yes, and so will everyone else. But not if you dress in tatters. The dressmakers are coming today," he added. "Your sister will soon be coming to see you, as will your half brother. You cannot look as you do. Now, we shall finish our meal."

She hung back. "*Monsieur*?" she asked softly. "The

artist . . . I mean, what did he look like? That is to say . . . " She hesitated, not knowing how to put it.

The comte raised an eyebrow. "I thought the English were straightforward. I see we shall have to teach you tact as well as the language. Do not trouble yourself to find a clever way to say it. He was not your father. You are my daughter, and no one else's. She flirted, as do all women. But she was faithful. At least, like women of our class, she had promised to be so until she had given me a son.

"That is to say," he added, his lip curling, "she was faithful until she met this wonderful artist. And she met him *after* you were born. She had given me three daughters; only one of them survived infancy. She was not eager to go through the *ennui* of the process again. The painting was an inducement, you see, because I promised her another, better one, when she gave me a son. She decided to give him one, instead. That is to say, the babe she carried might have been a boy. We shall never know. But that was why she fled, the note she left told me so. Charming of her to admit it, wasn't it? At least my second wife gave me my heir before she left me, and she did so honorably, by dying while doing so. And now, shall we finish our breakfast?"

Amber followed him back to their luncheon, but her appetite was gone.

It did not return.

She was too anxious to have an appetite. She had to

stand hours for fittings of gowns, capes, shoes, and undergarments. The comte also ordered a hairdresser from Paris to dress her hair. She was evaluated and made over by a gaggle of others whose professions she could only guess. None of them spoke English, or at least none attempted to talk to her. She'd never been so still and mute for so long in her life.

Her hair was done in a charming style, sleek in front with a cascade of curls at the back. Her new gowns were lovely: simple and elegant. She supposed she looked very fashionable. But fashion had never meant much to her. The process took weeks, and the comte told her she couldn't meet the rest of the family until it was done. So she bore it.

It wasn't pleasant being unable to speak the language. The comte hired an instructor for her, and she began to learn, but wondered if it mattered if she did. She only saw the staff at the comte's great house, and most of them were supercilious. The fact that she couldn't understand them made them more so, or so at least she imagined. She saw too many sparkling looks exchanged between them when they spoke to one another in her presence that never happened when the comte was present. She didn't mind that so much as the crushing loneliness.

She missed Grace and Mr. Tremellyn, and worried about her old dog, too. Ness had been too old for travel, and she missed him as much as she did St. Edgyth and all the people in it. She even missed her usual chores, since she had nothing to do but stand for fittings or wait for the comte to summon her. Her nights were long and lonely. The comte dined with her sometimes, but never said much to her. After dinner, he disappeared. She suspected he had a mistress, because he would ride out after dinner, if he bothered to stay for it, and not reappear until past noon the next day. So her nights were spent reading, writing letters home, or pacing until she grew weary. She sometimes went early to her bed, and that was even worse.

The nights when rain blew in from across the Channel were the worst. Her bed was huge and soft, but she couldn't find a comfortable way to sleep because she couldn't help thinking about another bed, on another rainy night.

Now Amyas St. Ives seemed like a dream she'd had while dozing one night by her fireside. It was a dream she wished she would have again. She remembered his voice, his laughter, his story, and his sorrow about it. She couldn't forget his remarkable face, his breathtaking kisses, his wonderful body, even his poor maimed hand.

He hadn't wanted her because she hadn't had a name or family. Now she had both, and riches besides. That would be something to fling in his face if she ever saw him again. What perfect irony. She was very fortunate, she supposed; not many women got such a deliciously fitting revenge. And yet the thought of that glorious revenge never made her smile. Instead, she'd bury her face in the pillow, and wonder, as she lay waiting for sleep, how anyone so lucky could be so sad.

* * *

Amber sat in the grand salon and tried to conceal her anxiety. When the guests were finally shown into the room, she rose from her chair on suddenly weak legs. Here, at last, was her real family.

"Here she is," the comte told the trio of newcomers. Children," he said, "I present to you your long-lost sister, Genevieve."

Amber inclined her head. She didn't think she had the strength to rise from a curtsey, and the way they were staring at her stiffened her back.

"Your sister, Clothilde," the comte told Amber, introducing her to a beautifully gowned, dark-haired young woman who looked very like himself. "And here is her husband, Maurice, le Duc Ambois. His title is an old and an honored one. His estates and properties, alas, were victim to the Revolution."

The thin, pale gentleman he spoke of raised a monocle and stared at her.

"And here is your half brother, Georges," the comte said, indicating the other man who had come into the room. He spoke with the same touch of pride in his voice that he'd used when showing Amber around his estate.

Georges was a swarthy young gentleman who looked almost exactly like the comte, down to having the same cold blue eyes. Amber could see Georges had also inherited his father's ability to conceal emotion. Or else he simply didn't care that he suddenly had acquired a new half sister.

Clothilde eyed Amber narrowly, and said something in French.

"In English, please," her father said. "It is only polite."

"I *said*," Clothilde said irritably, and in perfect English, "that she looks similar. But it is said that everyone has a double somewhere. There is no proof."

Amber was startled. Clothilde was older than she, and would certainly remember her mother. Whether or not she believed Amber to be her sister, wouldn't she be at least moved to something other than annoyance by the sight of a woman who looked like the mother she'd lost?

"I never knew the mother, of course," Georges said calmly. "So I would not know. The picture in the salon is wretched, but still, she looks very like. So, what are you going to do?" he asked his father.

"What I would have done had she never left us, of course," the Compte said smoothly. "The reason I asked you here is to discover if you have any objections."

Georges shrugged. "It is all the same to me."

"And you?" the comte asked Clothilde.

"Would it matter if I did?" Clothilde said bitterly. "But it is a gift she doubtless did not dream of and more than she deserves."

"Now, now," her father said. "It is not Genevieve who ran from us."

Amber frowned. She still could not think of herself as "Genevieve" and doubted she ever would.

Clothilde shrugged.

"And you, *monsieur le duc*," the comte asked Clothilde's husband. "Have you any objections?"

"It is not my place, or my business," the man said in a high, light voice, waving a hand as if to brush the whole matter away. "So what does it matter what I care?"

"It matters because you have a name and a title, and your voice would be heard," the comte said patiently. "Can I rely upon your using neither against her?"

"Whatever you wish," the duc said.

"Of course he will do as you wish, Papa," Clothilde said, giving her husband a scathing look. "He has the title and the name, as you pointed out when we wed. But you have the funds, and believe me, *mon père*, this one, he does not forget it."

"Very good," the comte said, as though hearing his son-in-law traduced was an everyday occurrence. "So it is settled. And now, shall we dine?"

They filed into the dining room. The food was excellent, as ever. But to Amber's surprise and sorrow, the conversation did not improve. Nor did it ever include her. If this was a family reunion, it was the strangest she'd ever seen. The brother and sister spoke English but only used it to slice at each other all through the meal, bringing up cruel rumor and innuendo, while the duc paid all his attention to his food and wine, and the comte looked on, seeming vastly entertained.

If this was her family, Amber thought, as the luncheon dragged on, it was one she didn't want to be in. She decided to send more advertisements to newspapers and periodicals in England. Cornwall had a long and rocky shore. Surely more than one child had been lost at sea.

It only took another week for Amber to make up her mind. She lived in luxury, without laughter. She dined on delicious foods that had no taste to her. She was surrounded by people and had no one to talk to, and had no work for her hands or mind. She'd been reunited with a family that left immediately after meeting her, and appeared reluctant ever to see her again. And she had acquired a father who seemed barely to tolerate her. She couldn't see this changing, even if she learned the language, even if she lived here for another lifetime.

She left word for her father, requesting an audience with him.

"And so," she concluded as she spoke to him that very afternoon in his study, "although I thank you for everything you have given me, and all your generosity, I find this is not the life for me, sir. I will, of course, write to you, and keep you informed as to what I am doing. It was good of you to take me in, and I do appreciate it. But we both know there is and could be no real bond between us, except for blood, if indeed there is such. I feel I must return to England, because that is where my life is."

She was nervous, because he'd let her speak her

piece without interruption, and without so much as a blink of reaction to her request. She pleated the side of her skirt in suddenly damp fingers. "Of course, I don't expect you to pay for me, sir," she said, when he only looked at her, his head to the side. "I am quite capable of supporting myself. And," she added hastily when he still didn't speak, "I promise I will never tell anyone of my connection with you, because I can see you mightn't like that."

He smiled. This time, it seemed genuine, even sympathetic.

Her spirits rose.

"But this is nonsense," he said. "I can see you have been *ennui;* you've been bored. And why not? Like mother, like daughter. Doubtless you feel the lack of a man's attentions. But don't despair, I haven't forgotten you, I have been busy in your behalf. I intend to take you to Paris with me next week, to meet your betrothed."

Her head came up. "What?"

"You have been betrothed since the cradle, my dear," he said. "To the son of an old friend of mine. Louis Armand is a charming young man, only a few years older than yourself, and though while not a *savant,* at least clever enough to hold a conversation. He is not an Adonis, but not unhandsome either. He is perhaps a bit plump, but as his father says, he needs a wife to nag at him and keep him away from the pastry. His fortune, however, is also quite plump."

The comte smiled at his witticism. "You will be

married at Christmas," he said. "We plan a great ball to celebrate it."

She stepped back in surprise. "That's impossible!" she said. "I don't know the man, I don't want to marry a stranger. The whole idea is absurd."

"You are too hasty," he said, as he rose from his chair. "This is a matter that was decided when you were born. Marriage is not a matter of roses and dreams, my child. It is a matter of fortunes and property. I was delighted to find you so we could satisfy this transaction. Your sister Clothilde was married in just such fashion. It is our way."

"It isn't my way!" Amber cried.

"Oh, but it is," he said. "You are, you see, underage, and so have no say in the matter. You will thank me one day. We shall leave for Paris in a week's time. Is there anything else you wished to talk to me about?"

Amber refused to go down to dinner that evening. She didn't sleep that night, and was hollow-eyed and empty the next morning. But she was too busy planning to think of eating or sleeping. It had all been too good to be true in the beginning, then too strange to be pleasant, and now too horrifying to allow. One thing she knew: She wouldn't marry the unknown Louis, nor be a piece of property to be traded away.

She'd made decisions. She would leave France, with or without her father's consent. She'd be safe in England. After all, the comte had no proof she was who he believed her to be, only the power to convince his countrymen he was right. Once away from France, she was sure the danger would be less.

The problem was how to do it swiftly and surely. She'd sat up through the night, thinking about it. Now at last, she understood her mother, and if her mother could escape this place with an infant in tow, so could she. Of course, her mother had an accomplice to help her. She'd just have to do without, Amber thought, because she certainly couldn't stay. Her lack of the French language would be a problem, too; but she believed she had enough money tucked away in her purse, and enough courage and outrage in her heart to get her all the way to the Antipodes.

"*Mademoiselle*?" her maid asked as she entered the bedchamber and looked at the untouched breakfast tray. She raised her eyebrows and pointed at the untouched pot of chocolate, and the now cold croissants.

"No, *merci*," Amber said sadly. "I mean, *oui*, take it away." She picked up the tray and handed it to the girl.

The maid shook her head sadly. Then she smiled, and balancing the tray on her hip, reached into her apron pocket. She handed Amber a thick letter. "*Pour vous, mademoiselle. Il est arrivé le matin.*"

Amber sighed. At least, this one maidservant had a smile for her, and better yet, a letter from home. "*Merci*," she said, and took the letter.

She was surprised to find that there were two letters; one had been included in the packet with the other.

The first she read was from Grace, and as usual was filled with stories about how she was, how Toby and her father were, and how they all missed Amber. Grace wrote that she and Toby looked forward to coming to visit on their wedding trip in the spring.

Amber laid the letter down. She prayed that Grace would never be able to visit her here. Then she picked up the other letter. Though unopened, it was battered and bent, as though from much travel, and was from a "Mr. St. Michael." She frowned. She knew no one of that name. But then her spirits soared. Maybe it was another answer to her advertisement, this one from an Englishman, telling her who her real family was! She eagerly unfolded it, and read. And then read it again. And then, for the third time, although scarcely able to see through her tears, read it yet again.

My dear Amber,

I've been a fool, and a blind man, a coward and a climber, and I am sick of it, and myself. I don't know how such a fool dare ask a woman such as yourself to forgive him, take pity on him, and forget his trans-gressions, those made both before he met you and af-ter. But this is what I'm doing now.

Amber, I do love you, and love you entirel . . .

The comte saw Amber again, at her request, after luncheon. He was as astonished at the transforma-tion in her as his servants had reported being. She glowed. She wore a gold gown, to echo the wilder tones in her glorious hair, and her eyes were bright. She reminded him so vividly of his late wife, he almost winced. Instead, he smiled.

"I see you have slept on the matter," he said, "and come to your senses."

"Oh. That. Oh, no," she said. "Indeed not. I've received a letter from home. My good sir, I have another offer of marriage! And this one from the man I love. He's not from St. Edgyth, he's from London; I can't wait for you to meet him." *Which will be after I write to him, and tell him what to say*, she thought, and added, "He has investments in England as well as in the Antipodes, and is extremely wealthy."

"How fortunate for him," the comte said dryly. "But it is out of the question. You are engaged to be married to Louis, and you will marry him."

Amber shook her head and kept smiling. "I'm sure Amyas is richer. You would do just as well with him as my husband."

"Would I? But it is not entirely a matter of money. It is a question of family honor. We had an agreement. Put the matter and the gentleman out of your mind, please. And let me hear no more of it."

"You can't dismiss him out of hand!" she said angrily.

"Oh, but I assure you I can," he said, turning his attention to some papers on his desk.

Amber thought frantically. If she could have, she would have stormed out of the room and this house.

But she knew that was a thing she couldn't do, so she had to tell him something to change his mind. She thought of what would revolt Mr. Tremellyn and make him wash his hands of any young woman he was thinking of being charitable toward. Though it pained her because she didn't want the man to think of her as a slut, she believed she'd hit on the right thing to say.

"I—we—we were lovers!" she said defiantly.

"Indeed?" he said, raising an eyebrow. "Congratulations. Do you think that makes a difference? Among the *bourgeoisie*, perhaps. Not among people of our class. Louis will not mind not having a virgin bride. You are obviously not *enceinte*, so it makes no difference. After you are married and have given Louis a son, you can perhaps come to some sort of accommodation and see your lover again. That is your business. Mine is to see you wed."

Amber caught her breath. She was humiliated and embarrassed, but also too angry to speak. As she turned blindly to the door, she heard the comte speak again.

"And if you wish to emulate your late *maman*, I advise against it. I do not make the same mistakes twice. You shall remain with me until I deliver you to your husband. You may go now. Oh," he added, "and for now, there will be no more letters coming to you, or going from you. This is, after all, my home. And you are my daughter and as such, my property. Until, of course," he added coolly, "you become Louis's."

Chapter 20

Amber's maid Marie shrugged, and sighed, and shook her head sadly.

Amber pursed her lips, and frowned.

Marie sighed again, sat down, and picked up her sewing.

And so Amber knew, without a word being exchanged, that she still wasn't allowed to leave her room, and that Marie felt very sorry for her. Amber didn't speak much more French than she supposedly had done when she was a toddler, and Marie didn't speak a word of English. But they understood each other very well.

Four days had passed since Amber had told the comte she would leave, and he had refused to let her go. Now she felt as though the little gilt clock on her mantel was ticking her life away. Marie brought her meals, because she refused to dine with the comte. He no longer insisted. And so pretty little Marie was her only companion, and a good one, Amber supposed, because she had become so clearly sympathetic.

They strolled the gardens together, and murmured comments on the fine weather, or a particularly pretty flower, and they understood each other well enough, just as they did when they made equally gloomy faces when it rained. They played cards together to pass the evenings, and because they were both young, they sometimes laughed and teased, and showed their cards, and won and lost without caring. Amber let Marie try on her gowns, and tried to give some to her; but Marie was clearly afraid to take anything from her, lest she be accused of stealing.

They learned each other's moods, and sometimes, when Amber looked sad, Marie would pick up a brush and tend to Amber's bright hair, and sigh with exaggerated envy. Amber would look at Marie's curly brown hair and sigh with equal exaggerated envy until they both laughed. When Amber was particularly sad, Marie would go downstairs and return with extravagant sweets for her. Amber had little appetite, but she ate to please Marie. If she didn't, Marie would twist her face into expressions of such concern that it was either eat her treats or feel like a monster.

Amber also realized her little jailer was obviously a romantic. Still, she was as adamant as her master and never agreed to anything he had not sanctioned, and likely thought the idea of a young woman being punished by her father not unusual. Or else, Amber thought sadly, she was afraid of losing her position in this great house. She would never know. There was only so much information that could be exchanged in pantomime.

Now, Amber sat by her window and stared out at the glowing morning. She was allowed to walk in the gardens after luncheon and before dinner. But there were always footmen and gardeners watching. They seemed indolent, but let her take one step off any of the crushed-shell paths, and they sprang to attention.

Last night, in the dead of the night, when she'd heard Marie's light snores coming from the dressing room where she now slept, Amber had made a real attempt to escape. She eased her door open and waited, her heart hammering. She planned to tiptoe out of the house and make her way to the coast. She'd sewn her purse into the lining of her cape and taken off her slippers. Opening the heavy oaken door without making a sound had taken her all of five minutes, and she'd been elated when she'd finally stepped out of the room and begun to creep stealthily along the corridor.

She'd discovered that the footman sitting by the stair was delighted to have something to ease his boredom. She'd nodded at him and walked back to her room, closing her door again. She hadn't realized she was watched both day and night. She was truly a prisoner.

Now she wondered if even Amyas, with all his experience of jails, could have come up with a way to escape this gilded prison of hers. Thinking of the man brought his image to her, clear as the bright morning.

She leaned her forehead against the diamond windowpane and stared out dully. Then she sat up abruptly. She stood, and pushed open the casement on the window, leaning out so she could focus on the distant horseman she saw riding toward the house.

"*Non, mademoiselle!*" Marie cried, rushing over to close the casement.

"Don't be silly," Amber cried, leaning against the now-closed window and staring out again. "I wasn't going to jump out, I just have to see . . ." She squinted. She stared. She thought she might be losing her mind, at last. Or it could be . . .

She watched, breathlessly, one hand to her heart. As the man she saw came riding up to the house, Amber gasped. Bizarre thoughts sprang to her mind. Could Fate be so cruel as to make this mysterious Louis she was supposed to marry be the mirror image of Amyas? Or could she really be going mad?

Her room was on the second floor, and as the rider neared she could finally see him clearly. She watched, mesmerized, caught between doubt and sudden leaping exultation. Had he actually come to rescue her, as he did in all her dreams? He wore a high beaver hat, that head held high enough for her to see that poor abused and blunted profile when he turned, the sunlight catching and highlighting the edges of the gold in his thick, overlong hair.

Amber stood and stared until he rode up to the front door, and she lost sight of him. And then she ran to her door, tried to turn the latch, then rattled at it like a madwoman and pounded with both fists.

"*Ah, non!*" Marie called, dropping her sewing to come running to her side. "*Arrêtez! Ne faites pas cela! C'est impossible, la porte est verrouillé. Vous vous blesserez seulement. Le maître vous a indiqué ne peut pas partir.*"

"But I must see him!" Amber cried. "He is . . . *il est* my . . . *amour!*"

"Ah," Marie said, tears forming in her own eyes as she held Amber's hands tightly in her own. "*Quelle tristesse! Je suis si désolé, mais j'ai mes ordres. Ah, la pauvre fille.*"

But he had come! Amber didn't know why, and it didn't matter, not now, she thought, trying valiantly not to cry. Weeping wouldn't solve a thing. She had to let him know she was here. Now she understood Amyas as never before. She'd thought being confined and losing your freedom was the worst thing that could happen to a person. Now she knew there was something even worse. It was being a prisoner and knowing your freedom and all you desired lay only steps away, and not being able to reach it.

"Mr. St. Ives," the comte said, as Amyas was shown into his study, "how may I help you?"

Amyas bowed. He was weary and felt ill. He hated sailing, and still suffered the aftereffects of his journey, because he'd come straight from the coast where he'd landed last night. It wasn't that he got seasick, in the usual way. Being on the sea upset him more than mere physical discomfort. Every time he stepped aboard a ship he remembered his greatest journey, the one he'd been forced to take. He had only to hear the slap of waves on a hull to remember sitting in the dark in the bowels of a great ship, breathing air shared with dozens of men, some sick, some dying, some dead. He remembered it so vividly that even if he stood on deck he found it as hard to breathe as it had been then, when he'd wondered if he'd die of suffocation, or drowning, or punishment. Because there'd been times when it had taken all his self-control, as well as help from Daffyd and the boy and man they'd allied with, to keep him still and sane.

So he still felt queasy. Worse, now he felt even sicker with shame, and belittled. He'd been a fool again. How dared he come to this magnificent house and ask Amber if she'd like to give up all her riches for him? How could he possibly expect her to leave her true family, all her newfound luxury, to come with a man who'd been a criminal and convict? A fellow who had certainly abused her trust, if not her body and spirit. A man who had no name to give her.

As he'd approached the great palace of a house, he'd thought he'd got a glance of her bright hair at an upper window, but hadn't been sure. Still, his heart had risen. Now, seeing the vastness of the estate, he felt it sink, and wondered if he ought to turn and head right back to the coast. But he'd come so far. He told himself he didn't feel like getting on board a ship again so soon.

The truth was that he had to see her again no matter what she said. If she only laughed in his face, he deserved it, and at least that would end it. He doubted he had a chance in Hell, as he'd told Daffyd when he'd left England. But if there were the merest chance, he'd take it, no matter the humiliation he risked. He'd known defeat as well as pain; he could deal with it. Not knowing would be worse. Because how could he ever be peaceful in his own mind if he never knew?

"*Monsieur le comte,*" Amyas said now, "I've come from England to inquire after the health and well-being of your daughter Genevieve, whom I knew as Amber. We were friends, you see."

"I think I do," the comte said, watching him closely. "I wish you would have written; it might have saved you a journey."

"Something happened to her?" Amyas asked in alarm, his heart racing. Had she fallen ill? He refused to believe that. Had this man decided she wasn't his daughter after all and cast her out? "Where is she?"

"She is here," the comte said, raising a hand to stop the flow of inquiry. "It is only that my daughter spoke of you to me. She said she did not wish to see you, under any circumstances. Ah," he continued, seeing Amyas's expression, "I see this is not a surprise to you."

"Indeed not. I had wished..." Amyas stopped, and frowned. He hadn't been invited to sit down, but the comte didn't look angry or annoyed with him, only blandly polite. The man was only looking at him quizzically. But if Amber had told Amber's father what had happened between Amyas and her, the fellow should have been frothing at the mouth. So she hadn't told him all. Now Amyas began to wonder if she'd told him anything. He thought he knew Amber, and he was certain that even if she hated him she would have told him so herself. He sensed a mystery.

He kept his expression smooth, but it took effort. He pretended to think for a moment, then let his expression lighten. He shrugged, and when he spoke he drawled, like a man trying to give a pretense of not caring. "Well, you know how it is, *monsieur*, when a fellow and his lady have a falling-out. She couldn't have known I was coming. I think, if I can speak to her, I can change her mind."

"Oh no, I think not. I gave her my word that this would not happen. She warned me you might say just such a thing. I fear I must ask you to leave, *Monsieur* St. Ives, and not return. After all, what would be the purpose? She is to be married within the month."

Now Amyas couldn't pretend. He stared. "I don't understand. To whom? If I may ask," he added. When he got no answer, he went on, "Because she's only been here a matter of weeks, and so knowing her, I doubt she could have given her heart so quickly. The only other gentlemen she showed a preference for was a fellow from St. Edgyth: a Mr. Pascoe Piper."

The comte hesitated. "Ah. And I take it you haven't been to St. Edgyth recently, Mr. St. Ives?" he asked carefully.

"No, I've been in London," Amays said, watching the compte just as closely.

His answer made the man relax. The comte shrugged. "Well, then, there you are. So," he said, impassive again, "if you would please leave now, sir? I fear I must insist that you go. The thing is decided, the arrangements are being made. She is a happy girl, and I would have her remain so. I don't want her upset in the least, you see."

Amyas bowed, assuming the mien of a man who had been hurt, but was hiding it. He drew himself up in his best imitation of an offended gentleman. "Indeed," he said haughtily, "it seems there is no further sense in my staying. It also seems I have been misled. Please give your daughter my best wishes for a long and happy life."

He turned to go. Then turned around again. "May I at least leave a note for her?"

"If you wish," the comte said. "There is a table in the hall; if you wish to compose it here, I will send paper and a pen. But then I ask that you leave, and swiftly. I give you good day, Mr. St. Ives."

Amyas nodded and strolled out into the hall. He waited until a footman gave him a sheet of paper, a tiny well of ink, and a pen, and then leaning on the table, after much thought, Amyas finally penned a brief note. He looked at it, frowned, but then handed it to the footman.

"For the comte's daughter," he said. "Miss Amber, no devil take it, for Miss Genevieve," he said slowly, as though talking to someone simpleminded, as simpleminded gentlemen of his acquaintance did when talking to foreigners who didn't speak English. And then he left the great house, not believing for a moment that the note would ever reach Amber's eyes.

Amyas squinted at the bright sunlight as he waited for his horse to be brought back to him. He swung up into the saddle, rode a few steps, then, grimacing, reined in and swung down again.

"Here, lad," he called, beckoning to a stableboy, "have a look at this fellow's foreleg. Seems a jot off to me. It was a long journey, he may have picked up a stone."

"*Comment?*" the boy asked.

"Blister it!" Amyas said in his most imperious gentleman's manner, "Isn't there anyone here who speaks the King's English? Fetch me someone who can, lad! Someone who talks . . . *Anglais*. Aye that's it: *Parlez Anglais*, as you Frenchies say!"

The boy hesitated, then ran off toward the stable that was to the side of the great house. Amyas took the horse's reins and, scowling mightily, walked the animal around the great circular drive, then toward the side as well. He stopped every so often and lifted the horse's foreleg, before dropping it, frowning, and looking around, as though for assistance.

An old man in a battered hat came shambling from the stables. "*Monsieur*?" he asked. "A difficulty?"

"Yes," Amyas said. "The beast is favoring his right front leg. Mind, he's a bag of wind. The stable owners near the coast think they can cheat every Englishman who wants to hire a nag, but I know horses. Well, I suppose they can be forgiven; half the horses in this land were main courses at dinner, weren't they? Those that are left didn't look good enough to eat, I suppose. I didn't want this jade, but they gave me no choice. Well, will you have a look at him?"

"The leg?" the old man asked, looking a bit confused at the flow of speech.

"Aye, dammit, the right front," Amyas said. The old man bent and ran his hand up and down the horse's foreleg. Amyas stood back and looked around, as though supremely bored. His gaze sharpened as he looked up at the windows of the house.

"I find not a problem, *monsieur*," the old man said.

"Then look some more," Amyas commanded. "Take him to the stables. Have someone ride him, and you'll see there is a problem."

The old man touched his hat and led the horse away, Amyas following, at a sauntering pace.

Amyas stood at the front of the stables, impatiently slapping his thigh with his riding crop, waiting, as a stableboy rode the horse around the drive. But he didn't look at the horse; his light gaze measured the house and the drive.

"*Monsieur?*" the old man called. Amyas looked into the shadows on the long stable aisle. There was a little maidservant standing with him, looking at Amyas anxiously.

Amyas strode into the stable. The maid curtsied.

"The girl, Marie, she says she is to give a note into your hand," the old man said. "But that this is not a thing you can tell anyone."

"I won't," Amyas said simply.

The maid hesitated.

"My honor on it," Amyas said, hand to heart, "I will not."

Marie looked at the old man, and when he nodded, she handed Amyas a crumpled note. She watched as he read it and saw his eyes growing alert, his expression becoming hard. "I thought as much," Amyas murmured to himself.

"*Maintenant je comprends,*" Marie whispered to the old man as she looked at Amyas. "*Pour un camarade si joli, j'essayerais de me jeter hors d'une fenêtre aussi bien.*"

"She says her mistress will be glad," the old man said hastily, when Amyas looked up.

Amyas smiled at Marie. "I'm glad you didn't let your mistress throw herself out the window, *mademoiselle*, as you said you, too, would do for such a pretty fellow. And thank you for the compliment, I'll treasure it. No one has ever called me pretty before. *Merci du compliment, je le prisera*," he translated, bowing to her. "*Personne ne m'a avant jamais appelé joli.*"

She blushed and curtsied.

Amyas grew serious as he spoke to the old man. "I take it you will not betray this girl?"

"But how could I? She is young and foolish. But she is my granddaughter. A fine thing that she must work in the house of an inferior. But she lives, and so do I, and that is something, at least. I had a title and funds once, and still have more learning than she, poor child, much good it did me. The Revolution," he said sadly, "it changed all our lives, *monsieur*. We ate not only our horses, but also our future. I would not betray her, never, no."

"Then you are well out of this." Amyas said. He paused a moment, then nodded. It meant trusting a stranger. But he was relying on his instincts, and they had always served him well. A man like the comte would have enemies, many who worked for him. "Just tell your granddaughter to have her mistress ready tonight, past midnight." He looked at Marie, and tilted his head toward the house. "*C'est que la deuxième fenêtre, vers la gauche, ne c'est pas?*"

She nodded, wide-eyed.

"The second window to the left," Amyas breathed. "Very well. *Monsieur*," he said, "call your granddaughter to your side this evening, on some urgent errand. That way she will not be involved in what happens, and neither will you." He reached into his jacket, withdrew a wallet, and took out a thick sheaf of banknotes. "These will hardly repay you for the favor you do me and the young lady in that room. But believe me, you do your master a great favor, too. Because if I cannot get my lady this way, the way I will would go much worse for him. Thank you, and *adieu*."

"You speak French well," the old man said as he hastily pocketed the notes.

"I speak whatever I have to in order to live," Amyas said. "Which is why I still live."

"Then do not attempt the house," the old man said. "The comte has the doors and windows guarded so the Englishwoman he says is his daughter doesn't leave him. He doesn't share his thoughts with servants, but we all know that though he has no great love for her, he has great plans for her."

"So do I," Amyas said. "Don't concern yourself about me or what will be done. Just don't speak of this to anyone, and all will be well. Don't worry," he said with a sudden wide white smile. "I won't cry rope on you, whatever happens."

He saw the boy who had taken his horse come cantering back toward the stables and quickly walked out into the light again. "Ah!" he said. "Finally! And so what was the problem?"

"None," the old man, who had come with him, murmured, "As I think you knew, *monsieur*."

"Anyone can be mistaken," Amyas said with a grin. "So, now I can go. I hope I can return," he said softly, "and leave again, in peace."

The old man shrugged. "I am paid to know horses, *monsieur*," he said. "And naught else."

"Good," Amyas said. And after circling his horse with a worried look, and giving the stableboy a few coins, he mounted, let his horse take a few steps, then nodded, waved, and rode off.

Chapter 21

The footman sitting in the front hall of the Comte Dupres's palatial home was on the job. It was true he was dozing, but it was the middle of the night, and it was boring work. Besides, he was only nodding off from time to time. Every so often his bent head would jerk upright, he'd look around as though surprised, then, with a sigh, relax, and blearily stare up at the great staircase again. The lamps burning in the niches on the sides of the stair showed nothing they hadn't when he'd looked a moment before. Within minutes his head nodded again. So the dark figure that stole up behind him didn't feel guilty when he tapped the back of that head with the weight-filled stocking that he carried.

When the footman's body slumped into a heavier

doze, Amyas generously settled him in the chair again so that when he woke he wouldn't be lying on the cold floor. Still, Amyas didn't move on until he was sure the footman wouldn't be able to speak or move when he woke either. It would be impossible because of the stocking now tied round his mouth and the way he'd been tied to the chair. He would breathe, though, and for that Amyas counted him lucky, even though the fellow's master would likely try to remedy that when this night's work was done.

Amyas moved like the shadows in the recesses of the great hall as he went up the stairs again. He didn't worry about the footman poised at the top, because he'd seen to him already. He reviewed his night's work so far: a kitchen maid bribed, a scullery maid winked at and handed a coin, too, a gardener working night duty as guard, tapped and tied, three footmen stilled one way or another. They all still lived, though it had been a near thing in the garden. Amyas's head still ached from that encounter. No one in the stables gave him trouble—the old man had probably seen to that.

But Amyas didn't celebrate yet. There was still Amber to collect, a hasty exit to be made, a considerable part of the comte's homeland to pass through to get to the coast. And then there was a ship to arrange passage on and a body of water to cross again. But if he'd learned anything during his years of crime and punishment, it was how to avoid thinking of obstacles and pay attention to each job at hand. He moved on.

Judging from the windows, he reasoned that Amber's room would be the third down the corridor to the left. Amyas moved stealthily, only stopping when he reached that door. He put a gloved hand on the door handle and turned it. It didn't move. Then he knew it was locked, and so it had to be her door. With a silent curse for the bastard who'd lock a door for any reason in an old house whose timbers were probably tinder after all the centuries since it was built, Amyas slid his hand into his pocket and produced a small, pointed tool. He slid it into the lock, moved it until he heard a quiet but distinct click, then pocketed the tool again. He carefully opened the door.

He stepped in and closed it behind him.

Amber shot from the chair where she'd been sitting. She gaped at him. Her face was white with fear, but just as lovely as he remembered. Her hair was down, and as tumbled as it had been when he'd last seen her. But there were tracks of recent tears on her cheeks. She stared at him. Her hand flew to her throat. Her plump rosy lips parted.

He sprang toward her and clapped his gloved hand over her mouth. "You were going to scream," he said into her ear. "Right?"

She nodded, her eyes wide as she looked up at him.

"You can't."

She nodded again.

"Can I take my hand away now?" he whispered, his lips near her ear. He took a deep breath of her scent as he waited for her answer.

She nodded again.

He removed his hand, and she fell into his arms and buried her face in his neck. "I thought you weren't coming," she murmured. "I thought I'd never see you again." She took a long shuddery breath that he felt down to his toes. Then she drew back. Her eyes flashed with fury. "How could you endanger yourself like this?" she asked in a fierce whisper. "Leave now! Go, go. You must. You can't stay here."

"I don't intend to," he said.

"Oh," she said, in a forlorn little voice.

It was too much for him. He took her into his arms and kissed her. She kissed him back with such desperation, and then cooperation, that he forgot the time and place.

But not for long.

"No time for that now," he said, holding her at arm's length, away from his own temptation. "We have to be going. Are you ready?"

"No," she said sadly. "I mean, I am, but I can't. If I'm caught, nothing changes for me. But if they catch you, the comte will see you clapped in prison again. I couldn't bear that. A French prison would be worse than anything you've known."

His smile was tight. "Any prison would be worst for me, which is why I don't intend to be caught."

She shook her head mournfully.

"Listen," he said, holding her shoulders tightly, "I was a criminal, and let me tell you, I was a very good one. I survived more prisons than most men know exist, so I know my way around them, and how to steer clear of them. I wouldn't take you with me if I thought I'd be caught, because what good can I do you if I'm in a dungeon?"

He glanced around the room and let go of her. He swept up her cape from the chair, draped it over her shoulders, raised the hood, and tied it at her neck as he kept talking. "You're right in one thing though. French prisons are said to be the very devil, because if you don't have enough food for honest folk, you're certainly not going to feed your criminals. So, we'll stay far from them. But that would have to be far from here. I went to all this trouble to get here, don't tell me you're turning me away?"

His face grew solemn. He tucked a strand of her bright hair back into her hood and took her hands in his. "Will you come with me now? We'll talk about whether you'll stay with me later, because I know there are apologies to be made, and forgiveness to be given—or not. But we can't do either now. Now, we have to leave. I've cleared the way for us, but it won't be clear for long. So. Are you coming?"

She turned from him. His hands fell to his sides.

But she only bent, picked up the carpetbag she'd packed, and faced him again. "Let's go," she said.

They left her room and stopped at the head of the stair, when she saw the footman bound and gagged, lying on the floor there.

"He lives," Amyas whispered in her ear. "Now listen closely. Take my hand and don't let go. We have to fly down that stairway, but even if you slip, I won't let you fall. Just run with me, on your toes, if you can. When we get outside, we have to go down the drive, but alongside it, not on it. We can't step on it because the crushed shells would crackle under our feet, and we'd be too easy to see silhouetted against the white in the moonlight. Then we have to run a long way, into a grove beside the road to get our horses. You won't be able to see much, and you might trip, but I'll always catch you before you fall. Ready?"

She swallowed hard. And nodded.

Amber thought her heart would leap right out of her throat to lie pulsing on the great shining inlaid marble floor as they tiptoed past the bound footman. She thought her legs would buckle under her, they felt so weak; but she ran down the steps and through the hall, and out the door, and fled into the night with Amyas.

"Tired?" Amyas asked.

"No," Amber said truthfully. She might be exhausted, but she was too frightened to be tired. They'd been riding for hours, or so it seemed, and the night had grown blacker because a cool wind had begun to drive clouds across the moon. Sidesaddles were more comfortable than riding astride, and she was grateful for it, but she wasn't used to riding much at all. She had to spend every moment trying to sit upright. Still, the discomfort was nothing to her terror of being caught. Every sound made her heart beat faster. She passed her time wishing. She wished she'd never left the comte's house whenever she wasn't wishing she'd never come to it in the first place. But that made her think of the reason why she had, and again, she'd wonder what had made Amyas change his mind. She wished she could talk to him. But he'd been silent for most of their wild journey.

"Soon," he said, as though reading her mind. "We're going a roundabout way in case anyone's following. They can easily track us to the west, toward the Mont, which is closest, and where they'd expect us to go. I made sure of it. But then we turned north on the high road, where we left no tracks. We're going to a port on a small town on the sea, used by fishermen and smugglers. You know, like St. Edgyth. It should do. I know a place there that deals with rogues, where the landlord wouldn't give up a guest for all the gold in the land, because he'd be giving up his livelihood if he did . . . not to mention his life." She saw his smile flash white in the remaining moonlight. "Don't worry. He only deals with the better class of criminals."

"We can talk now?" she whispered.

"We can talk later. Now, just keep on keeping on beside me."

They rode on. When Amber scented the sea in the wind her spirits rose. For the first time, she really believed they'd be able to sail to England, where she'd be free. That thought kept her warm, as a thin cool rain began to fall. She held on to the saddle with both hands and tried to keep her balance, although she could finally feel her strength ebbing. Soon, she was struggling to keep her eyes open as well.

"Here, at last," a voice said, and Amber's head snapped up. She felt hands at her waist, then was lifted down until she felt the ground under her feet. She staggered. "And not a moment too soon, eh?" Amyas said, and swept her up in his arms.

"I can walk," she protested. "I just need to get used to it again."

"I know you can," he said, with a smile. "But I need the excuse to hold you. Come, our landlord's getting nervous. He wants us inside and our horses away before anyone knows we've been or gone."

The inn was ancient. Amber got a brief glance at a dark entry, and saw light and heard masculine voices coming from the taproom on the right, before Amyas carried her up a dark and winding stair.

"*Voilà*," the man who led them up the stairs whispered, holding his lantern high.

The room was small, and held only a bed, a table, a bureau, and a looking glass. It smelled of woodsmoke and damp, though a fire burned fitfully in the grate on one wall.

Amyas set Amber on her feet. "*Bon. Apportez-lui l'eau, les serviettes, et un certain dîner. Où est la chambre?*"

The man shrugged. "*C'est lui. Il n'y a pas des autres à avoir. . . . Vraiment!*" he exclaimed when he saw Amyas's expression.

"Then I'll sleep in the stables," Amyas muttered. "But I'll dine with you," he told Amber. "The fellow says he has no other room. It doesn't matter; we'll leave in the morning. Bring us dinner, then," he told the landlord. "*Apportez-nous le dîner, puis.*"

The landlord nodded and hurried off.

"Well," Amyas said, as he took off his cape and rubbed his hands together. "Not much, but it will do. Here, I've ridden you into the ground! Take off your cape."

Amber found her fingers too chilled to work the ties on her hood. Amyas frowned and untied her cape, then led her to a chair by the fireside.

She looked up at him with widened eyes. "We can talk now?" she asked. "I have to talk with you."

"We'll have time enough and more for that," he said. "First, warm up and wash up. I have things to see to downstairs. But I'll be back soon enough."

He went to the door, and then looked back at her. "Or we can talk in the morning if you like."

"Now," she said.

He nodded, and left.

"The inn might be small, and rather smelly, to tell the truth" Amber said with a sigh of pleasure an hour later, "but dinner was delicious."

"It's a French inn," Amyas said as he put his own fork and knife down. "They could make their boot-laces taste good, and I don't doubt they've had to in recent years."

She grinned at him. The warmth, the food, the absolute joy of actually sitting at a table with Amyas had restored color to her face and hope to her heart.

"So now," he said, as he leaned back and looked at her, "we can talk."

"I did fall on that food, didn't I?" she said. "But yes, please." She looked at him candidly. His glamour remained. He was still golden, and so handsome to her that it made her want to be shy with him. But her recent terrors had taken her beyond that. "How did you get into the house?" she asked.

"I told you, I was a very good criminal, and those are skills you don't lose."

"But why?" she asked. "I mean why come to France, especially when I didn't answer your letter? I couldn't, you know, I didn't get it until I was already here, and I wasn't allowed to send letters. If it weren't for Marie, my maid, I couldn't have gotten that note to you, and I don't even want to think about that. But what made you write me that letter? And why did you decide to rescue me even though I didn't answer it?"

He looked at her with an expression that made her pulse race. "You have to ask?"

She took a breath, but persisted "Well, but I do. I mean, you left me last time, remember?"

He scowled. "I wish I didn't, but yes. That was before I knew my own heart. I didn't know I had one, in fact. All I had was ambition, and I soon found that a cold bedfellow."

Her face turned pink. She rose, walked to the hearth, and looked down into its fire. "I see. Well, as to beds . . . I hope you know you don't have anything to worry about. I mean, we didn't do anything. That is to say," she said, turning to look at him, clearly embarrassed but equally determined, "we didn't do *everything*. Even if we had, no one knows."

"I do," he said simply, stretching out his long legs, leaning back in the chair and watching her. "But no, that's not why. Although," he added with his usual skewed smile, "it's a very good reason, actually."

He rose to his feet in one swift move, went over to where she stood, and took her hands in his. His eyes blazed bluer than the heart of the fire they stood next to as he went on, "Amber, or Genevieve, whatever you want to be called now, the thing is that I love you, have loved you and still do love you. We match in mind, and body. At least, you suit me as no other woman has ever done, and I doubt any other could ever half so well. I don't want to find out about others. I want you, now, and for the rest of my days."

He shook his head. "I know. I had this stupid notion of rising in the world by marrying well. You knocked it right out of me. Please remember, I sent that letter to you before I had any idea of who you really were. Don't forget that! It should count in my favor. I came to see you because even after I knew you had a title, and was sure you wouldn't want me because of it, I had to try once more.

"At least, as it turned out, I could be of service to you," he said. "The comte wanted to trade you like a milch cow. I couldn't allow that even if you don't want me as a husband. By the way, I hope you understand you don't owe me for rescuing you. Don't worry about that. You're safe even if you decide to throw me out right now. You'll be watched over. I belong to a very exclusive fraternity, don't you know," he said with a twisted smile. "I know the best sort of criminals in every land.

"People don't think much of criminals, for some reason," he added, with a wider grin. "But we do have our rules and standards. That's not nobility, it's survival. And one thing is sure, we don't peach on each other or let each other down for love or money. The comte won't find you. If he does, he won't get you. You're as good as home already—wherever you choose to make that home." He looked down into her eyes. "I'd like it to be with me.

He heard her sharp inhalation, and added, "But don't feel you must, unless, of course, you must."

She smiled.

"Thing is," he said, his gloved thumb caressing the back of her hand, "Can you forgive me? Will you believe me? And why the Devil would a titled beauty like you want a mongrel like me?"

She snatched her hands from his. He looked down, surprised.

"The Devil indeed!" she said angrily. "You say you're done with that nonsense, and there you go again! First, you didn't want me because you wanted a woman of social standing. Now, you don't expect me to accept you because I suddenly am. What the Devil do you want, Amyas?"

He smiled, and showed her. He touched his lips to hers lightly, barely grazing them. And then he pulled back and looked at her.

She stared at him gravely, steadily, then flung both arms around his neck and kissed him back. She heard the chuckle low in his throat, as he put a hand in her hair. His other hand went around her waist to pull her close, and he kissed her with all the skill and passion he was capable of.

He was capable of so much that she was soon breathless. She'd always loved to look at his mouth, and now it was soft against her own. His embrace was gentle, too, and yet for all his gentleness, she felt ravaged. Every sense she possessed felt as though it was burning. She wanted to go up in flames, but had to pause to take a breath.

He chuckled again. "Love," he said, "you have to learn how to breathe while you're at it."

"It's not that," she said. "It's you. You take my breath away."

"I'll give it back," he promised, and kissed her again.

His hand cradled her breast, as his mouth met hers and his tongue silently promised love she'd never known. If he didn't give her breath, he made her forget she had to breathe. She didn't want to stop, and didn't have to, because in a few minutes, he bent, scooped her up in his arms, took her the few steps to the bed, and followed her down to the feather mattress.

He paused only to pull off his jacket, loosen his

neckcloth, tear it off, and toss it to the side, then he joined her again. He kissed her lips, trailed kisses down her neck, and bent to her breast. She was surprised to discover he'd moved her gown down, but very glad of it. She touched his hair, marveling at how clean and silky it felt under her fingers, reveled in the feeling of the pulse pounding in his strong neck, and dared to run a hand across his hard chest. And then his lips found the peak of her breast, and she gasped, and sighed, and squirmed. He drew back to see her expression, before he kissed her again.

His hand moved up her leg, to her inner thigh, toward the innermost part of her that he knew would give her the greatest pleasure. But she tensed and frowned. He still wore his gloves, and however soft the kidskin leather was, the touch of it was alien. It recalled her to the moment. Her eyes flew open.

He didn't know what troubled her and so only tried to reassure her. He drew back, saw her confusion, bent his head to her again—and then stopped as reality hit him, too.

He scowled. "Damn me for a villain!" he said, pulling away with a jerk. "I wanted to do it right." He sat up and looked at her. "Will you do me the honor of becoming my wife, Amber . . . Genevieve, whatever the bloody hell your name is? It doesn't matter, because I want it to be mine, that is, whatever one you want me to use."

She stared at him. Her lips curled. A giggle escaped her. "Yes, of course," she said. But then she paused, her expression suddenly solemn. "Amyas," she said, her lashes covering the expression in her eyes. "I hope you know, whatever I am now, I mean, whoever I was born to be, I'll probably never see my real father and my family again, nor will I want to. Does that make a difference?"

"You think it would?" he asked.

She didn't answer.

He swore under his breath. "I suppose I deserve that. But hear me well. What you are is what I want as my wife. What you will be is my love, forever. If anything," he said in a gentler tone, "this is better, because it makes us equals, and we can make our own world together."

She looked up and smiled. And lifted her arms to him.

His breath hitched, but he pulled farther back. Her face was flushed, her plump mouth was deliciously pink from his kisses, the firelight glowed in her tumbled hair, he saw her high firm breasts, their tender pink nipples peaked; saw the gentle swell of her rib cage, the smooth skin of her stomach . . .

Amyas swore under his breath, and spoke what he thought aloud. "Aye, that's the right way to start a new life, you bloody fool," he muttered. "I mean to make a decent man of myself," he told her seriously, the passion in his turquoise eyes still gleaming, though they were no longer half-lidded, but now clear and sincere. "And so I can't make an indecent woman of you. I may not be a gent, but I want you to have all the rights and privileges of any fine lady. I'll wait until we're wed."

"But . . ." she said, sitting up, "we're here, and alone, and I said I'll marry you, so it doesn't matter."

"Yes, it does," he said simply. "To me. I may be no one and nothing, but I wanted this to be right. And yet here I am, about to take you, unsanctioned, in a low inn in a foreign land, as though you were . . ." He stopped, and shook his head. "This is altogether a hurly-burly affair," he said instead. "Not worthy of you. But I can only be so much of a gent. I can't wait another day. Still, I can make it right, anyway."

He rose from the bed and hastily tucked his shirt in.

Amber stared at him in surprise, watching as he found his discarded neckcloth and wound it around his neck, grimaced at the effect in the looking glass, and then cast it aside before he shrugged into his jacket again.

"Where are you going?" she asked. "What are you doing? Is it something I did?"

"Yes, you bewitched me," he said. "Made me forget my resolve. Wait right here. Don't even think of going downstairs. Rest, relax. I'll be back. Though you might want to fix your hair, or something," he added, with a sigh for how desirable she looked in her disarray. "Because I'll be bringing back company."

He took one last regretful look at her. "I'll be back," he said again, "as soon as I can be." He hurried from the room before he could change his mind.

Chapter 22

"**I**t is not possible," the innkeeper said sadly, looking at the coins Amyas had laid on the tabletop. "*Ce n'est pas possible*," he repeated in French.

"Why not?" Amyas demanded.

"*Parce que* . . . because, *monsieur*, the clerics are all in their beds now. It is night," he added, speaking slowly and distinctly, as though to a dangerous madman or a sot, because in his trade, he dealt with both. "And because you are a foreigner. Are you even a Catholic, *monsieur*? Not that it matters, *comprenez-vous*? It is near midnight. No decent cleric would attend you and your lady."

The word "decent" seemed to convince Amyas. He scowled, and rapped a steady tattoo with a gold coin he had just offered on the tabletop, as he thought about what to do next. They were in the taproom of the inn. Amyas glanced around and saw the last few customers in the place, who had been busily pretending not to be listening to the wild-eyed stranger and their host, quickly look away. This studied inattention wasn't unusual in the sort of inn it was.

"There is no sense asking any of them either," the innkeeper said, inclining an elbow at the suddenly disinterested spectators. "This time of the night, *vous comprenez*, we have only the local fellows and stray sailors from the sea, and *certainement*, none are men of God."

Amyas cocked his head to the side.

"Well, but, we are a stone's throw from the beach," the innkeeper explained. "It is nice little harbor, if you do not wish to be seen coming or going from it. Thirsty fellows from the boats, they can roll right in here. Tonight, because of the inclement weather, there are not a few ships at anchor."

Amyas contemplated this. His eyes brightened. "Yes," he said thoughtfully. "Aye! That would do. *Merci!*" he said briskly and, tossing the coin down on the table, leapt to his feet and strode from the place.

Amber was dressed, her hair brushed and tied, her cape at hand, and her fear and anger growing by the minute by the time she finally heard the knock on her door.

"Amber?" Amyas called urgently. "I have a visitor to see you. May we come in?"

Her heart sank. Had he changed his mind? She

froze. Had he been forced to? The only person she knew in this country who would want to see her was the comte. The comte had money and influence, and Amyas sounded nervous. But there was nothing she could do by hiding now. She rose from the chair and raised her head. "Come in," she said, and steeled herself.

The door opened. There was a man with Amyas.

Amber stepped back, her hand on her heart.

"Hello, Amber," Pascoe said.

"But I don't understand," she breathed, looking to Amyas.

"It's Fate," Amyas said, with a smile.

"You think he swam here?" Pascoe asked, his dark face watchful as he looked at her. "He hung about St. Edgyth waiting for word of you. We didn't get any. You didn't answer any letters. Tremellyn got nervous and asked me to find out what was happening. As if I had to be asked once he told me," he said scornfully.

"This is the nearest port to your father's palace. Well, not really. But the likes of us don't go to the bigger harbors near the Mont, not if we know what's good for us. And we do. He," he said, hitching a thumb toward Amyas, "insisted on coming. His mad brother, Daffyd, came nosing around looking for him and stayed to keep him company." He made a grimace of a smile. "I think the fathers of all the girls in town would have hired me just to be rid of that one, so I let him come, too."

Amyas grinned. Pascoe saw it. "Ship of fools, we

had," he muttered. "But might be we need them now. We thought he was just going to talk with you, so we let him go alone. Now St. Ives says he had to rescue you. So, what's toward?" he asked Amber. "He says you want to marry him. Any of it true?"

Amber nodded, then looked at Amyas. "May I have a few minutes alone with Pascoe?" she asked.

His smile faded. "I'll be just outside," he said, and left the room, closing the door behind him.

Pascoe didn't move from where he stood, feet apart, hands deep in the slashed pockets of his dark coat.

"All of it is true," Amber told him. "My father is a count, but he didn't care about me, he only wanted me to marry for his profit. When I refused, he locked me in, made me a prisoner until he could take me to Paris. Amyas came, thank God, he came in time. I still don't know how he did it, but he subdued all my guards and carried me off here."

"I can imagine how he did it," Pascoe said, frowning. "He has a dark past, that one."

"Yes. But a bright future, I think. At least, so I pray. Because, yes, I do love him, Pascoe. And I do want to marry him.

"Aye, makes sense," he said, nodding. "I couldn't see why else you turned me down."

"I never told him about your offer," she added, wondering if he looked grim because he thought she might have belittled him to Amyas.

"Of course you didn't, think I don't know that? You're a fair-minded female, else I wouldn't have wanted you myself. Well, then. I hope you know marrying a criminal isn't the best wager a girl could make?"

She stared at him, then put her hands on her hips. "Pascoe," she said with a touch of asperity, "what do you call sneaking wine and silks past the revenue men then? Charity work for French orphans? Smuggling's a crime, and no mistake. He only stole a pound note when he was a boy, and was clapped into Newgate and sent to the Antipodes for it. You have boatloads of goods going back and forth regularly. Now, if you factor in age at the time a crime is committed, and value of goods taken . . . Think on, Mr. Piper."

He smiled at last. "No fooling you, lass. That's what I liked about you from the start. Well," he said on a sigh, as he clapped his cap on again, "there are other fish in the sea, and don't I know it. So, I'll do it."

"Do what?" she asked, suspiciously.

"Why, marry you, of course," he said.

The hour was late, the night was black, the rain was constant. The groom had a hard time standing on his feet, and the invited guests were also staggering. No one had indulged in one drink, though, except for the man who was to perform the ceremony, and that was just for his nerves because he'd never done it before. It was just that the ship kept rocking in the storm-tossed waters.

They stood on deck because the captain's quarters

were too small, especially filled with contraband as they were.

"You sure this will hold in a court of law?" the best man asked the groom again.

"No," Amyas admitted. "But I've always heard a captain can marry a couple aboard his own ship, and there he is and here we are. At least it will hold until morning, when we can sail, and be good enough for that damned French father of hers if he finds her. It doesn't matter beyond that. We'll be married again in London when we get there. Do you think the earl would allow me to live if I didn't let him in on the doings?"

Daffyd grinned. "No. You're a wise man, Amyas. And you have a beautiful bride. Now I know why I couldn't pry you out of Cornwall. Ah, here she comes."

The bride, dressed in a borrowed sailor's oiled cloth coat, came staggering toward them, on the arm of Tobias Bray. Her bright smile could be seen in the light of the flickering torches Pascoe's other crewmen held. She joined Amyas and took his hand—then grabbed his arm as the ship pitched forward and back again.

"We'll make it quick," Pascoe said. "I'm not a flowery-spoken man, but I am captain of this vessel, and I can marry you if I like. Anyone say different?" he asked.

The only sound was of the wind and the waves.

He nodded, sending water sheeting down from his hat to the holy book he held. "Aye. My thoughts exactly. Well, then, Amyas St. Ives . . . is that your legal name?" he asked Amyas.

"It is," Amyas said proudly. "Signed and certified by the courts, too. I own land, shares, and property, all in the name of St. Ives, so no one can take them from me. My friend the earl saw to that."

"Then, Amyas St. Ives," Pascoe said, "do you take this woman, Amber, Genevieve Tre . . . no, Dupres, to wife?"

"Absolutely. I do." Amyas said.

"Amber Genevieve Dupres. Do you take him to husband?"

"Absolutely, I do," she said.

"Then you're spliced, by my command, as captain of this vessel, and no man alive better try to gainsay me," Pascoe pronounced. "Well, it's done," he told Amyas. "Legal as I can do it. I think you're supposed to kiss her."

But Amyas couldn't. The moment he bent to her, the ship tilted up to the right, then fell left, and the bride, groom, and guests all had to hang on to each other to keep upright.

And all that could be heard above the rain and the wind was their laughter.

Amber and Amyas had shared a drink with the crew and left Pascoe smiling, at last. They drank with Daffyd and the two other crewmen who were going to stay in the taproom until morning with him, on alert for any minions of her father's. They'd even shared a toast with the two lads snugged in the stables, also on alert for any of the comte's men. Amber hadn't really drunk that much, but she'd wet her lips at least a few times. It should have made her merry. But the enormity of the night had occurred to her, and now she stood in her bedchamber at the inn and marveled at what had happened.

Amyas strode into the room after bidding Daffyd good night, closed the door behind him, hung his greatcoat on a hook, turned to his bride, and the smile died on his lips. She was still dressed, standing in the middle of the room, looking warily at him.

"What?" he asked, stopping where he stood.

"Nothing," she said. "Everything," she added. "Weren't you there?"

He smiled, and was at her side in two strides. He took her in his arms, and buried his nose in her neck. "You smell like rum," he said. He drew back to look at her. "Are you bosky?" he asked.

"No," she said. "Not a bit. I didn't drink that much. Are you?"

He shook his head.

She raised a hand to his hair, and looked at him. "You're so very handsome." She sighed. "I can't believe I can look at you every day and every night forever now."

"You *have* had too much to drink," he said. "I'll go down and get some strong coffee. The landlord's brew is bad enough in the morning; it ought to be strong enough to sober up a friar by now."

"Amyas," she said, "I'm not drunk. I'm happy. I'm amazed. And I'm so grateful. But I'm not drunk."

He looked at her quizzically. "Your eyes are clear enough. They're very bright in the firelight, and that could be the influence of the rum, but they are clear." He leaned forward and solemnly brushed a light kiss on her right eyelid, and then the left. "And your nose looks straight enough," he said thoughtfully. "It would be wandering all over your face if you were drunk, you know." She grinned as he placed a kiss on the tip of her nose. "But you're smiling like a simpleton," he said with a frown. "That does worry me." He kissed her lips.

Her mouth was warm and welcoming, and sweet, and she'd learned to answer his questing tongue with her own.

"It's very warm in here," he finally breathed. "Would you like to take off your coat, wife?"

"Wife?" she said, wide-eyed. "Wife," she said, and smiled.

"Aye," he said, with some difficulty, because he was trying to untie the knot in the ties of her cape. She'd traded back the oilskin for her own cape, but had tied it tight to keep it on for the journey back to the inn.

"Let me," she said, and hurriedly undid the knots, as he stood waiting. The moment after she threw off the cape, she cast herself into his arms.

"No, let me," he said, raised her in his arms, and bore her to the bed.

Sometime after he'd gotten his shirt off, and after she'd tossed her gown into a corner, and as he was proceeding to kiss her senseless, she grabbed on to reality again. "But," she gasped, as his mouth resumed that long-past journey that had been interupted by a wedding, "what about your brother, downstairs?"

He paused. "What about him?" he asked, confused both by desire and her strange question.

"I mean," she said, "he's downstairs. He'll know, won't he? I mean, what we're doing."

"Oh," Amyas said on a laugh. "No worries there. He thinks we've done this many times before."

She didn't know whether to be mortified or gratified. But when his lips met hers again, she knew.

He had little experience with untested women; but he knew women well, and loved this one as he had no other. And so he was very slow and deliberate. He inched her along, taking each new step carefully, then going back to the last one so she wouldn't be alarmed. He tried mightily to keep this first experience of hers entirely hers.

But though she was overwhelmed with the newness of it and the closeness with him, she was still attuned to his every breath. "Why do you turn from me?" she finally asked, when she noticed that every time he moved, he was careful to keep his lower body angled away from her.

"I don't want to alarm you. You're not used to men . . ." he faltered, trying to find words that were flowery enough to describe what he was hiding from her.

She thought a moment, and realized just what he was trying to keep from her. He felt her smile against his lips. "I'm not used to making love," she said with a tender smile, as she ran a hand down his back and felt his shiver of response. "But I grew up in a village of fishermen and their women. So I know how men are made, and what happens when they make love. Don't worry."

"I've heard that some women are alarmed," he said, and hesitated. He didn't want to sound like he was bragging about his size any more than he wanted to make her wary. Most of all, he didn't want to talk now at all.

"I won't be alarmed," she promised, her smile growing. It faded as a new thought occurred to her, one that chilled her. "Unless, of course, if there's a problem . . . I mean, if you were . . ." Her voice dwindled. She didn't know how to complete the thought. His hand was mained, and he limped, she suddenly wondered if he could he have suffered a more intimate injury, one he was embarrassed to tell her about.

He propped himself on his elbows. He cupped her face in his hands. "Love," he said, as he moved his lower body against hers, "there's nothing wrong with me except that I may die from wanting you. You see?"

He moved away, so she could literally see as well as feel his arousal. She drew a quick breath in surprise.

She'd known about men's bodies, but not that they could achieve what his did. She told him so.

He smiled. "Shall we find out what else mine can do?"

She dared to explore him, and was fascinated at his reaction to her touch, then thrilled at the power it gave her to give him pleasure. She only gasped in dismay once, when her hand discovered the long, knotted scar on his thigh.

"Only a souvenir," he said huskily. "I got a guard angry. The leg was broken, it mended; it only bothers me when it rains, or when my wife doesn't kiss me."

Then she didn't gasp with anything but pleasure. And that she felt in plenty. His body was clean and well made, hardened by years of toil, yet his touch was gentled by years of self-control. She would never know how much of that it took for him to remain controlled. Finally, even his iron will relented.

His hand moved from her inner thigh, to cup her, and at last, he parted her. Her heated skin was perfumed, or at least it was to him. Her naked body was all he'd wished; he only wished he could see her more clearly now, but the light of the guttering fire only showed him glimpses of her loveliness and her reaction to him. But he could feel her eagerness and hear it in her rapid breathing. Which was why he was stunned when her hand reached down, and she stopped him.

"No," she said suddenly. "Please."

He drew back. They were both damp with longing, skin to skin; they'd been close to closing and he stopped with effort. He'd prepared her so carefully, she'd been with him all the way.

"What?" he asked, frantically wondering what he'd done wrong, what she didn't like, what impediment there was now, at the last gate. "Amber, it's all right for me to touch you there. It will feel good, and then make the rest feel so much better. You'll see."

"Amyas," she said softly. "It might. But you're still wearing your glove."

"Oh. That," he said, and felt his desire ebbing. "But only the one, and it's finest kidskin, love."

"Do you always wear it when you make love?"

He hesitated.

"You *have* made love before?" she asked, with a straight face.

"Aye, well, yes. But not without."

"Then take it off," she said, "so I can have something of you no woman has had before."

He thought he might overflow with love. "You have," he whispered, "You have my heart."

She said nothing.

"But the hand," he said patiently, "is grotesque. Disgusting."

"I've seen it," she said. "It's not so bad."

"You don't want to feel it on your skin, believe me. I don't."

"I do," she said.

"But I've never . . . no women has ever minded . . ." he stopped, reluctant to speak of other women while he was in his marriage bed.

"Maybe not," she said. "But they weren't your wives. I am. I'll get used to it. And as I'm going to do something with you that I haven't done before, won't you give me something new of yourself, too?"

"Then, yes," he said. "I'm yours, competely."

He peeled off his right glove and held up his disfigured hand.

She could feel his frame suddenly knotted with tension, and felt his indrawn breath as he waited for her response. She took his hand in hers, and then brought it to her lips. "Such a fuss," she murmured against his mutilated hand. "It's not beautiful. But it's not half so bad as you think."

"It's half, indeed," he said.

"Do you never stop jesting?"

"Sometimes," he said as he bent to her again. "Want to see when?"

"Yes," she said, with a shudder as he touched her intimately.

He would never know if that shiver was from the newness of his touch, or from revulsion at the nakedness of it. Because he was shivering, too. But soon enough, he knew for certain that her shudders were from desire. And only then did he come to her at last.

When he entered her, she breathed, "Oh, yes, Amyas, my love." Then she could say no more, because the surprise of his entry and her body's resistance to it silenced her. And then she couldn't speak because of the strange and slowly growing pleasure of it.

He steadied himself, holding himself on his elbows. He used all his hard-won control to wait and watch for when she was ready for more. The muscles in his shoulders corded, but he strained to be still. It was the most difficult thing he'd ever done. But he wanted to move mountains for her, and so it was the least and the most he could do.

She was astonished. He fit within her perfectly, the burning pain eased, and her body slowly relaxed against his. When he moved again, she tensed again, but soon, she began to move with him, suddenly desperate to find the place he was moving to as well. They rocked together and held each other tightly.

"My wife," he breathed into her ear.

She was too involved in sensations, too moved by him, heart and body, to reply in words. She could only try to hold him closer.

Then, both experiencing love for the first time, they finally gave themselves to each other, again and again, and completely.

Late in the night, nearly to morning, they were still murmuring to each other. They were weary and sated and yet neither could bear to leave the other, even to go to sleep.

"I never know why you picked me," Amyas said softly, as he held her close, "but I'll never make you regret it."

"I know," Amber said, her head on his chest and her hand on his heart. "I picked you because I like bent noses," she finally said. "And I can't count to ten." She felt his rumbling laughter as well as heard it. "But you know?" she said thoughtfully. "Apart from that, it might be because you are the only man I've ever known who doesn't think I'm different because I'm female."

He raised an eyebrow. She couldn't see it, but heard his silence as a question. In these few intimate hours alone together, they'd discovered they could understand each other's meanings from silences and sighs.

"I meant, you think of me as a person in my own right and treat me as such," she went on. "Pascoe, my father, all the others, even if they liked me, which my father did not, merely thought of me as female: a creature only useful for their purposes. Someone fit to cook and clean for them, bear children, or take pleasure from. My father wanted to use me as property. You were the only one who wanted me for what I am, whatever that is. So how could I help loving you?"

"Well, but you're wrong there," he said. "Soon as we get home I want you to scrub the floors, milk the cows, and have triplets. And then I'll think of trading you for some prime property."

She laughed.

"But what about Tremellyn?" he asked.

She was still. She'd never told him of Tremellyn's offer, and wondered if she ever would. It had changed her bond with Mr. Tremellyn, but she didn't want it to mar Amyas's friendship with him, if that friendship were even possible. But she'd hopes. Maybe, one day she'd tell him, she thought. She told him another truth instead. "But Mr. Tremellyn was like a true father to me."

Amyas was silent a moment before he spoke again. "I don't know if I'm different from other men, in what I think of women," he said, as he gently stroked her hair. "But it's true some fellows think of females as different, weaker, or less clever then men. Some may do so because they need to feel superior. Now, a poor man, I can maybe see it. He probably needs something he can be proud of because he's got so little. And as for rich men, I confess I don't understand. Maybe it's because they don't even see women for years on end when they go away to school. So how can they know them? I can't imagine doing that to a boy, and mind, I don't want that for my sons." He paused, his hand stilled. "Would you?"

"Certainly not," she said with a smile in her voice.

"Good," he said. "Now, though I don't know how I survived to adulthood, still, the hard life taught me a few things. I learned early on that women could work just as hard as men, and they were as ill-used as men, too, if not more so. They might have wiles that could take a fellow's breath away; but they could kill and betray you just as easily, so it didn't pay to worship them. They could be as kind as angels for no reason, too; so it didn't make sense to fear or dislike them.

"Crime levels the playing field: When you see men

and women hanged together for the same game, you understand that. You also come to see they can aid and comfort each other equally. So a wise fellow soon learns that people are people, and their sex doesn't matter. It's lovely to use, of course." He moved, lowering his head so he could whisper in her ear. "Speaking of which . . . I estimate we've an hour 'til dawn, so shall we? I mean, use the time creatively?"

"Oh, yes, please, Amyas my life, my love," she said on a sigh, as she raised her lips to his.

Chapter 23

❦

The wedding was tasteful, and the wedding party that autumn evening was lavish. Any party held in the earl of Egremont's vast London house would be, but this one was especially fine, because it was for the man he thought of as a second son.

Flowers were everywhere, the champagne flowed, the guests were of the highest caliber, and there were rumored to be not a few of the lowest in attendance, too, to give the event extra savor. The aristocracy loved consorting with the lower classes, so long as they were safe doing it. The gossip about the returned earl's adventures in the prisons and the Antipodes gave the event a special cachet, and ensured every invitation was prized and accepted. The guests would dine out on this experience for weeks.

The groom, for example, was a dangerous-looking fellow, madly attractive, in a battered tomcat sort of way, as one society matron remarked behind her hand.

The bride was said to be French aristocracy, and very beautiful. Her family from France wasn't in attendance, though they'd been invited. But with the state of the world in such flux, no one was surprised.

The bride's friends from Cornwall were well represented. The gentleman said to have acted as her adoptive father was there, solemn and utterly respectable, as was her adopted sister, who was glowing, her own fiancé by her side. There were delicious rumors of some sort of daring adventure the bride had experienced; talk of a recent rescue from France, which was odd, since France and England were at peace for the first time in memory. Still, with such intriguing folk in attendance, few doubted it. The dark, rough-hewn fellow who watched the proceedings narrowly was whispered to be a sea captain who had aided in the adventure.

The best man, as dark, sleek, and excitingly attractive as a maiden's dream of a Gypsy lover, was rumored actually to be a Gypsy himself. And the other man the groom called brother was the earl's own son, an elusive but much-admired ornament of society, although unfortunately, at least for the matchmaking mamas, he was married, and happily.

The host, the elegant earl of Egremont, was rich,

good-looking, and a scholar who had been a convict and bore the traces of both in fascinating ways.

In all, it would be an event to remember. Especially, of course, for the bride and groom. But not exactly in a way they had expected.

"Amyas," a white-haired gentleman guest said, after he offered his congratulations to the smiling couple. "A famous name, and not one commonly heard these days, Mr. St. Ives."

"Famous?" Amyas said, raising one eyebrow.

"Ah, well, at least to me," the gentleman said apologetically.

"This is Professor Robert Holland," the earl explained, "a noted authority on ancient music."

"Then you mean the Cornish song," Amyas said. "Yes, I've heard it. Sung it many a time, too."

"In all three parts?" the professor asked.

"Three parts?" Amyas asked.

"Yes, for three voices," the professor explained. "As Cornysshe wrote it."

Amber, at her new husband's side, stopped chatting with her other guests when she overhead that. "Cornish *wrote* it?" she asked.

"Indeed," the professor said. "Sir William Cornysshe, musician to His Majesty King Henry's court; interestingly enough, both Henry VII and VIII. However, we believe he wrote it in 1515, so he would have composed it for Henry VII. It's an interesting piece, isn't it? No modern person knows to whom his references allude; but I believe he was commenting on a scandal of the time, as such songs often did. It's a bit naughty, to be sure, but in the context of the time, so few modern listeners understand . . ."

"It's not a Cornish folksong, but a *Cornish* one?" Amyas asked in confusion.

"C-O-R-N-Y-S-S-H-E, yes," the professor explained. "Sir William Cornysshe, the man who wrote 'You and I, my life, and Amyas.'"

"The Devil you say!" the groom's adopted brother Daffyd exclaimed, staring at Amyas.

Amyas looked as though the professor had struck him. "All these years? Not Cornish? Not from Cornwall, but by 'Cornysshe'? Then my name—the whole journey, all my questions and investigations, everything I thought . . ." He didn't seem able to go on.

His bride began to giggle. "Oh, my. Thank God his name wasn't Sir William Kentish," she cried, looking at her husband, "or we'd never have met!"

The professor watched the young people dissolve into laughter, and smiled. He didn't understand why they were all helpless with mirth, but weddings were, after all, merry events.

Especially this one, and so was the marriage, to no one but the bride's and groom's constant surprise and continuing delight.

Put some Spring in your step with these delightful new releases from Avon Romance coming in May!